TO DROWN THIS FURY IN THE SEA

THE PANTHER CHRONICLES, BOOK THREE

T. THORN COYLE

"Serve the light and seek the truth resting in darkness. Aid those in need, to the utmost of your power. Learn the avenues of magic and protect the secrets of the Association whenever possible. Risk your own life before putting the life of another in danger."

– The Oath of the Association of Magical Arts and Sorcery

*"I think what motivates people is not great hate,
but great love for other people."*

—Huey P. Newton

"Radical simply means 'grasping things at the root'."

— Angela Y. Davis

PROLOGUE

He paced the cage, big paws padding on the concrete, from the metal toilet bowl to the bars and back again.

He didn't look at the terrified eyes of the guard on the other side of the bars, but he could smell the man's stink. The guard's nervous sweat was sour and acrid. And his crotch stank of a long night in spent in jail, encased in a gray polyester uniform.

How they stood it, he would never understand. His panther form could not comprehend how any creature would voluntarily place itself in concrete walls and bars that clanged and stank of oil and cold.

His man's mind could not comprehend how any man could oppress another. Eking out a living with a truncheon and a gun. Lording it over people, treating them like they were vermin, when your life was little better. A small house or apartment in a depressing neighborhood with a few scraggly trees. Barely paying the heating bill come winter. Wife and children complaining, if you were lucky enough that the wife and children stayed.

Prison was still prison, even for the pigs.

Everyone except the ones who put the people there. The capitalists. The overlords. The oppressors. The Man.

He was in jail without bail. On trumped-up charges.

He'd spent too long here already. They'd botched his trial, separating him out from the the white cats, turning the Chicago Eight into the Seven.

Wasn't that always the way. The white hippies and yippies got a proper trial, while the Black Panther was carted off in shackles.

The judge had ordered him gagged during trial, and they'd literally chained him to a fucking chair. His shifter form had roared in his head at that, but the Party told him to be cool. They would try to get him out. Don't show his skin.

Not yet.

But after Fred killed those cops, and Roland shifted in front of a crowd in South Central LA? All bets were off. And once the Panthers busted Huey out, there was no need for him to hide his nature anymore.

So, in the service of getting free, or at least an actual fucking trial, not the farce they'd forced him through, he shifted now. Every single day.

Every morning, he turned into his sleek, massive, black-furred self. Every day, he trained his orange eyes on the guards. He yawned and licked his lips. He gave a low, terri-fying cough from the back of his throat.

The guards couldn't see that he was smiling.

All they saw were jaws filled with sharp teeth. And the razors on the ends of his black paws.

Today was different. Today, a white man in a black suit, with movie-star hair and glasses dark as midnight, stood outside the bars of his cage and stared.

A fucking Feeb.

The man had some kinda magic, that was for sure. He was one cold motherfucker. Something slippery about him. Something the panther recognized as a threat.

Riding just on top of the papery magic smell the man gave off, he could smell something else. Something familiar. He smelled it from the guards here every day.

The acrid, sweaty stink of fear.

The panther licked his lips and spread his jaws again.

Let the fucking pigs be scared. They should be. They couldn't gag him now.

He was a shifter.

A member of the Black Panther Party, in good standing.

Freedom fighter. Revolutionary.

Motherfucking actual panther.

1

JASMINE

My worn black lace-up boots marched through Oakland's Chinatown, supporting my feet and legs the way they must have supported whatever poor small-footed soldier had them before me.

I wasn't a middle-class, eighteen-year-old sorcerer fresh off the bus from Southern California anymore.

One year later, I was a soldier now. Fighting in an army of liberation. Looking for freedom for my people. For *all* oppressed people: black, brown, white...whatever. If they were struggling, poor, and oppressed, the Black Panther Party was there for them.

As Huey said, "Black Power is giving power to people who have not had power to determine their destiny."

I hadn't been to Father Neil's church to work the Free Breakfast for Children program in what felt like too long. The Party had taken me off duty, to free me up to train folks in community magical defense. That was cool and all. I liked it.

But days like today? I needed something simple. Something good.

A reminder of why we were doing all this revolutionary action in the first place.

My boots took me up to busy San Pablo Avenue, where the delivery trucks rolled by. To Saint Augustine's. The old, red-brick church that was home to so many of us.

It took us all in, believers or not. Embracing us in warm, forgiving arms.

Even though I knew my work was righteous, I felt a little bruised all the same.

Some forgiveness, a warm kitchen, and the faces of some little kids?

That would suit my day just fine.

"Hey Tanya!"

I walked into the steamy kitchen through the back door. The rust-colored tiles and long steel countertops embraced me, as did the humming fluorescent lights, the crashing of the scrambled egg pans coming out of the oven, and the cinnamon oats in the big pot on the battered gas stove.

"Jasmine! I thought you weren't coming here for a while." Tanya was a marvel.

Pressed hair with perfect edges, always dressed for her bank job, Tanya was the most dedicated Panther I knew. Not part of leadership, and a person too many others over-looked, Tanya pretty much kept the Free Breakfast for Children program running, often starting and ending her day in the kitchen, between getting her own two kids to school and putting in her time as a bank teller downtown.

Today she wore burgundy slacks and a cream-colored blouse under a flowered apron. She set the shallow baking pan of eggs on the stove top and kicked the heavy oven door closed.

"I wasn't, but I missed it too much," I replied.

Tanya took off the battered gray oven mitts and ran the

back of her hand across her forehead, smoothing down the edges of her hair.

"Come here, girl," she said, arms opened wide. I dropped my big fringed leather purse on the counter and walked into her arms.

I smelled cocoa butter, a whiff of pressing iron, and eggs. Her arms were bony despite all the kitchen work, but her chest was soft against mine. The hug was quick, but surprising all the same. I'd never had a hug from a party member besides my boyfriend Jimmy. And Tanya and I? We liked each other, and respected one another, but weren't particularly close. She was a woman I always wished could become a friend, but there was never enough spare time.

"Thanks for the welcome, Tanya. What can I do to help?"

"Start serving up the food. The kids'll be here any minute, and then you know how things get."

I grabbed paper plates for the eggs and melamine bowls for the oatmeal and stacked them on the counter next to the long metal serving trays.

Tanya's hug was strange, but a lot of things were strange these days. Ever since the standoff at DeFremary Park, people had started treating me different. And then word got out that I'd taken part in busting Oakland Party founder Huey Newton out of prison. People were either terrified of me, or wanted to take care of me somehow.

I was grateful that some folks just treated me like a friend. Maybe Tanya and I would get there. Seemed like it.

"Who else is here?" I asked.

"Leroy and George are setting up the dining room, but that's it today. We're a little short, so..." She scooped eggs onto the paper plates with a metal serving spoon and handed them to me to set onto the trays. "It's a good thing you stopped by."

"Tanya." I stopped myself. Wasn't sure exactly how to ask what I needed to.

One tray was full, so I scooted the full one aside and started on a second.

"What?" she asked, still scooping egg onto plates.

I kept up with her pace, trying to think. How in the Powers could I put this?

"Have you ever noticed anything strange here at the kitchen?"

She snorted at that. "You mean, besides finding out that honest-to-Goddamn shape-shifting panthers are bringing in the powdered milk and oats and spouting off about Frantz Fanon?"

I grinned at that. She had a point. She also seemed to have the eggs under control. I set out a couple more empty trays, then moved over to the ten-gallon pot of oatmeal on the stove, grabbing a ladle from the hood overhead.

"No. I mean like that snake thing I was battling at HQ. Or white spiders."

Tanya's brow wrinkled at that. "White spiders? That's strange. The only spiders I see in the kitchen are daddy longlegs or the little brown ones. We shoo those outside. Should I be watching for white spiders now?"

I stopped ladling out the oatmeal, because even with my back to her, I could feel Tanya had stopped scooping eggs and was staring at me. So I turned. Sure enough, hands on her aproned hips, small scowl on her face, Tanya was waiting for an answer.

Hoping I hadn't just blown it, I took in a big breath and dropped into my center to steady myself. As much experience as I had with this sorcerous shit, talking to mundanes about it still made me feel uneasy. But we were all part of this army now.

Children's voices filtered through the swinging wood door that led into the church hall where breakfast was served. Damn. I could hear Leroy and George greeting the kids. Hear the voices, excited for a warm meal, happy to see their friends, excited even for the little lecture that accompanied breakfast. Black history. Black power. Black pride.

What we all needed right about now. I dug it. And I had other work to do here. And I still had to figure out the right way to talk to people about it, and to make sure danger wasn't creeping around behind my back, undermining everything the Panthers worked for.

"Let's get this breakfast ready. I'll keep talking as we work."

Tanya nodded and turned to scrape the last of the eggs onto plates. Then I felt her at my side, sliding the bowls I'd filled onto more serving trays.

"So. There's a weird cosmic battle going on. And we've seen white spiders appearing in strange places where spiders had no right to be. We think they're magic. Maybe even spies."

I could smell Tanya's nervousness rising. Couldn't blame her.

"This is so not what I signed up for, you dig?" She shoved a full tray down the counter next to the stove and slammed another down, grabbing more bowls.

Great, Jasmine. You've terrified your comrade. I shook my head. Should be used to it by now. But I likely never would.

"None of us did. But it's what's happening. The cops are killing people and the Feds have us under magical attack."

"The Feds?" She backed away from me. "The Feds have magic?"

I nodded. "Straight up Solomonic Temple magic. Old. As strong as my sorcery. Maybe stronger."

"I don't know what any of that means...but... How do you know? And is leadership hip to all this?"

"Doreen and I told them just last night. We had to. It's part of what went down when we broke Huey out. And part of how me and Fred got attacked at HQ."

"The snake thing," she whispered.

"The snake thing. And these white spiders are part of it, somehow. I've got a pretty good handle on the snakes, but the spiders need watching. And we need more help with that."

We loaded up the last of the bowls onto the trays. The children's voices had quieted down; there was just George's voice, rising and falling through the kitchen door. They were going to be ready for breakfast any minute.

"So I got permission from leadership to talk to you about it."

Tanya clutched her arms in front of her chest. "Why me?"

"Because I trust you, Tanya. You work hard for the Party. But more than that. You watch. You listen. And you keep your mouth shut."

She nodded at that, face tight, mouth small. "Yeah."

"You now have security clearance, Tanya. Leadership told me I could give it to you."

"But you're not..."

"I'm not leadership exactly. But I am in charge of sorcery. And I say we need your help."

Leroy came loping through the swinging door, his shoulders practically filling the whole doorway, crammed into a tight red turtleneck shirt tucked into bell-bottom jeans cinched at his waist with a tooled leather belt and hammered brass buckle. The man was just big, from his raggedy red-tinged natural and impressive sideburns on down to his boots.

He nodded at Tanya and then grinned wide when he saw me. It was good to be back at Father Neil's church for breakfast. I really had missed it.

"Breakfast ready?" he rumbled.

"It is," Tanya replied. "But"—she looked at me—"can I ask him, Jasmine?"

"He knows."

Tanya just looked up at Leroy, who dwarfed her. He put a hand on her slender shoulder and looked her in the eyes.

"I know, sister. And it's about damn time."

Tanya took in a jagged breath, then shook out her hands.

"Okay. I'm gonna ponder this, Jasmine."

Then she nodded at the trays lining the counter.

"Let's get this food out to the children," she said.

We all grabbed a tray. Leroy led the way through the swinging door.

In the church hall turned into dining room, three dozen bright faces looked up from the long tables and turned our way, smiles and all.

Take that, Federal Agents.

The revolution begins with breakfast, your spiders and snakes be damned.

2

CAROL

Carol tossed the straight sheet of long blond hair over her shoulder and settled into the creaky chair, dumping the heavy, patchwork leather shoulder bag at her feet.

There was usually open floor between the wooden shelves holding everything from jar candles, to books on sorcery, witchcraft, saints, and magic, to jars and jars of herbs and shells, porcupine quills, and the richly painted walls covered in gleaming metal milagros. Not this afternoon.

This afternoon, watched over by a blue-mantled Guadalupe backed by golden rays of light, the little shop was crowded with folding chairs. Las Manos was in session.

Rosalia shot her a look from across the crowded shop. Carol winced and shrugged her shoulders in apology. She knew that she was late, but she'd fought traffic all the way because of an accident on the freeway.

At least she didn't need to take the bus anymore. Terrance had seen fit to give her his three-years-ago-model Oldsmobile. Likely to keep her placid. Shut her up. And as a bribe to get her to back him instead of Jasmine and Cecelia.

As though any of that was going to happen.

The challenge they'd given him was pretty clear. Either he got his shit together, or the Association sorcerers were in rebellion.

Ernesto looked back at her and smiled. That warmed Carol up inside. She was glad she had dressed well, but not Mansion well. No A-line skirt and demure nylons today. Under her short, rust-brown leather coat, Carol wore a flowered peasant blouse that exposed her collarbones and a dangling, white-gold tree of life pendant Helen had given her as an early Solstice present. The blouse flowed over a new pair of bell-bottom jeans.

Nothing had really "happened" between her and Ernesto, but they inched closer to it day by day, calamity by calamity. The hotter the sorcery and the higher the stakes, the more their bodies and souls responded to each other.

Busting Huey Newton out of jail had brought them to their first real kiss. They'd needed to do something to ground the wild sorcerous energy they'd raised on that hill above San Luis Obispo. Energy that had blown the gates right off of California Men's Colony, where the Black Panther was being held.

And the kiss was great. Sweet. Sexy. Liquid.

But they hadn't had a chance to repeat the act. Not yet.

Rosalia cleared her throat and Carol blushed. Damn. She really needed to get a grip on herself. Too many psychics packed the little room today.

Las Manos had invited Ernesto and Carol as honored guests, making it even worse that she had traipsed in late. Las Manos never let in outsiders. At least, that was what Rosalia said.

Rosalia was the only member of the secret society of magas and hechiceras Carol had ever seen.

Paying better attention, she zeroed in on the man speaking. He was tall, gangly, with a nose almost as sharp as Rosalia's, though his eyes were rich brown instead of her arresting citrine. He had a subtle accent, not as pronounced as Rosalia's was to Carol's ears, but still marking him as a native Spanish speaker.

Dressed neatly in chocolate-colored hopsack trousers and a beige-and-brown Western-style shirt, his voice was in contrast with his plain attire. It sounded like a trumpet of war.

"La Raza is uniting. Rising up! They must have our help. The Brown Berets are doing the work of all Chicanos in Los Angeles."

He looked at Rosalia, Ernesto, and Carol then. Scanning their faces. Everyone in the room was silent, but for the slight squeaks and groans as bodies shifted in the wooden folding chairs. Carol could almost hear the room breathing. These were magic workers who knew how to pay attention.

She could feel their magic, pressing on her skin. Disciplined. Contained. Potent. With an undercurrent of something ancient that she couldn't quite place.

The gangly man spoke again, gesturing toward her. Then at Ernesto and Rosalia.

"These people have stepped up to help the revolution! They gave aid to our sisters and brothers in the Black Panther Party. Should we not do the same? What good is our magic, if we do not use it in the people's time of need?"

Slowly, a young woman, not much older than Carol, stood. Strong thighs strained against khaki trousers. A brown beret was perched on her wavy fall of dark brown hair. Her skin was darker than Ernesto's, but not as dark as

Jasmine's. She was clearly what Carol now knew to call mestizo. Largely indigenous, with some of the Spanish conquistadores in the mix. Ernesto had explained one night, over a second glass of forbidden wine, that the mixture usually happened because of rape. The spoils of colonization.

Her Minnesota background hadn't quite prepared her for this world. But she was glad she was here now.

"For those who don't yet know me, my name is Verónica. I thank you for inviting me here, Rosalia. Mi tío"—the young woman gestured at the man who had been speaking —"he knows I don't have much use for magic. Perhaps because I was too lazy to study as hard as he wanted me to."

There were chuckles around the room at that. The woman smiled. "But he is right. La Raza needs you. The Brown Berets are being beaten in the streets. High school students are having their eyeglasses smashed by the batons of la policía."

Rosalia walked behind the chairs and rustled behind the counter. Carol smelled copal and frankincense rising up. And then roses. The hechicera must be making an offering to Guadalupe. The Virgin. The one the indigenous Mexicans still called on as Tonantzin. The incense hovered over the room, which Carol swore everyone inhaled collectively. As one body.

Everyone needed a reminder of the grace blessing their sorcery. And a reminder that, as the Virgin watched over the people, so should they.

"Thank you, Rosalia, for reminding us we are under La Virgin's protection." The original speaker said. "This is why we honor you, no? You remind us of what is important." He turned to the rest of the room. Heads were nodding.

Rosalia had once told Carol and Ernesto that she was

the unofficial head of a leaderless organization. This must be what she meant. Rosalia knew what was needed. So her words and actions had weight. Carol tucked that thought away in one of the folds of her mind. It felt important. Like one of those things you couldn't really be taught, but had to learn somehow anyway.

If you wanted to become a person who got respect.

And Carol had never really been that person. She'd been fighting her diminishment the whole time, ever since she first came to the Mansion, plucked out of her ordinary working-class Minnesota home at the age of thirteen. Everyone in the Association had discounted her. Passed her over. Underestimated her worth.

Everyone except Jasmine, her best friend. And Ernesto, who was Professor Alvarez, now her former teacher.

And Rosalia. Rosalia had seen exactly who Carol was the first day she pushed through the door to this shop in East Los Angeles.

Carol was finally starting to believe she had power. So yeah, she would tuck this new bit of information away.

The young woman was speaking again.

"We heard stories about what happened up in Oakland, with the Panthers. A sorcery that can stop la policía, and keep our people safe from harm. What the Brown Berets want to know is, will you do this for us? Will Las Manos join your hands with our fists? We need you. The people need you. Now is the time."

Then the young woman nodded and picked up an army surplus book bag, which she slung across her chest.

"I'll leave now, Tío. I've said what I needed to say. I hope you will consider my words." She looked at Rosalia, who met her gaze with firmness. A look of respect and a small jolt of power crossed the space between them.

"Thank you, hechicera," the young woman said, "I am proud to have been here today. The Chicano Moratorium Committee thanks you. La Raza thanks you."

Then she walked out the door. Clear and sure as anything. Not waiting for a response. Not looking at anyone else.

Carol sat back in her chair, not even realizing she'd been leaning forward, toward the young woman. Captured by her. That was power.

Carol wanted some of that.

And seeing it in someone her own age.... Someone who hadn't been around for years. Someone who...didn't even use magic, but used everything else she had with great authority, even in a room streaming with power?

It wasn't just Jasmine who could have that.

That made it seem possible that someone like Carol could have that power, too.

"I'll be damned," she whispered to herself. Then looked up.

Rosalia was staring at her with those citrine eyes. Smiling.

3

DOREEN

The flower shop smelled good.

Day lilies and green fern. Pink and red carnations. The slight spice of orange marigolds. They were all in buckets up front, visible through the big plate glass windows, enticing people in off the street.

Smokey Robinson crooned softly from the little shop radio behind the counter. Occasional street noises joined the mix, but mostly, the shop was quiet in the mid-week, post-lunch lull.

The roses were in the refrigerated case, along with the orchids for corsages, but every time Doreen opened the case, their subtle scent wafted out to join the rest.

Of course, hothouse roses were grown for looks, not scent. Give Doreen wild garden roses any day. The white ones that smelled of licorice in mid-June were her favorites.

"What do we need to organize next?" Patrice asked.

Doreen's longtime friend and new lover peered over the notebook she'd started carrying in her purse ever since they'd formed their little training group with Drake, the thirteen-year-old boy who was turning out to be really something, magically. Patrice sat at the end of the long, high table Doreen was working at.

Patrice was in Doreen's favorite orange dress today. It matched her lipstick and set off her dark skin. The knit clung to her lush curves.

Doreen looked back to the red roses and white calla lilies she was arranging in tall vases, getting an order ready for a pre-Christmas party. She filled out the base with green fern. No baby's breath, the order specified. Fine with her. People were paying a lot of money for these arrangements. They could get what they wanted.

And she couldn't let Patrice distract her. Flowers and magic. That was the focus of the afternoon.

Doreen liked arranging flowers, and she certainly needed the money, but it was hard to work when it felt simultaneously like the world was on fire and her people were drowning.

"Doreen?" Patrice prodded.

"Sorry. We need to get more spell bags made. That one group that's been coming to the attic is good enough now that they can help Drake get other people working on it. We just need to find the space, since Father Neil still feels uncomfortable about us doing magic in the church hall."

Patrice made some notes with a small silver pen.

"Okay. I can get them working on that. We have enough supplies?"

Doreen tucked a curl of fern so the frond fanned out around the top of the tall vase, forming a green skirt around the stand of white and red flowers.

"We should. But if not, let me know. I'll see what I can rustle together. Meanwhile, I need to get people back out to the playground to practice moving energy together."

"You think it's worth it?" Patrice asked.

"The more magic that people are confident in working regularly, the more help they'll be in another battle."

Doreen thought back to DeFremary Park, and the way people had rallied, lending their bodies to the magic Doreen and Jasmine wove into a big web of protection.

"Although sometimes it just seems like too little, too late."

Patrice nodded, thoughtful, and looked across the shop and out the window onto the street. A woman in a tall green headwrap and a black wool coat walked in front of the store, carrying shopping bags.

Doreen set her ferns down on the table and walked over to her lover, putting a hand on Patrice's shoulder.

"You're right. It is too little, too late." Doreen said.

Patrice didn't look at her, just put a hand up to cover Doreen's. Doreen knew this was hard. It was hard for Doreen, too, and she'd known sorcery and magic her whole life.

"But everything is too little, too late. College kids are getting their heads bashed in, Patrice. We're getting magically attacked behind our own wards right now. All of our organizations have been infiltrated."

Patrice took her hand away and turned to look at Doreen. Her eyes were angry.

"You think I don't know that? You think I haven't lived here my whole life, and seen what happens?"

Doreen pulled up a tall stool and sat next to Patrice, bumping her orange-wrapped thighs with her own more sensible navy skirt.

"Hey. I didn't mean that. I just meant that we have to work with what we have. Like we always do. We're masters at making do. And that got us through at DeFremary Park. And it's gonna get us through again."

The shop phone jangled from behind her.

Doreen gave Patrice's arm a squeeze and went to the golden-yellow wall phone and picked up the receiver.

"Oakland Blooms, Doreen speaking."

It was Helen. Sounding frantic.

Doreen rooted her feet and drew up some of her fire. Patrice's head jerked at that. She could feel when Doreen did the smallest amounts of sorcery now. Even Doreen just calling up her Element had an effect on Patrice. That was good. Meant she could be trained even more deeply than Doreen had thought at first.

All of that flashed through Doreen's head in a single thought. Meanwhile, Helen was still squawking in her ear.

"Helen. I need you to stop talking for a moment. Take a breath."

Doreen felt for her connection to Helen, felt the Fire struggling to get through to Helen's Water, which always manifested itself as ice. There it was. Erratic, but still there. Doreen reached out over the distance, trying to stabilize her friend.

Something was really wrong.

Terrance Sterling. Doreen shook her head. The current president of the Association of Magical Arts and Sorcery was proving to be both a loose cannon and an obstruction. She and Jasmine had been battling him for the last month, and reports from Carol down in Los Angeles were very troubling.

The man was falling apart.

Helen was confirming that now. Doreen had seen it for herself when she was in LA, but apparently the problem had escalated further. Doreen wondered why no one else in the Association seemed to have noticed. Or maybe they had, but didn't care.

"Do you need me to come down?" Doreen asked.

Patrice mouthed, *What's wrong?*

Doreen shook her head again.

"Helen. Helen. Take a breath. Do. You. Need. Me. To. Come. Down?"

Doreen waved for Patrice's notebook and pen.

"Send it to me." Doreen closed her eyes. Opened up her psychic field. A wash of emotion hit her, followed by a sheet of Helen's Ice. Doreen swept those aside. She could feel Patrice at her side, waiting, smelled the combination of cocoa butter and Aqua Net, but she couldn't concentrate on that right now.

She needed to open to what Helen was sending.

The images were muddled at first. Confused. Terrance, writhing on the floor. Scratching at his arms. The spiders in the Mansion temple room. A flash of Carol's blond hair.

A sense of foreboding. Something big. Watching. Waiting. Biding its time. A big, fat, white something. Spinning out a web.

There. There it was. The sigil Helen was trying to send her with her mind. The one Jasmine said Carol had been channeling? It turned out Helen had found a notebook of Terrance's. The book was covered with this sigil. Page after page of it.

Doreen's eyes snapped open and she gestured for a clean page. Patrice flipped her notebook open and handed Doreen the silver pen. Doreen nodded to the clipboard used for orders, hanging from a nail on the wall. Patrice shoved it under the notebook.

Doreen began to draw. The sigil practically drew itself. As though it was connected to her blood and breath. As though it had taken over the synapses sparking in her brain.

It grew large in her mind as she drew. Over and over, she traced the shape, until she was sure she had it right.

"Okay. Okay. Stop sending. Helen. I'm done. I'm done." The silver pen fell from her right hand, clattering on the black-and-white tiled floor. Patrice gently took the clipboard and notebook from her and set them on the long, tall table, then bent to pick up the pen. The metal pen shocked her, and Patrice dropped it again, looking up at Doreen, fear in her eyes.

Doreen felt sick to her stomach. She wanted to run down the street, far away from here. The sigil had poisoned her. Poisoned this little shop that had been such a refuge all these years.

If this was what they were up against? It was even worse than she already imagined.

"Helen. I need to. I can't. I'll call you tonight. I'm sorry. I'm sorry. I can't right now. But I will. I promise. We'll get through this, too."

Doreen hung up the phone. And walked into her lover's arms.

She needed all the comfort she could take right now.

Then she needed to close up shop, take a shower, and wait for Jasmine to get home.

4

———

SNAKES AND SPIDERS

The room was dim, as always. Samuels was grateful. He could finally take his dark glasses off, and slip them into his breast pocket.

It was funny, he'd gotten used to always wearing them, to protect his night-sensitized eyes, but sometimes he had to admit, he missed the light. And the weight of glass, wire, and plastic on his face grew tiresome.

But he'd thrown in his lot with the shadowed spaces built by the increasingly crazy Master.

J. Edgar Hoover.

A man who had almost had him killed last week, after an hour of what would have seemed like extreme torture, if Samuels hadn't been in charge of much worse torture and interrogation sessions himself. The sigil tattoo still burned and ached on the soft skin under his right arm. A little magical reminder that his soul was owned by the FBI.

He would be dead now, Samuels knew, if the Master didn't think Samuels was still useful to the Bureau.

The Master ruled the Bureau. Ruled them all. He was the

Temple builder. The puppet controller. The white spider at the center of their massive web.

The slightly portly white man with the square face sat behind a giant, polished wood desk in the lead-lined room, white shirt still crisp, black-and-burgundy-striped tie knotted just so under the thickening chin.

Black-suited sentries in dark glasses guarded the doors and the one window in the room. The window that always had heavy velvet curtains closed.

The Master had his right sleeve rolled up, rubber tourniquet banding his bicep as he plunged his daily "vitamins" into an engorged vein.

The shots kept him going, day and night, despite his age. Samuels always wondered when the Master was going to have to pay the price for years of use. A man couldn't get by on methamphetamine, coffee, rich food, and no sleep forever. Even with the aid of magic.

"Samuels."

He was summoned. The Master rolled his sleeve down, carelessly threading a silver link through a white cuff.

"Report."

The tattoo under Samuels' arm flared with pain. An ordinary tattoo would have healed by now, but the magic had been twisted to give him constant pain. Proximity to the Master increased the reminder that, powerful magician or not, Samuels was still owned.

He stilled his mind, ignoring the pain and the sense of prickling under his own snow-white shirt and black suit coat. He lightly gripped his left wrist with his right hand, keeping his hands from combing through the black sweep of pomaded hair on his head.

No one ever rattled Samuels. Ever. Except the Master, who almost *always had, in these tiny, subtle ways. Samuels had to figure out a way to get his discipline back. And regain his position in the Temple. Those damned Panthers kept botching his assignments. What should have been simple was ending up a tangled mess, again and again.*

So Samuels was not currently in the Master's favor.

The Master grinned slightly, a temporary grimace on his smashed-potato-like face.

Samuels locked his mind down more sharply, then found the words the Master needed to hear, even though the report he had to give would make a weaker man want to off himself in his garage rather than speak the words about the very situation that had already ended with Samuels chained in the middle of a magical circle, the Master sweating over him, drawing sigils in the air.

Samuels cleared his throat, and focused on the seal above the Master's head.

"As you know, the new infiltrator is dead. I have no idea how it happened, sir. He disobeyed all orders, and the compulsion he was under must have been insufficient."

Samuels felt the Master staring at him, and his spidery probing of Samuels' defenses. Samuels breathed a small personal sigil into his aura, hoping to shore up his wards. There were things in his mind the Master needed to never see or hear.

"And why did the compulsion fail?" the Master rasped.

"Well sir, we're looking into that. He was very tightly bound, and the compulsion was set to inflict extreme compression around his lungs and vital organs each time he even thought of escape. It should have felt like he was suffocating to death."

The Master just stared at him. Samuels could feel it, even as he studiously trained his eyes on the shield.

A single finger tapped the wooden desk.

"There are some things a man fears more than death," the Master said. "I think you understand that, now."

Samuels swallowed. "Yes sir."

"Yes, Master," Hoover said.

Okay. That was a new demand.

"Yes, Master."

"What I need from you, Mr. Samuels, is to find out why these fucking Panthers do not fear us anymore. And why we never knew they could change shape."

5

———

JASMINE

The old, ramshackle white Victorian that held the Panther's West Oakland headquarters was never quiet, no matter what time of day it was.

I was sitting in an afternoon meeting with a bunch of leadership. It was funny how quickly my role in the Party had changed. Once they figured out Doreen and I were actual assets, with real power, even the most skeptical members treated me with more respect.

That was kind of weird, but felt good, too. And if it meant fewer folks to get in our way, I was cool with that.

Cigarette smoke filled the air. Leroy was in the room. Tarika. Barbara. Carlos. And my love, Jimmy, slim, muscled, and handsome, sitting in a rickety wooden chair, left ankle resting on his right knee. He wore my favorite burgundy turtleneck today, over black bellbottoms, and was a real distraction.

Huey Newton should have been there, but like Fred Hampton and Deborah, he was in hiding. For now at least.

Until we knew how the Feds were going to react to these

Panthers not only being alive, but free, everyone was laying low.

We couldn't even talk about it in HQ. No matter how many times security swept the place for bugs, no one ever felt secure. There were always bugs they didn't find. And infiltrators and provocateurs that seemed like the most committed Party members ever.

But leadership had to keep meeting, despite security concerns. We were always circumspect on the phone, and didn't talk about patently illegal operations—like busting Huey Newton out of prison—inside four walls.

I stood in front of an old rolling blackboard, white chalk making my fingertips gritty. I was trying to not wipe them on my jeans or touch my black sweater.

I'd drawn the sigil Helen sent to Doreen up on the board. It made me feel queasy just to look at it. That was one bad sigil. And not bad in a good way. Just. Bad.

"What does it mean?" Leroy asked, stroking his ruddy sideburns. "And how do you know it comes from the Feebs?"

Jimmy leaned back in his chair, trying to look relaxed, but I could see the tension in his whipcord muscled arms under the purple turtleneck sweater, and his jaw looked tight.

"We're still working on what it means." I tried to wipe the chalk from my hands on a tissue, but the drying grit wouldn't go away. I'd need to wash them when the meeting was over.

I blinked away some cigarette smoke.

"But it's pretty clearly something from the Feds. Too many of us are getting the sigil and it always seems to trace back to other events."

"Like what?" Jimmy asked.

"It shows up when the spiders are around in Los Angeles. It's been seen connected to the main Fed Doreen and I think is sending out the snakes. The guy controlling Lizard."

"How'd Lizard fight him, then?"

Lizard had been a soldier with the Los Angeles Panthers. He'd fought beside Roland, Peaches, Geronimo, and a man called Cotton during the shoot out with the brand new LAPD SWAT team...and then something happened.

He got taken over somehow. Turned into an informant. He was supposed to kill Huey when we busted him out of jail. Instead, he killed some guards and ended up dead himself.

Another sacrifice to the cause. Eighteen damn years old.

Carol had been able to piece that together from the connection he'd somehow forged with her. Lizard had appeared to her, asking for help, but she didn't know who he was. And before she could figure out how to free him from whatever magic bound him, he was dead.

It was tragic that we hadn't made the connection before we did the huge operation to free Huey. Maybe Carol could have helped Lizard before we went in. But we frankly hadn't spent much time with the LA Panthers helping with the operation. There simply wasn't time. We had coordinated the magic and the prison break in two separate groups, only planning together briefly, to make sure our plans meshed.

Besides, Doreen and Ernesto said that sometimes magical sendings didn't look or feel the same when you were standing in front of the physical form.

Which was another piece of lore to tuck away and examine when I had time. If that day ever came.

"I wish we knew, exactly. I did my best to trace the energy signatures, and from what I could feel, Lizard was dedicated enough to the revolution to fight the magic even though it must have been crushing him to death."

I swallowed.

"And I mean that literally. He was being squeezed until he couldn't breathe, every time he tried to get free."

Leroy tapped his cigarette out into an already overflowing amber glass ashtray.

"But he was killed by a shot to the head," he said.

"That's right. When he was running away. After not killing Huey. Our theory is that the magic slowed him down."

If I stopped and thought too much about it, the reality was terrifying. Bullets and magic, both controlled by the State. Both being used against us.

Whenever I wished we could just feed kids, plant gardens, keep people healthy with our ambulances and clinics, and provide safe escort for our elders, I remembered that *they* had magic and guns.

And that they wanted us all dead.

"And you think the sigil has something to do with it," Tarika said.

I looked at her, focusing on the thin wrists emerging from the cuffs of the deep green blouse with the sharply pointed collar. A magnificent natural bloomed around her head.

Despite their youth, these people all outranked me. And not being able to give clear answers was making me uncomfortable.

What in all the Powers was wrong with me? I would have thought my confidence would have increased alongside my sorcerous power and my position. Instead, I simply felt the burden of it all. And the holes in what I could do, and the questions I simply couldn't answer.

Barbara cleared her throat. The fine eyes and silver glasses, that yes, seemed to see through me, as though she had magic of her own.

She did, of course. All the shifters did.

"I do. But we don't know what all the connections are, yet. There are a lot of pieces to the puzzle. All I can promise is that we're working on it."

"You and who else?" Leroy asked.

"Doreen. And some sorcerers in LA."

Leroy ran a hand across his mouth.

"You trust these people?"

"With my life," I said. The ocean inside me rose up toward high tide, making me restless. I needed out of the smoky room.

"Look," I said, "I've known these people for years, all but one of them, and she's vouched for. They risked themselves to break Huey out. If that isn't proof enough that we can trust them, there's nothing else I can offer."

I couldn't stand it anymore, and wiped my damn chalky hands on my pants.

Leroy stood up, signaling that their meeting with me was coming to a close.

"A lot of infiltrators risked their lives, too. Including that man. Lizard. And who knows how many other people." He held my gaze. "You dig what I'm saying?"

For the first time since coming closer to the inner circle, his eyes drilled into me as though he might not trust me one bit.

"Yeah," I replied. "I dig."

And it worried the hell out of me.

6

———

JASMINE

After the meeting at HQ, I was jumping out of my skin. The fact that Leroy clearly didn't trust me now made me angry, frustrated, and a little bit afraid.

I had to move some damn energy, so I laced up some sneakers, threw on some sweatpants I'd stolen from Jimmy, and headed out for a run.

Doreen argued about me going running on my own at dusk, but there was no way I was settling in at home. Despite the December chill, sweat beaded my upper lip and slid across my lower back. My T-shirt grew soggy with it. I'd need to hit the shower when I got home.

I felt like garbage, but needed to run anyway.

One more mile to go.

Sneakers smacking the cracking sidewalks, I avoided tree roots and dog shit. Two brothers in berets and leather jackets walked slowly together, spines straight, just being a visible presence under the neighborhood streetlights. Letting folks know the Panthers cared.

Police had increased harassment since the standoff at DeFremary Park, stopping people for no reason. Frisking teens coming home from school. Taking men in for questioning, only to release them three hours later, after they'd missed their clock-in time at work.

The cops were freaked. I'd heard a brother was living in panther form in his jail cell. And the fact that Huey had escaped, and Fred, Deborah, and Ronald were still alive, had them extra scared.

When cops are scared, they get angry. Angry cops harass whoever they see as weak, in order to get to the strong.

So, the cops increased their patrols, and the Panthers did, too.

Old folks came out on their stoops to say hello on occasion, or to lodge a complaint.

A group of kids ran up to the men, shrieking, asking for who knows what. That made me smile.

I liked that people had learned to trust us. That there was no fear. That's how it should be. Community safety. Food. Medicine. Education. Someday maybe we'd even get to shelter, though we didn't quite have the resources for that yet.

I trusted that would come.

People were very nervous. Drake and Doreen had been working overtime with the training.

I was still trying to keep my shit together. It was really a good thing the semester was out, because no way was I dealing with the Association, the Feds, the cops, the weirdness with leadership, *and* the new emotional upheaval on top of writing papers.

Running was all that was saving me. I'd been having visions of Mr. Black Suit. That snake. They were freaking me out.

I hadn't told anyone about the visions, and was still trying to figure out if they connected to the mood swings. I should have asked Doreen for her help, but that just wasn't gonna happen. No way did I want her rooting around in my head right now.

There was just too much going on.

And if that snake really was attached to me, the Panthers would never trust me to help them again.

I shooed those thoughts, and the lingering, papery feel of the snake, to the back of my head.

Turning the corner, I let my feet take me by the boarded-up windows of an abandoned home, past the liquor store on the corner. The barbershop door opened; a burst of male laughter emerged on the winter breeze.

Coming up on one of the little back streets—not quite alleys, but narrower than the street I was on—I heard scuffling, yelping, quiet *thunks*, and what sounded like a boy's voice.

I ran past the street opening, then slowed to a stop. Listened. Regulated my breathing. Closed my eyes for a moment and reached out with all my senses.

The smell of oily asphalt and cracked chicken bones. Grease. Cooked cabbage. Spilled beer. Sweat. The tang of gun oil.

And fear. Drake. It was Drake. And he was trying to use magic.

I pulled on the waters of the bay and planted my feet. Since working with the Panthers, I knew enough to assess first. It was good sorcery training, too.

What in all the Powers was happening?

Cops. Three cops. I could smell them, now. Smell their tobacco and polyester and yeah, the gun oil was from them.

Looking around, I didn't see the two brothers from the Party on this block. Damn. Just me, a concrete wall, and a chain-link fence across the way.

I turned into the small, side street. One cop had his nightstick under Drake's chin, forcing his face up, grinding Drake's head against a wooden fence. The cop's other hand, pink with scars, and huge, was twisting at Drake's brown jacket, holding him still.

Drake was waving his right hand around, trying to zap the guy. But he wasn't connecting to the spell bag bulging in his jacket pocket. The cops must have moved too fast.

"Think you can do magic on us, boy? Think you niggers can teach us a lesson?"

The other two cops stood back a little. One of them smoked a hand-rolled cigarette. They both laughed, watching Drake struggle against the fence. Against the white cop's hands.

"Think those Panthers are gonna help dirt like you?"

"Teach him a lesson, Chuck," the cop with the cigarette said.

The power of Water rolled through me when I heard that. How dare they?

My fury tasted of salt and the deepest silt in the bottom of the bay. There was no part of me that was not water.

The third cop saw me.

"Hey look, someone came to save you, boy!" he laughed.

I became a massive wave. A wave of furious energy that slammed the cop against the building, and tumbled everyone and everything in its wake.

Drake, the cops, the garbage cans, a kid's bent-up banana seat bike. They all rolled and tumbled and slammed against walls, fences, and asphalt.

The waves inside kept building. The energy of water kept slamming out and forward. I was the only one who knew it was water. By their shouts and grunts and squeals, I knew there was just shock and human pain at being slammed and lifted through the air.

In ways I never even knew I could.

In ways that felt so good to me, I could taste that, too, alongside the salt and silt, and the taste of rotting alley garbage at the back of my throat.

"Jaaaaasssmmiiinnnnnne!"

Drake's voice. Drake. Right. Fuck.

I had to get a grip. Slow the tide. Dam the rolling waves.

Closing my eyes, I felt my body begin to rock, back and forth, front to back, my breath syncing itself to the motion, gentling the waves of blue energy and fire, slowing them, until they were small waves slapping the pylons of a pier or lapping at a sandy shore.

And then the blue fire was gone. I fell to the ground, slamming my face into asphalt, right wrist smacking the metal of a tipped-over trash can.

Footsteps running toward me.

"What the hell?"

"Who is that?"

"It's Jasmine, man!"

Hands gently shook my shoulders. "Hey, sister. Wake up."

I struggled to lift my mind back to the surface, enough to talk. Enough to blink. I couldn't do it. Too much.

"We've gotta get them outta here before those cops... what the fuck happened here?" a voice said.

"Damn, man. I don't know. You right, though. Gotta get these two away."

"How's it gonna look then, us carrying two unconscious people outta here?"

The voices paused.

"I can stand." Drake's voice again. Weak. What had I done?

Drake's soft breath on my cheek. "Jasmine. You gotta wake up. If we don't get out of here, the cops are gonna...I don't know."

Drawing one huge breath up from my belly, I felt it barely raise my chest. But it was enough. I pried open my eyes. It was full dark now.

My mouth was dry as dust. And I felt...blank.

"Water?" I managed to croak out.

Someone put something against my lips. Metal. Tipped it against my mouth. I coughed. Brandy.

But it was moisture. I took another sip.

"Help me."

Two strong sets of arms hoisted me to my sneakered feet.

"We got a car around the corner we can borrow. Let's get you there."

Someone else picked up Drake and carried him. He wasn't doing as well as I was.

We picked our way out of that little side street, leaving the wreckage behind.

Wincing as my battered body limped to the car, I couldn't even care.

Stumbling onto the main street, my nose caught the papery scent of snake.

The black-suited man was out there.

7

DOREEN

After Jasmine left, slamming the front door behind her, Doreen decided to do some work.

It was getting late for supper, and she should have been cooking. Then winding down, getting some rest. The florist shop still needed to be opened in the morning, and she was the one to do it. Her boss was barely there, now that the Thanksgiving holiday was over and before they got slammed for Christmas. She trusted Doreen to take care of the few orders coming in and the customers who walked through the door.

That was good. Except when Doreen had a lot of other things to take care of.

But after forty-three years, she knew herself. She was too distracted to cook, or read, or watch the news, not while Jasmine was running around in whatever state she was in.

Doreen's bedroom was her refuge, and had been for the decade since Hector had been killed by the sheriffs in the Los Angeles hills. She'd hidden there, at first. Then made it a place of rest.

And lately, the white coverlet had been pulled back to welcome Patrice's lush body and her smile.

That was a good thing.

No Patrice tonight, though. The bed was neatly made. Doreen's navy coat was hung inside the closet. The Ponds cold cream and L'Heure Bleu were on the nightstand.

And on top of her dresser, a small altar waited. Creamy white tapers ready to be lit. Incense stand with a charcoal disc inside. Matchbooks in a glass dish. Momma's ruby wine glass, filled with water.

Doreen palmed the metal disc that rested just beneath her collarbone. Momma's moon amulet. It had only recently surfaced again, after having been buried in all the boxes of stuff Doreen had simply shoved up in the attic when she moved to Oakland after Hector's death.

Well, clearly it was needed now. Like the big Chokwe mask from Angola, and Momma's crystal ball, both of which were on the big ancestor altar in the newly cleaned and blessed attic. What once held boxes was now a ritual space.

Like everything else in Doreen's life, space had been made, and the sorcery was coming back, full force.

"It's time now, Doreen. Get to work and ask for help."

She flicked on the two lamps on either side of her bed, turned off the overhead light, and took a deep breath.

With a snick against the cardboard matchbook, a match flared to life, and she touched the tiny flame to the waiting tapers. Candlelight bathed her hands. She shook out the match.

Doreen could have lit the candles with her own powers, but over the years had found that continuously connecting to her Element in small ways increased her sorcery and meant that when she needed to draw on Fire, it was more readily available.

There was harmony in touching one's Element whenever a sorcerer could.

"Besides, it keeps your magic clean," one of her early instructors used to say. Having returned to magic after her grief-stricken absence, Doreen had found this to be true.

"Hail Fire. Hail Air. Hail Water and Earth. I give thanks to my ancestors, to the Powers, and to sorcery itself."

The agitation inside her settled at the words. Doreen's sorcery needed to not be so bound up in whatever was happening with her niece. Jasmine had to walk her own road. The simple rituals were a reminder: Doreen had her own work to do.

Choosing one of the twin flames of the tapers as a focus, she settled into candle gazing, standing in front of the dresser altar space.

Her breath grew soft against her lips. Her belly and chest rose and fell in longer and longer cycles. Her eyes unfocused, filled with the orange and yellow glow of the flame.

Then she dropped her gaze to the glass of water, ruby crystal refracting the light of the candle flames.

"Momma, hear me please. You've helped me in the past, and I ask for your help now. We need guidance. A clear path through the thicket of violence, fear, and indecision. Won't you come?"

Tiny flames danced on the crystal facets. Doreen's eyes were drawn to the water itself, lit gold and red in the glass.

Touching the amulet resting on her chest, she breathed across the water. Momma appeared then, round face illumined by the ruby glass and flames, growing larger and larger until she rose up from the glass, and looked at Doreen's eyes with her own.

"I am here, child. What exactly are you asking me?"

Doreen gasped, then got her breath back under control. What was she asking?

"I thought I knew where we were going with all of this. But it's grown so complicated all of a sudden. From too many directions. Snakes and spiders. Federal agents. Shapeshifters. The revolution. The Association. That niece of mine..."

She stared at her beloved mother, who simply gazed back. Silent.

"There's something I'm supposed to be looking for that I'm missing. Or some words I'm supposed to hear, that I can't. Or maybe..."

"Something you are supposed to be doing that you have avoided up until this moment."

Oh no. Not that. Doreen felt the cramping of refusal in her belly. There wasn't anything good that was going to come of this. Why in all the worlds had she even thought to ask?

"Because you know it's right, child."

Momma Beatrice's eyes were kind, but her mouth was firm.

"So what am I supposed to do?" Doreen asked, in some frustration. "If I knew already, I wouldn't be asking. So how can I know what's right?"

Petulant, she knew. But damn it. Sorcery wasn't supposed to be this obscure. If the Powers wanted something from her, they could damn well be more clear about it.

"You weren't ready, child."

Doreen knew that was true. It wasn't so long ago she was still refusing her magic altogether. Wasn't even training Jasmine the way she said she would.

Well. She'd changed all that, at least. And after facing

down the Oakland Police Department, the California Men's Colony gates, and the Black Panther Party?

Doreen could face this.

Whatever it was.

So what was it?

Momma Beatrice's face flickered and wavered in the flames. Doreen held out her hands, and increased the strength of the image with her own Fire.

Suddenly, she knew she needed bare feet on the floor. The crocheted slippers were getting in the way of the flow.

Bending, she snatched them from her feet, tossing them aside. The small, nubbly, hooked rug under her feet was better, but still not enough.

Wood. She needed wood. Even though she wasn't one-hundred-percent sure why. Earth wasn't her element, but as soon as she kicked the small rug away and felt the smooth Douglas fir planks under her heels, she knew why.

Every tree held the fire of the sun within its whorls. That was how they grew.

Just like she had the Fire inside herself, the very wood that built her house held flame.

"Closer to the truth." Beatrice said inside Doreen's mind.

So. Doreen flexed her toes and sunk the balls of her feet more firmly on the floor, letting her ankles, knees, and hips adjust themselves, then lengthening her spine.

Okay. Right. Breath coming more easily, fanning her inner flame.

"Every person holds this fire," Doreen said to the image floating above the ruby cup set on her altar. "I just have to find a way to make them believe that."

"That is your larger task, Doreen. You thought you were here to do sorcery, and you are. Then you thought you were to teach the people magic for their own protection. That is good, too."

"But..."

"But child, people need to touch their fire if this damn revolution of yours is going to do any lasting good. Otherwise, they'll just look to you forever."

Doreen paused. The words still hovered on the edges of her mind, not quite sinking in. But she *felt* the meaning. She felt it all the way down to her bare toes.

And she knew it was a key.

Touching the amulet again, she felt it buzzing.

Then Momma was gone.

8

CAROL

"I can't even sense where it is," Carol said.

The fireplace in seating area of the library crackled. When Carol had first moved to the Mansion from Minnesota, she thought the fireplaces were ridiculous. Times like this, she found them comforting.

The whitewashed fireplace was on the edge of the large room, with comfortable green and blue chintz chairs in the space between two cream damask sofas that faced each other. The chairs faced the fire.

Ernesto sat across from her, in the second barrel chair. The firelight made his seal-brown hair shine with umber tones. She wanted to kiss him. But they were still not familiar enough with one another for her to break into a working session like that. And they were still so new to kissing each other, that it was hard to think of anything else.

Carol's stockinged feet curled under her bell-bottom jeans. Leaning against one of the stuffed arms of the chair, she toyed with the leather thong around her wrist, strung with one blue glass bead knotted in the center. Rosalia had given it to her before the working above the California Men's Penal Colony.

She said it would act as extra protection if Carol ever needed it. That the glass would deflect bad sorcery back at the sender.

But it would only be useful once.

Luckily, the rescue of Black Panther Huey Newton had gone off without a hitch, and the bead was still intact. Carol was still troubled that Rosalia had felt it was a necessary gift. She also knew she needed all the backup she could get, especially now.

"I mean, he was always such a strong presence, you know? And now, even when I try to read him...I don't bump up against his shields, I bump against nothing."

Ernesto nodded. "I know what you mean, maga." He pitched his voice low, so it wouldn't carry far. They'd made certain the big library room didn't have anyone hiding in between the tall walnut shelves, seeking some obscure text for research.

The place was empty, but they needed to be careful. They probably shouldn't have even been having the discussion in the Mansion, but they both felt the pull to stay in familiar territory after all the strangeness of the past weeks.

Posh and weird as it was, the Mansion was still home to the working-class girl from Minnesota and the Chicano not-quite-radical from LA, along with a dozen students, two other teachers, plus Helen Price and Terrance Sterling.

"His form is still present, but the animating force is clearly absent," Ernesto continued. "There's something missing from his eyes."

"So, I don't know if I told you this yet. Actually in all the weirdness it slipped my mind until now. But you know Terrance's fancy tie tack?"

"The Tree of Life?"

"Yeah. Well, one day when we were meeting in his office, I saw it sitting on his desk."

Ernesto leaned toward the long, low, walnut coffee table and poured some water from the pitcher into his glass. He gestured at the other glass, eyebrow raised in question.

"Sure," Carol said.

He poured the water into the second glass and set the pitcher down with a heavy thunk.

"What about it?"

"One of the gems that represent the planetary spheres on the Tree was missing. And it was Malkuth. That tiger eye that represented Earth."

Ernesto let out a slow whistle from between his teeth.

The door slid open. Helen stood there, Jackie O bob neat and sleek as always. This evening's Chanel suit was deep green, with matching low-heeled pumps.

"I thought I would find you here," Helen said. "May I join you?"

Carol gave a slight shrug to Ernesto. No way was she going to say no to Helen Price. Even if she was a little pissed off at her.

She knew Helen was protecting Terrance. Even though, for a while, it seemed as if she was siding with Jasmine and Doreen, and was going to help the cause.

"Of course," Ernesto said. "Please, come sit with us."

Helen's heels struck the wood floor until they reached the large Turkish rug that muffled her steps.

"Would you like my chair?" Ernesto started to rise.

Helen waved him back with one slim, pale hand, gold bracelet flashing from beneath the green sleeve.

"The sofa is fine with me," she said, sliding down into

the cream-colored embrace of the cushions, arranging her legs at an angle.

Carol instantly felt like she should put her feet back on the ground and her shoes back on. She had to force herself to stay exactly where she was. Carol was an adult now, and had done sorcery Helen couldn't sneeze at, whether or not she agreed that it should have been done at all.

"What are you two talking about?" Helen asked.

Carol's shoulders stiffened, and she saw Ernesto freeze slightly before taking a sip of his water.

"Would you like some water?" he asked Helen. "I can get another glass."

"No. I'm quite fine," Helen said.

And waited.

Carol sat up straighter in the cozy barrel chair, wrapping her arms around her knees. The blue glass bead dug into her wrist. Despite her feet not being on the floor, she could feel the wood everywhere in the room. Blanketing the floor. Wrapping the coffee table. Rising with the bookshelves. Burning on the hearth.

She drew the power of wood, the power of Earth more deeply into herself. Something clicked, as though the wooden pieces of a puzzle all found their exact spot, in harmony with one another.

In that moment, Carol was in harmony with herself.

"We were talking about the fact that Terrance's soul is missing and he still hasn't agreed to a soul retrieval or any kind of healing work," she said.

Ernesto choked on his water. Helen's eyebrows rose.

Carol should have felt cowed and ready to backpedal. But she didn't. She only felt strong. As strong as the trees that had formed the wood making up the room.

As strong as the manzanita and palms rooting themselves outside.

She looked at Helen. And saw fear in the older woman's tastefully made-up eyes.

Helen pulled a thin white handkerchief from her left sleeve and held it to her lips. It was almost as though she was trying to hold back words. Or tears. Or stifle a scream.

"Helen," Ernesto asked in a gentle tone. "What else do you know?"

"It was those spiders!" burst from Helen's mouth.

Carol flushed with anger.

"How long have you known?" she asked.

Helen looked at her, white-faced. A log snapped and sparked on the grate.

"How long, Helen?" Carol asked again.

"Two months."

"His soul has been gone for *two months*?" Ernesto asked.

"May I have some of that water now?" Helen asked.

Ernesto began to rise up from his chair to get a third glass, but Carol gave him a look.

"She can drink mine. I haven't touched it yet. And I want you in the room for this."

All of a sudden, the hesitation Carol had lived with her whole life was just gone. Crushed in an avalanche of anger and betrayal. These people who had been her teachers, who had made her feel so insignificant and small? They were just as stupid and messed up as anyone else in the world.

They weren't some fine sorcerers, so much better than the unwashed masses down the hill. They were cowards. And clearly flawed in ways Carol couldn't even begin to comprehend.

How in all the Powers did a person like Terrance Sterling lose his soul?

And how had none of the other one hundred sorcerers in the Association noticed or cared?

"When did you think you were going to tell the Association, Helen?" Carol asked.

"Never," Helen whispered. "I tried to tell Doreen, but then I couldn't. I just couldn't. I even went up there...and I called her. For help. But..."

"You just thought you could what, pretend nothing had happened while we all watched him foaming at the mouth? You didn't even say anything when we stood in his office and challenged him!"

"Carol," Ernesto said, then turned to Helen, whose shoulders were slumping slightly, affecting the cut of the fine green suit.

"Helen, you said it was the spiders. Do you know what happened?" he asked.

The older woman shook her perfect bob, then swallowed. She was shaking. After a moment, she went and stood in front of the fire, thin arms wrapped around herself.

"All I know is, he started having visions. Before *your* visions started, Carol. And these symbols came to him. He was excited by those at first. But they never felt right to me. I tried to get him to slow down. To take it easy. To bring in some of the other Association members who had different skills..."

She stopped then, hands covering her face.

Ernesto picked up the glass of water and brought it to her, gently nudging her arm. "Here."

Carol just sat and stared, feet finally on the Turkish rug. She felt so angry. More angry than she'd ever been before.

"But he refused, didn't he?" Carol asked. "He wanted to do it himself, didn't he? That's why he acted so strange toward me when the visions started to come."

Helen drank her water, eyes flicking to and from Carol's as though she couldn't stand to look at her for long.

"Terrance was jealous, wasn't he?" Carol said.

Ernesto and Helen were silent. A lawnmower coughed, and began to hum outside the windows.

"Terrance Sterling, head of the Association of Magical Arts and Sorcery was jealous. Of me."

Carol gave a snort of disbelief.

"Well," she said. "How are we going to force him into healing, or force him out of the Association?"

"How dare you?" Helen said.

"What? You think we haven't come to this, *still?* You think we're not going to need a conclave to discuss this? You had a chance, Helen, to do the right thing. And you failed."

"Carol," Ernesto said.

"No. I'm done. Helen, when you went up to Oakland to meet with Doreen, we all thought you'd come to your senses. And you know what? If you had, things may have not gotten this bad. So tell us, what happened?"

Helen sat down heavily on the sofa, almost dropping her water glass. Ernesto caught it in time, and placed it back on the coffee table.

"He convinced me it was all going to be okay. That he had a long term plan, and it hadn't come to fruition yet..." Out came the white handkerchief again. This time, she worried it in her hands. "He convinced me to give him one more moon cycle. To prove that what he was doing would benefit the Association. But I want to get him help now. I do."

Carol threw herself out of her chair with a huff. If she'd been a panther, she would have roared. Anger shook her bones. She held it in check only with sheer force of will and sorcery.

"You're going to pay for this, Helen. I don't know how yet, and I don't think it will come from me, but yeah. You're going to pay somehow."

And she walked out of the room.

9

JASMINE

Jimmy's room in the ramshackle Victorian looked the same as usual. Queen size mattress on the floor, two thin pillows raising lumps under the purple Indian bedspread. Stack of books next to it, under an old lamp with a ratty shade.

Paint that had likely been bright and cheery once, had weathered itself into muddy tapioca color. Too many years of cigarettes, handprints, and sheer time.

Political posters on the wall. And his pride and joy, a turntable that perched on top of the long, salvaged, blond-wood dresser. It was silent that morning. No Marvin Gaye or Sarah Vaughn. No Lost Poets.

Just the silent sun streaming weakly through the window, past the tied-back Indian bedspread.

Usually the room made me smile. Since we'd started having sex, we'd spent a fair amount of time on that mattress. But not today. For one thing, we both had work to do. Meetings to go to. People to train.

For another thing, I was angry. Mad at the cops. Mad at the Feds. Mad at my magic. Mad at Jimmy.

I was also still in a lot of pain from the alley. My body healed pretty quickly, but even so, my muscles ached and my skin felt tender from the amount of magic I'd poured out. Too quickly. Not enough buildup.

Shit like this kept up, it looked like I would need to practice doing full-on magical assaults with zero preparation.

I just hoped Drake was doing okay. Must have scared him pretty bad.

I licked my lips, and it tasted like salt rimed them. I shook my hands, and water practically flew off my fingertips.

I knew that no one else could taste the salt or see the water, but still, I had the whole goddamn ocean stuffed inside me, and it had nowhere to go.

"I don't know what you mean, babe." Jimmy sat crosswise on the bed, back leaning against the wall, legs stretched out. "How have I not been supporting you? And why aren't you lying down?"

I began to pace the cracked wood floor boards, ignoring the pain in my right hip. The floors seriously needed some stain and wax. Whole patches were bare and scarred. The revolution didn't have time to keep up the floors.

"You were there when we busted Huey out, Jimmy. You know what happened! And now leadership isn't trusting *me*? And you don't say one word to give me back up. Not. One. Word. It's almost like you don't want to say anything because we're having sex. You afraid they'll call you out for favoritism? That it?"

Jimmy's eyes darkened at that, but he looked genuinely confused. That pissed me off even more. Water roiled out into my aura. I could hear it hiss inside my head.

Hissing like a teakettle about to boil. Hissing like a

snake. Like a Powers-damned, Federal-agent slithering snake.

"I still don't get it," he said. "Leroy and Tarika? They're the same as always. Security is security, for me, you, them, everyone. It's all the same. With the cops and the Feeb breathing down our necks, and weird shit coming in with you to HQ, you think they don't have a right to be a little concerned?"

"How dare you! You're accusing me of bringing the cops and the Feds down on the *Panthers*?"

"Jaz. Can you calm down a minute? Take a breath or something like you do?"

I wanted to punch one of the dirty cream walls. I wanted to sock the picture of the revolutionary with the rifle slung over one shoulder, right on the nose. I wanted to scream. But you didn't scream in West Oakland unless you wanted a bunch of folks running in on you. That was for sure.

Yeah. I still had discipline enough not to scream. And not to actually start punching the walls.

I also had enough discipline to not drown the old Victorian and every person in it, ruining the piles of party newspapers, and rusting all the guns.

"Jimmy. Don't talk to me like I'm ignorant. Like I don't know how things run, or *what's at stake*. You treat me like that, and we're over."

A flash of hurt crossed his face. Then his cheeks and mouth and eyes set themselves in stone. Which was a good thing, because the scent of musk was thick in the air now, when it hadn't been before. I didn't know if Jimmy was about to shift, and didn't really want to find out.

"I'm sorry," I said. "I don't actually mean that."

The ocean inside me roared, drowning out the other voices in my head. The ones that whispered maybe I was finally going crazy. Maybe I wasn't trustworthy. Something had breached my aura and I couldn't even figure out how. I mean, that Fed had hooked into me, but Doreen had done an extraction, right? It felt like something was still in there, and that bothered me. And if the snake *was* still attached, maybe I *was* a security risk..

And maybe I couldn't do this shit after all.

"I think I'm just scared now, Jimmy. And I don't know what's going on."

Suddenly, he was at my side. I felt the man there. Felt the shifter, too. The big, dark, pelted cat poised inside my lover. Smelled his musk and amber scent. Even with my eyes closed, I could still see his own gold-rimmed eyes.

Jimmy. My Jimmy.

Then the ocean roared over my head and took me under.

I fell. Slammed up into the rolling water. Slammed down into the earth. Slammed up. Slammed down again. Tumbling over and over and over and over and over.

And came to on the mattress, a warm blanket covering me. Fully clothed. Except he'd taken my shoes off. And shoved a pillow underneath my head.

Which ached like anything.

I touched my temple.

"You okay, babe?"

Blinked open my eyes. Ouch. Too much light coming in.

"My head hurts, and my mouth feels weird. Dry. It's like I'm getting a fever. Sick."

The feel of knuckles. The back of Jimmy's hand on my forehead.

"You do feel hot."

"I'm freezing."

"I'll get you another blanket. Stay here."

The feel of his body shifting off the mattress. Sound of the door opening and closing.

I drifted. Far out on the ocean. So damn cold. Working with my Element didn't make me cold. Not ever. Why was I cold now?

The door opened again. I kept my eyes closed.

"You tying my brother up in knots?" It was Leroy's voice.

Every muscle in my body tensed again. Screaming.

Opening my eyes, I squinted up at the ruddy sideburns framing Leroy's face, wincing in pain at the light from the ceiling fixture haloing his head.

He crouched over me, squatting on his heels next to the mattress. He must have just come in from outside. He had his black leather trench coat on. It strained around his shoulders as he leaned in.

"Look, Jasmine. Your magic don't work like ours. And I don't trust whatever that snake thing is that follows you around. But you've done right by us, and you're still a Party member. So until you prove otherwise—and as long as you keep blasting cops in the streets—we got your back."

"Is there a problem?" Jimmy's voice asked from the doorway.

"No man, we're all cool here. Just checking in on the sorcerer here. I heard you talking in the kitchen, saying she fainted or something."

"Or something," I croaked out from my tight throat.

Leroy turned and held my gaze for a moment. Then gave a nod.

"Take care of yourself, Jasmine Jones. We need our revolutionaries healthy and on the street."

Then he stood. I heard his footsteps cross the floor.

"Talk to you when you're done here, man?"

"Sure. Let me just make sure she's settled," Jimmy said.

The door closed.

Jimmy spread a second blanket over me. The slight weight felt good. As if it would protect me from whatever was out there.

"I brought you aspirin and some water. Think you can sit up enough to drink?"

I struggled up to my elbows, almost passing out again with the pain that spiked my head. Jimmy rushed to support me. I opened my mouth then, felt two bitter aspirin touch my tongue. He held the glass of water, tilting it until it bumped my lips. I drank. Swallowed the hard round pills.

Then started to cry.

"I'm so sorry, Jimmy. I just *really* don't know what's happening to me."

He wrapped me in his arms, blanket, tears and all.

"S'alright, babe. I got you. Shhh. Shhh. Shhh."

The ocean tugged me under once again.

10

DOREEN

It was afternoon, the day after Jasmine and Drake's nasty encounter with the police. The Oakland playground was busy with children arriving after school.

Doreen watched thirteen-year-old Drake, carefully studying his face. She'd tried to get him to go home after school, but he had insisted on coming by the playground to help.

"They had me up against the wall, Doreen! I couldn't touch the spell bag." He practically spat, anger, shame, and disgust warring for prime position on his face.

She knew he had passed out in the alley from the onslaught of sorcery, and likely some amount of fear. Shutting down was natural. So was belligerence, she guessed. At least his body seemed uninjured.

And he was clearly more determined now, than ever.

The boy had grown up so much in the last month. Doreen didn't know whether to feel proud or sad.

A chain basketball hoop swung and creaked at the other end of the court, where a boy and girl played one on one.

The kids didn't have to learn magic to come to the playground. Those who didn't want to, or whose parents were still undecided, did homework on the long, battered wood benches lining the court, or played games.

The only rules were, the south half of the court was for magic class. No interrupting. No making fun.

Parents took advantage of the adult supervision and the impromptu play and study groups. Doreen and Patrice encouraged it. Knowing the children and teens were under their watch meant they were safer. And it also meant more of them would end up learning magic than not, once they figured out it was an okay thing to do. Maybe even cool.

At any rate, Doreen could tell Drake was a little stiff and sore. He didn't move with his usual bounce, and his usually smooth brow had an extra furrow in it.

He flung his book bag on one of the scarred wooden benches near the cyclone fence and approached a group of waiting nine- and ten-year-olds.

He got the children into groups of three to throw energy "balls," getting them used to sensing what they might not be able to see. More importantly, training them that there was power available to them. Even if their bodies were too small to go up against adults, they could think and magic their ways to safety if they needed to.

The Panthers taught the children how to think, how to feel pride in who they were. Those were the two baselines for all good magic, anyway. With that covered, Drake, Patrice, and Doreen could focus on other magical basics. The things non-sorcerers could learn.

Energy sensing. Mind protection. Making protective spell bags. Linking to their friends.

And if the Powers were right, Doreen was going to have to start teaching them about the deeper magic the ancestors insisted they all carried.

She just hoped she could figure out how. And do so in time, before whatever was coming next slammed into their community.

"He's doing well, isn't he?" Her lover's voice cut through Doreen's reverie.

Patrice had just arrived from work, all lush in a purple skirt suit today, with fake pearl earrings and a necklace that matched. Her lips were a deep burgundy that echoed the color of the suit.

As usual, she smelled of Doreen's current favorite things. Miss Helene's Cocoa Butter, Aqua Net hairspray, and an undercurrent that was just Patrice-scent.

Doreen smelled her own cinnamon Fire scent increase in response to her lover, and smiled. Just being around Patrice made Doreen's magic rise.

"Drake is a marvel, actually. Most kids would have run screaming after yesterday. Between the police and Jasmine, he has every right to be quivering under his blanket. But here he is."

The two women watched the thirteen-year-old boy, with his button nose and old brown jacket, patiently starting the younger children over and over with the exercise. They must have gotten the hang of it, because he pulled two groups together to form a circle, starting them in on a round of energy hot potato.

He must have sensed the two women talking about him, because he glanced up and gave a small wave.

Patrice waved back.

"How's Jasmine?" she asked.

Doreen clucked her tongue against her teeth and shook her head.

"That girl. She's not well, Patrice. I'm actually debating whether or not to call Cecelia. But dragging my sister into this mess? I just don't know about that."

Patrice put a warm hand on Doreen's arm. "But having her mother around might help her."

"Or it might push Jasmine further away."

One of the children Drake was working with shoved the child across from her with the energy ball.

"It looks like Drake needs backup," Patrice said, striding across the basketball court like a queen.

Doreen still felt unsettled by it all. Unsettled by the fact that Jasmine's boyfriend, Jimmy, had been worried enough to call her. Unsettled by the fact that the girl was still barely present, so far down in elemental Water that Doreen had trouble reaching her.

Apparently, it had been a hard evening. The Panthers had wisely brought Drake back to HQ, and gotten him cleaned up in the bathroom, while Jimmy wrestled Jasmine into bed.

Thank the Powers the boy was all right. And that he wanted to continue learning magic.

"If I let the pigs stop me now, Doreen, it means they won."

"Don't call them that, Drake. They're human men, just like you. If they want to turn themselves into something else, let them. But the longer we insist they're human, the more they have to be held accountable."

He just shook his head at that. But then, Doreen didn't expect many people to agree with her view.

A group of young teens that had been bent over a book on one of the benches loped toward her.

"Mrs. Doreen?" One of the young girls, hair in big puffy twists secured with purple and pink ball rubber bands, hands on her wide hips, asked. The teens all looked so young. And they were. Around Drake's age. Thirteen. Fourteen. Wearing scuffed-up shoes, sweaters and bell-bottoms on some, uniforms on a couple of others. All of them kids from the neighborhood.

"Yes, Kimberly?"

"We found this book in the library," Kimberly said, nudging one of the boys forward. Ramon, his name was. A light-skinned boy with waves in his close-cropped natural.

He held it out to her. Red, black, and white dust jacket, with black, hand-drawn sigils on the front. *A History of Secret Societies* by Arkon Daraul. Doreen flipped the hardback book over. *Life in the World Unseen*, the back jacket read.

Doreen coughed. Books like this were dangerous. They were filled with speculation, wild titillating "facts," and just enough truth to get someone in trouble.

And the sigils on the cover were real. She could feel it. And that was *not* good.

"Is this like what you belong to? A secret society?" Kimberly scrunched up her face and asked.

Doreen fought down a smile.

"Something like that. Though if they're in a book, how secret do you think they are?"

The teens all paused at that.

"You all want to study some books?" Doreen asked.

"Yes ma'am," Ramon replied. "We figured it might help us learn some of what you're teaching us better."

Oh, to send these kids to a place like the Mansion in LA. Doreen wished she and Jasmine had the time to form their own organization. One that wouldn't just train born-sorcerers. But a place to take in kids like this, whom no Association member would give a second thought.

The ancestors whispered at the base of her skull. Yes. This was what they wanted.

But damn it, how?

She looked around the basketball court. At Patrice and Drake with the younger ones. At the faces of this group of teens.

Doreen guessed this basketball court was it, for now. These afternoons didn't have to only be for triage. They could build something.

"Magic for the people," Jasmine was calling it.

Two kids across the way gave out loud yelps and shook their hands. Then the group Drake and Patrice were with burst into laughter.

"I've got better books to show you," Doreen said. "Get permission, and we'll start a study group one evening a week. Your parents, or aunts and uncles, whoever takes care of you, they're all welcome, too."

She didn't know where she would possibly find the time, what with Jasmine out of commission and needing who knows what, and the self-defense training, and whatever was going on with Terrance.

But life in Oakland was always that way.

Life didn't stop.

You had to learn to meet it.

And if cops were attacking kids for no reason?

You had to learn to meet it from every front possible.

And Doreen had to help these kids and their families do that.

Right away.

11

CAROL

Carol parked her green Oldsmobile in front of the peeling white Iglesia de Cristo, which stood next to a pink stucco house and across the street from the old Romanesque Revival building. The Church of the Epiphany, Carol's destination.

Running across the street, bell-bottom jeans threatening to trip up her boots, Carol paused for a moment to get her bearings in the Los Angeles sun, then walked past the old fieldstone walls holding up what must have been the original old church, which had been added to over the years.

In their phone call that morning, Rosalia had said that was where the church hall was. Up the steps, there was a portico lining the "new" church, built sometime in the early 1900s, and sure enough, as soon as she entered the shaded portico, there was a heavy wooden door to her left, leading into the older building.

The noise hit her first. Twenty sets of boots stamping out a pattern on the wooden floor.

The Brown Berets were practicing in formation. Rows of mostly men, with a few women, in tan and brown, faces shining from exertion, lit by a round glass window high up on the smooth, beige wall.

Carol saw the young woman who had spoken at Rosalia's shop. Verónica was her name. Ernesto had told Carol that Verónica was one of the few women in Brown Beret leadership.

Their spines were straight as the group moved with precision, forward and backward, left, then right.

"La Raza!" the leader shouted.

Arms snapping upward, "Por la gente!" the group responded.

Stomp. Stomp. Stomp. Stomp.

"La Raza!"

"Por la gente!"

Carol saw Rosalia, citrine eyes squinting a little in the light from the round window, just across the floor. The older woman stood, her own spine erect, in a soft purple skirt and her usual black jersey blouse, with a flowered shawl wrapped around her shoulders.

Carol made her way carefully around the marching Chicanos in their tan trousers, chocolate brown berets on their heads.

Rosalia looked at her and smiled, which filled Carol with relief. Some tension she didn't even realize she'd been holding left her shoulders. The discomfort of a blond white girl in a sea of brown. She'd been working on it, but clearly the old fears still crept in.

"What are they saying?" Carol asked. "I recognize *la gente*. The people, right?"

"Si," Rosalia said.

"And La Raza?"

"They both mean the people," Rosalia said. "But La Raza is la raza cosmica. The Cosmic Race. It originally meant the mixing of people who would show us the way. The blending of the people into one. Indigenous. Spanish. Mestizaje. Now though? It means 'our people.' Mexicanos. Part Indian, part Spanish. Our ancestors. Us."

"Our people for the people," Carol said.

"That is right," Rosalia nodded. "Something you sorcerers up at the Mansion need to learn, claro?"

"Claro," Carol said with a sigh.

Things at the Mansion were so not good. It was why she'd called Rosalia today. Ernesto should have been with her, but he had students to attend to, he said. Sometimes Carol forgot that, what with everything else going on. The classes she had taken went on, with a new crop of people training their Elemental powers.

The Brown Berets paired off and began sparring. Carol winced at the fists coming so near faces, barely deflected with a palm or a forearm. She knew she needed to get physically stronger, but violence scared her.

She and Jasmine fought about that. About the guns in particular. The Black Panther's insistence on self-defense was one thing, but guns felt too much like *offense.*

Jasmine scoffed at that. "How do you want us to defend against guns, Carol? With kisses? You think no one's ever done offensive sorcery before? You are dreaming, girl. When they come for you, you better hope someone like me is around."

"So, why have you come to see me today, maga?" Rosalia asked.

Carol shuffled her feet, stomach twisting in a tight knot. She was so damn uncomfortable talking about this still, despite all she'd been through.

She had to reign the old, timid Carol in, and let the new Carol take control.

"Terrance. You know we can't find him. His soul."

Rosalia kept her eyes trained on sparring Chicano warriors, but shook her head.

"That man. He's bad news. He's in El Mundo Malo."

The Brown Berets stopped sparring and began pushups on the wooden floor. Right. Another reason not to join the Brown Berets. Besides being a blond Swede from Minnesota, sparring and pushups were right out.

Though she really should start jogging at the very least. Yeah. Someday.

"What do you mean?" Carol asked.

"Walk with me," Rosalia said.

The two women skirted the back wall of the church hall, inching around a hulking printing press in the corner.

Rosalia caught Carol looking at the behemoth.

"That is where they print La Raza newspaper," she said.

The paper Carol had seen Ernesto hiding, what seemed like a year ago, but was really only a month ago.

So much had changed since then.

"Father John is a good man. He helps la gente."

Rosalia opened a wooden door and stepped into the sanctuary.

Sanctuary it was. Peace washed over Carol as the sound of boots faded behind the closing door. Red carpet beneath carved wooden pews. Stained wood beams held up the vaulted wood ceiling. White walls set with stained glass rose on either side. To the right of the simple wooden altar, a pipe organ gleamed. A small crucifix was on the back wall, under another round window.

"It's beautiful in here," Carol breathed out. Traces of frankincense permeated the air. Everything that had been troubling her for weeks left, rising toward the wooden beams.

"Come. Sit." Rosalia led her to a pew.

Carol thunked her patchwork leather purse down and sat on the smooth wood.

"So..." Rosalia said.

"So. Terrance. You know we've been worried. You were there for the confrontation. And you know about the seizures. And not being able to sense him... But with everything going on, I can't remember what else I've told you. Plus, he's still refusing to get help."

"And now you don't trust him. And no, you shouldn't."

Carol played with the strap of her bag, then looked up at the cross. A sigil flashed across her mind, and she inhaled sharply.

"What is happening, maga?"

"Being here. I don't know. I just made a connection, I think. Terrance and the sigils. All his seizures. My visions."

Rosalia took Carol's hand in hers. Carol realized she was shaking. The peace of the church still surrounded her, throwing all the roiling mess of sorcery and emotion she'd been living with into stark relief.

"The sigils took Mr. Sterling somewhere, Rosalia. I can feel it. It was part of why they scared me so much. The Bad World..."

"El Mundo Malo."

"Yeah. He is there. His spirit is. And the spiders, the snakes...it's all connected somehow."

Rosalia nodded, citrine eyes grave, mouth tight.

"It's what I've been afraid was going to happen to me. How could it happen to someone like Terrance?"

There was the sound of a heavy door shutting at the church entrance. Soft footsteps on the red carpet. Rosalia dropped her hand and looked over her shoulder.

Carol dug a handkerchief from her purse and wiped

some perspiration from her upper lip, and dabbed her eyes. When had they teared up?

"Father John, buenas dias!" Rosalia said.

"Rosalia. What brings you to church?"

The priest stepped in front of their pew. He was a tall, fair-haired white man in black framed glasses, wearing black trousers and a black long-sleeved shirt with a clerical collar.

"This one here." Rosalia gestured to Carol. "She needed an epiphany."

Father John laughed at that, a high and joyful sound.

"This is the right place for it. Did it work?"

Carol couldn't believe this conversation. The hechicera and the priest, talking about her. She wiped her nose.

Then realized the priest had directed his question her way. Her face flushed and she cleared her throat.

"Yes. Yes, I think it did work."

"Father John Luce, meet Carol Johansson. You are both mystics, I think. But Carol is not yet as revolutionary as you are, Padre."

Carol rose to shake the priest's outstretched hand. His skin was warm. His presence the calmest thing she'd felt in a while. No wonder the church felt so good.

Rosalia beamed up at them.

"Father John, I think we may need your help."

By all the Powers. What was the woman up to?

12

SNAKES AND SPIDERS

The sting of the small stones tied into the hemp ropes ripped tiny bits of flesh from his back.

Samuels welcomed the pain.

Any pain that was self-inflicted was pain that someone else could not deal out to his body or his soul.

Samuels knew why the Panthers didn't fear them anymore. Whatever shifter magic they had formed a strange protection against the ceremonial powers the FBI had built up over the past decades.

Staring at that damn shifter in the Chicago jail was proof. Every time Samuels had probed the beast, his magic had just bounced off, as if there was a force field around the animal's body.

That judge had been right to chain the Panther in the courtroom. Samuels wondered if the judge sensed it somehow. That the black man was something other than a man.

And the Panthers had some other magic helping them. A sorcery so strong it shouldn't exist. That damn girl. Samuels needed to crack that, crack her, just the way he was cracking his own weaknesses right now.

He'd tagged her, but something was going wrong with that,

too. The tag was still there, but the signal was weaker. And he couldn't really get inside her defenses as easily now.

He needed to keep his own defenses strong. The more he tortured himself, the less the Master's torture could get through.

The more information he kept to himself, the more power he had that the Master didn't.

The Master had gotten to him. And Samuels wasn't going to let that happen again. He needed to be stronger. So out from the bottom drawer had come the Penitente's tools. The crude flail. The barbed cincture that bit into his thigh. The vise that would be the last resort for him.

He didn't think he had need of it just yet.

Training his body also trained his mind. Training his mind, trained his soul.

He needed to train his soul to face the fucking Master.

And he needed to train his mind to keep up with that Panther bitch.

Kissing the flail, he placed it on his tiny bookshelf altar, and settled more deeply into the recesses of his own soul. He did his best thinking that way, devoid of distraction. Body humming with endorphins. Mind clear of the world.

So. As for the lovely Panther with her slim hips and rounded breasts, so far, so good.

The slight tear Samuels had managed to inflict on her energy field hadn't quite healed, regardless of whatever repair operation she'd done on herself.

And since she'd zapped him at the same time, he had a stronger taste of her. He knew what she felt like. Moved like. And now he had an in.

She was so preoccupied with everything the Bureau was sending at her, there was no way she was going to notice she had failed to fully shore up her massive shields.

They were good ones, he had to admit. Shiny like chrome to his eyes, and rippling like the surface of a pond. Good deflection.

The flare of anger she'd sent at him along with her blast had given him the opening he needed to tear that tiny piece of aura between her shoulder and her head. His barb had struck something in there. He just hoped it still lodged in her body, needling its way into her flesh.

Something had taken root, that was certain.

He could feel her emotions every time he gave the slightest tug of the serpentine thread. She was still hooked.

Samuels whispered to the serpent ring around his finger. He crooned magic words into its silver ears. The astral serpent that rode within him responded, sending out tendrils of itself along the magical line. He built it up slowly, day by day, kneeling on the hard boards of his bedroom floor, in the space that ringed the Turkish rug that was his one concession to comfort in the spartan room.

His knees and the bones in the top of his feet had grown used to the hard surface, but still ached enough to remind him to pay attention to the work that was at hand. It wouldn't do for a man such as Samuels to grow too comfortable, too complacent.

Comfort was death. His adversaries would ferret out any weaknesses, undermining his power. And the Master would exploit the smallest failing to his death.

Samuels fought the bile back down his throat. The memory of the torture rose up again, despite his attempts to drive it forth. It was still too fresh, the way it was intended to be. He couldn't let that happen again.

Samuels grimaced, then smoothed his face of all emotion.

He picked up the flail again.

13

JASMINE

My head was splitting open and I swear, my brains were about to fall out. My ribs felt bruised, my wrists ached, my thigh muscles screamed. I swear, even my ass hurt.

My bed was usually just a bit too soft for me, but it felt hard as a stone, and the white chenille coverlet topped by the bright Indian bedspread were heavy on my bones.

Don't dump the elemental power of a whole ocean through your body if you expect to survive. Surviving is a drag. Noted.

I had a full jelly jar of red wine. The acid of it stung the cuts in my mouth where my lips had hit my teeth. But the wine was helping everything else. At least, that's what I told myself.

Sorcerers don't drink much alcohol. But I didn't want to be a sorcerer right now. Not with the way things were going.

The breeze moving through the cracked-open window casement smelled like the bay. Usually my favorite smell, today it made me feel a little ill. I kept waiting for the wine to settle my stomach, but it wasn't working on that, either.

I took comfort in the purple inked sheets within reach on my desk. I couldn't lay them all out on the bed like I wanted, because I'd catch it from Doreen if the mimeo stained my coverlet. So, one sheet at a time, I was soaking in the words of Chairman Fred.

Just like I used to in the days when I thought I'd never meet the man. Before I knew he was a shape-shifter. Before I knew much of anything.

Before I even knew about my Uncle Hector. That he was more than a handsome black man who loved my Aunt Doreen.

Since finding out about the shifters, I had more questions than I had answers.

Like, it turned out shifters were pretty much unkillable. Recent events with the Panthers had proven that.

So what had tipped the white men off about my uncle? How had they known they should kill him? That he was something unusual, and maybe a danger?

How had they known he wasn't just a California mountain lion, drawn in closer to the city lights from hunger or for other reasons unknown?

How in the hell had they figured out they needed to chop off his head?

Had they panicked when all the rain of bullets did was slow him down?

And why had Hector gone out running at moon dark without the protection amulet Aunt Doreen kept charged up and put on a long enough leather cord to fit his lion's neck? As it was, the sheriff's men also knew to cut the gold ring from his softly furred ear, leaving the tip on a rock near his body.

At least that's what I was told.

Swirling the wine in my mouth, I winced. All this

thinking wasn't getting me anywhere. But thinking was better than the emotional upheaval that got me in this condition in the first place.

Doreen telling me about Hector had busted something inside me. The betrayal of not knowing. The horror of his death.

And it seemed strange to me that someone like Huey Newton had been captured by the state. Not that he had been framed, because even a sheltered middle class girl like me could see how that would happen, but how the hell had he got caught?

I set the wine down on the small desk under the window, next to the stack of mimeo'd speeches, thoughts, and other Panther material. I picked up a fresh sheet of paper. It crackled in my hands.

"A lot of people get the word revolution mixed up and they think revolution's a bad word. Revolution is nothing but like having a sore on your body and then you put something on that sore to cure that infection. And I'm telling you that we're living in an infectious society right now. I'm telling you that we're living in a sick society."

That was truth, and I knew it. We were all infected. Me, with my middle class black Crenshaw upbringing. Doreen. Hell, even Jimmy and Huey. Even Fred.

I got it then. We were all sick, and all fighting the illness. That's why the power moving through me felt so wrong. I couldn't accept who I was. Not really.

Funny, I thought I accepted myself just fine. Then things really went down and it scared the shit out of me.

Putting down the paper, I sipped at more wine. The anger struck my core like a hatchet hitting an old tree stump. There was nothing anyone could really tell me about all this. And I didn't know how to learn it myself.

The way Carol always bowed her head and thought she wasn't good enough? I had some of that inside me, too. And the power was warping my emotions. Until I got clean, until I felt the revolution in my bones, the sickness wasn't going away.

I looked toward the window, at the white curtains blowing softly in the breeze. Some kids were playing kick-ball in the street. Why weren't they in school? What time was it, anyway?

Something heavy moved against my legs. A weight that shouldn't be there. Like a cat had jumped on the bed. It started moving up my left calf, toward my thigh.

"Shit. Shitshitshitshit." Breath heaved in my chest, and I groaned at the movement of my bruised ribs. The pressure up my legs hurt, too. Whatever it was, it was heavy as fuck.

"Use your sorcery, Jasmine," I said.

The wine made it hard to get clear enough, but I had to *see*. Gripping the jelly jar in my right fist, I strained against the pain and the alcohol fog inside my head.

Sssssssss. I heard it then. And smelled the dried-out, paper-skin smell.

"Snake," I said, gritting my teeth as if I could bite the word in half.

The curtains flew out from the window as I reached past the pain and the fog and the wine and found the bay again.

"Come. *On!*"

The water rushed inside me, and I opened my mouth to scream from the agony of it. The jelly jar shattered in my fist. I felt the heat of glass slicing my fingers and my palm. Felt the wetness of wine and blood on my arm and chest. The wine stung my fingers like the devil.

"By all the Powers!" I grunted out. My legs thrashed,

trying to get free of the blanket. Trying to stand. The snake was too heavy. I was in too much pain.

Squinting my eyes, I could barely make out the astral form, crawling toward me.

"You bastard!"

My bedroom door burst open.

"Jasmine!" Doreen shouted. I could smell her cinnamon Fire over the wine and ocean and snake.

Then I saw the serpent's head, ready to strike.

Clutching my hands together to make one fist, I poured all the blue, ocean-fueled fire into my aching palms and *sent*.

The snake exploded in a flare of light. A loud clap thundered in the air and ozone reek filled the room.

"Jasmine." Doreen spoke, softly. I could barely hear her through the ringing in my ears. She touched my wet, bloody hands.

I fell forward, weeping, into her soft arms.

14

JASMINE

It all happened so fast.

The snake. The glass shattering. Doreen.

Jimmy and Doreen rushing me to the hospital, hands wrapped in an old bath towel, glass shards cutting into me at every breath of pressure.

The hard chairs in the crappy, cracked-linoleum-tiled, piss-and-disinfectant-stinking emergency room waiting area. The long wait, hands and body throbbing. I must have been keening low in my throat without realizing, because Jimmy started saying "Shhh. Shhh," over and over.

Finally, there was the concerned look on the white doctor's face as he pulled the glass out of my hands.

Like I'd tried to harm myself on purpose.

The hushed conversation about whether I needed the psych ward. Doreen's louder insistence that I was just fine.

The tiny stitches in the webbing of my right hand.

Jimmy, tucking me into my bed, then removing his shoes to lay beside me, on top of the fresh blanket Doreen had gotten from the closet. It was golden brown. My white coverlet and the Indian bedspread were ruined.

Everything hurt.

Doreen's voice from the kitchen. First talking with Patrice, then conferring with my parents on the phone. I heard her say my mother's name. Cecelia.

Jimmy, snapping off my desk lamp.

Then it was morning. Gray light filtered through the curtains over my desk. Jimmy was gone, but I could hear him in the kitchen. Doreen and Patrice's voices.

The smell of coffee and bacon. Jimmy loved bacon. Doreen must like him. It all sounded so homey out there. Plates on the table. The sound of forks and knives rattling in the drawer.

Patrice's voice coming from the kitchen was growing to be a familiar sound. Jimmy? Not quite yet. Most of the time we spent at his pad. My bed was just too small.

Speaking of which, I wondered where he'd actually slept. If he had.

Wincing, I scooted myself up in the bed with my elbows. I couldn't really adjust the pillows with my swaddled hands, so I just shoved at them with my shoulders. That hurt, too. Everything hurt.

Testing, I tried to send a thought out to Jimmy. Damn it. Cotton wool. My skull started to pound. But I heard soft footfalls in the hallway, so something must have gotten through.

The door squeaked open.

"Hey babe. Want some coffee?"

He looked so beautiful, I almost started crying. So. My emotions were still doing that thing. *Keep it under control, Jasmine Jones.*

"Can you help me with these pillows?" I asked.

He set the heavy white mug in one of the clear spots on

my desk, glancing at the pile of mimeo'd sheets that had cascaded to the floor.

Adjusting the pillows behind me, he put his hands under my armpits and helped scoot me up some more. The scent of him was all I wanted. All I needed. The feel of his warmth.

His strength.

I felt so weak all of a sudden. I couldn't remember the last time I felt weak. Carol would wonder what in all the Powers had happened to me.

"Jimmy, I don't think I can do this anymore."

His weight, depressing the side of the mattress. His hands on my face.

His gold-rimmed eyes.

"Jasmine, you can. And you will. You're strong, babe." We both laughed a bit at that. "Yeah. Maybe not this minute. But you'll heal up, dig?"

He grabbed the white mug, took a sip of the fragrant coffee, then tipped the heavy porcelain to my lips.

I winced as the heat hit the tiny cuts in my mouth.

"But?" I asked.

"But we think you need a break. To heal without so much pressure. Doreen's been on the phone with Cecelia. They got that Association of yours to pay for a plane ticket again. That lady—Helen, I guess. Said she's feeling guilty about something."

"A ticket?" I didn't understand, and was struggling to get my bandages out from under the blanket and the sheet. I needed some air on my arms for some reason.

"To LA, babe. So your parents can take care of you."

"You're sending me away? You're all sending me away?" My voice was rising and I could feel the water trying to pool itself at my feet.

But I wasn't strong enough to do a proper draw of my own damn Element.

"Jasmine." He set the mug back down on the desk, and ran a hand down my shoulder. "You're on overload right now. You need care."

"So you're putting me on a plane. How's that good?"

He stood up then and began to pace my small room, eyes grazing the posters and the stack of books on my desk that I never got around to putting away once the semester was over.

The scent of something baking came from the kitchen. That was both an advantage and disadvantage of my room being where it was. The coffee was close, but sometimes I just wanted to be further away from the heart of the house.

Besides, if Doreen was baking, it wasn't good. She only baked if she had time—which under these conditions? She didn't—or she was upset.

Finally, he stopped and turned. The look on his face was slightly harder. Like he had to spit something out of his mouth but didn't want to.

"Just say it."

"Jaz...you know leadership is worried. Not that they don't think you've done good. But you know, Doreen's worried. I'm worried. We're all a little worried. And frankly, babe, I'd rather you got taken care of 'til whatever this is...I don't know!"

My stomach muscles ached with tension. The few sips of coffee turned sour in my stomach. I didn't want to hear this shit. But my body was telling me I needed to listen anyway.

What's your training, Jasmine? What's the first lesson?

Breathe. Then find your center. Then get ahold of your edges, girl.

"Jaz?"

"Give me a minute," I replied.

Breathe first. Okay. Three long breaths later, I was ready to find my center. My core strength. It was smaller than it should be. And riding up too high. But I could adjust that. Three more breaths.

I checked in again. Better.

Closing my eyes, I felt along the edges of my aura. Yeah. That wasn't so hot. There were holes along the back edge. Tears. Not large, but big enough. And my aura should have been oval, like an upside-down egg. Smooth.

Instead, the edges were wobbly and ragged, like I was sure my hair was right now.

In other words, I was a wreck. They were all right. I needed help.

"Yeah. Okay. I don't like it, but just tell me what to do. When do I leave?"

"There's a flight out of SFO tonight. You up for it?"

I would have to be.

Glancing at the pile of papers, I nodded, even though it hurt my head.

"Fred says, 'If you dare to struggle, you dare to win.'" I tried to swing my legs off the side of the bed, and the pain punched me back down to the mattress. "Damn it!"

Jimmy came to help ease me up. If I was going to get on a plane, I better get cleaned up and dressed.

"Yeah. Fred says that," Jimmy replied.

"Well, I guess figuring this shit out"—I waved my bandaged hands—"is my struggle right now."

"We all got struggles, Jaz. You aren't alone."

That didn't make me want to cry any less.

15

———

DOREEN

Cecelia had called the night before, saying Jasmine arrived just fine, though the flight had been hard on her. She was sleeping in her old room.

Cecelia also said that William was worried sick. Doreen wasn't surprised. That man loved Jasmine and Cecelia like the moon loved the sky, but he didn't have a lick of magic in him. So anything that ran the risk of hurting his women that he couldn't taste or punch or reason with or see?

Even after all these years around sorcerers, he didn't like it at all. He was supposed to be their rock and their safe harbor, not a helpless wreck when his daughter was attacked and hurting.

Well, Doreen didn't like it either. She didn't like where Jasmine's emotions were taking her. And she didn't like it when Jasmine told her that snake had been in her room.

Nothing should have been able to get past the ancestors *or* the house wards. Doreen and Patrice had just boosted all the protections around the building the week before. That snake kept going places it had no business being.

And now that they figured it was tied to the Feds, the danger felt even worse.

Doreen clucked a bit. What in all the Powers were they going to do with her niece? The strongest sorcerer to come out of the Association in years, and the power of her own magic was busting her apart.

"What are you clucking at, Doreen?" Patrice asked. "We have people waiting on us."

Doreen blinked. While she'd been woolgathering, Father Neil's church hall had filled up with all the parents of the kids and teens they'd been training. Folks greeted one another. Some of the younger kids raced through big room, shoes squeaking on the old wood floors, voices shrieking with excitement.

Doreen and Patrice stood near the swinging kitchen door, sipping at coffee, waiting until everyone arrived. Drake was on greeter duty, and doing a great job of it.

These meetings were not what Doreen thought she'd ever be doing, but as Momma used to say, *"You look at what's in front of you, not what might be coming on the wind."*

Well, sometimes a person had to pay attention to what was coming, but what was in front of Doreen right now was a community that needed more help than she was sure she had to offer.

"We do what we can," Doreen murmured.

Patrice heard her.

"It's more than they have now," her lover replied.

The men and women shuffled around, opening the wooden folding chairs that were stacked against the wall, forming a makeshift circle.

Drake brought chairs for her and Patrice, too.

"Thank you," Patrice said. He just nodded his head. He'd been more serious since the encounter with the Oakland police officers. Doreen knew he'd just been trying not to let on when he was around the smaller kids.

As always, a long, white cloth banner reminded church-goers what the focus of Father Neil's ministry was. *God is Love* was spelled out in red cloth letters, sewn with care by some church women, Doreen was sure.

Doreen wished more people actually believed it.

Love didn't always drive the Association, that was certain. And the Panthers? Jasmine had quoted Huey Newton himself, saying, "I think what motivates people is not great hate, but great love for other people." So she guessed the Panthers weren't so off from Father Neil's church.

Father Neil must think so, or he wouldn't allow them to meet here.

Once the men and women were more or less settled, Doreen adjusted her spine a little straighter, took a breath, and began to speak.

"You all know the police are retaliating for the success of our protection of DeFremary Park, and our continued efforts to protect our community."

She touched Momma's moon amulet. The bronze felt warm under her fingers. No matter how many times she'd had to do this of late, Doreen was still not used to speaking in front of groups. Especially not about anything other than magic. But the ancestors were clear.

She had to do this.

Looking out at the faces gathered, the bus drivers and maids, the shopgirls, schoolteachers and dockworkers, the nurses, even the one doctor, who had propped himself up against a wall, as though he wasn't willing to commit enough to sit down...looking at all of these people, she touched her own Elemental Fire and reached out with her senses to feel the smaller fires in each of them.

"As a consequence"—she took another breath in—"we want to expand our teaching. We've been giving you protection spells, and teaching your children some basic self defense. But we want to offer you more. We think this community is ready, and could become a model for communities all over the country."

"What do you mean?" a woman asked. One of the nurses, still in her white uniform and thick-soled white shoes.

Drake stood up, shoving the wooden chair back with his legs. Doreen looked at him, startled.

He cleared his throat, then looked at Doreen. She just looked back, waiting. Everyone was waiting.

"Excuse me, Mrs. Doreen, but I've been thinking about this. Can I tell you all what I've been thinking?"

"Go ahead, son," someone said.

He cleared his throat again, and tugged at his shirt collar.

"I got attacked this week. Three cops came up to me and started asking me about the Panthers, and the meetings. When I wouldn't say nothing, they slammed me up against a fence. One of them had his stick against my throat. I was trying to get to my protection bundle in my pocket, you know? But I couldn't reach it."

He tugged at his collar again, and looked at the floor.

"You know what got me out of that? It was Jasmine. She came and filled the street with magic. She stood there and whirled those cops right through the air. Hit them with a wave of magic. Uh, sorcery, I guess you call it." He looked to Doreen for confirmation. She just gestured at him to go on.

A few people coughed. Clearly uncomfortable.

"Well, Huey Newton says, 'No party or organization can make the revolution, only the people can.' And I think we've been putting too much on the Panthers. I think they been helping us as much as they can. And I think what Doreen is saying is, it's time for *us* to help the revolution."

He sat down suddenly, as if the breath had left him, scraping the chair on the wood floor.

Doreen felt tears in her eyes. By all the Powers. He'd just given her marching orders, hadn't he? A thirteen-year-old boy.

She touched the amulet again. That was what Momma and the other ancestors had been trying to tell her, that Doreen had almost gotten, but not quite.

Doreen rose to address the gathering again, when there was a disturbance at the side doors of the church hall.

An older black man burst in, shouting.

"You're doing the work of the Devil! You are in God's house! How dare you bring your sorcery in here!"

The doctor walked quickly toward him, and so did another man and a woman.

"Sir, we're having a meeting here, and you're disturbing us," the woman said.

"You are doing the work of Satan!" he shouted, and began struggling to get past the three bodies trying to shield the group.

"Doreen!" Patrice said her name sharply, like a slap. Doreen realized she'd become frozen in place. Shaking herself, she began to walk slowly toward the man, sending a calming, soothing energy outward from her core.

When she reached the the ersatz security force, she saw the man's face. He was around sixty-five, with grizzled stubble on his cheeks and chin, and deep creases over his dark eyes. His tight curls were close-cropped and mostly gray.

Where his voice was angry, his eyes were terrified.

"Brother, thank you for coming to speak your concerns," Doreen said. "May I help you?"

She sent a calming breath his way. If he was open at all, he would feel it. The tension in the other two men and the woman receded. That was good. The older man clenched up; then, looking into Doreen's eyes, he relaxed. Just a little bit. But enough, she hoped.

"You can help me by telling me what you mean to be doing here in Father Neil's church. Those Panthers feeding children is okay, but I heard you're teaching people sorcery. That isn't right. I've lived in this neighborhood for twenty years, and never seen anything like this before."

Doreen nodded.

"I can't make you less afraid," she said. "Magic doesn't belong to the Devil or anyone else." She pitched her voice louder, making sure everyone in the room could hear her. "Magic belongs to all of us. It rests inside us. Magic is power."

Doreen turned to face the group then, and the protectors moved aside, letting the man into their circle.

"What Drake was trying to tell us, and what I'm offering you now, is the chance to take your power and pool it together. To become a force of protection and strength for everyone who lives in our communities. To protect our children and our elders. Our churches and our schools."

She placed a gentle hand on the older man's arm and led him toward her seat. Surprised, he followed her.

Even the doctor grabbed a chair and sat down.

"We'll talk about sorcery. And magic. I know this man

here isn't the only one who might feel afraid. But I want to say this to you all..."

She touched the amulet again. It buzzed beneath her fingers. She felt Momma standing right behind her, and her Chokwe ancestor, the woman from Angola with her missing eyetooth and red mud in her hair.

"The Panthers have been doing their best. Feeding our children. Gathering shoes and coats for those who need them. Staffing our clinics and escorting our elders so they get home safe. And yes, protecting us from the police. Well, Drake is right, it's time we started to help the Panthers. Don't you agree?"

Damn. She was turning into some middle-aged revolutionary, talking like Jasmine now.

She just hoped her niece was going to be okay.

16

____

CAROL

They drove from the Mansion into southwest Los Angeles. Ernesto and Rosalia in the front seat of Ernesto's car and Carol in the back. Carol cranked her window down. The handle stuck a little, so she had to push. She really needed more exercise. Maybe doing pushups with the Brown Berets wasn't such a bad idea after all.

The smell of car exhaust blew on the cool wind that whipped Carol's straight blond hair around. She should have brought a scarf. Cars honked and tires screeched. The engine rumbled, shaking Carol's feet in her rust-colored boots.

She'd worn a granny skirt today, long and forest green. Wanting to dress nicely for Jasmine's parents, she supposed. Her peasant blouse was smocked with green threads. She played with the ties at her collarbones. Nervous about seeing Jasmine for some reason.

Like Jasmine wouldn't understand that Carol was different now.

Or was she? If she was so different, maybe she wouldn't have butterflies crashing in her solar plexus.

Or maybe she was scared to see that Jasmine was different, too.

They passed a weird circular building the color of cream. The top bowed outward. "The Chili Bowl," the sign read. "Grill Burgers. Tamales. Egg Royale." She had no idea what Egg Royale was, but smiled at the bowl-shaped building all the same.

Crenshaw. A place she'd never been before. Only a few miles from the Hills, and yet, it felt as far away to Carol as East LA.

Ernesto turned down off the main drag and onto a series of residential streets lined with green lawns and parked cars. Newer single-story, ranch-style homes made way for WWII bungalows as he navigated down the streets.

Rosalia had a thick Thomas Guide map book open on her lap. "It's the next street. Turn left."

And, turning the corner, more bungalows and a couple of Tudor-style homes.

Ernesto pulled over and parked in front of a neat home painted sea green, with a tall white chimney on the side. A peaked roof shaded the small cement slab of the porch.

The door was painted a deeper blue-green.

Carol slid out of the car and let the heavy door thunk shut as she looked around. The neighborhood seemed pretty quiet. Some of the homes had red doors. Most were white, with a few colors or brick inlay brightening the facades.

A Japanese-looking woman in a yellow coat pushed a baby stroller up the next driveway and gave them a curious look.

Strangers in the neighborhood.

Rosalia waved.

"Hello!" she called out.

"Good morning," the woman replied, before bumping the stroller up the two steps to her own porch.

Ernesto and Rosalia went up the walkway. Carol held back a little. Something felt strange. Off. And she didn't quite want to face it.

The door opened. Cecelia. She looked trim and fabulous as always, in a white dress that skimmed her figure, with a wide orange cloth belt encircling the hips. Wide pleats fanned out around her thighs. She wore stockings. Orange, patent-leather, low-heeled pumps.

How she looked so good after what must have been a late night getting her daughter from the airport, Carol had no idea.

Then she looked again. The creases at the edges of Cecelia's mouth seemed deeper than before. And her skin seemed slightly dull.

"Welcome! Please come in."

The house was as neat as Cecelia. A stuffed navy sofa. Family photos on the walls. A white-painted brick fireplace.

And Jasmine, walking slowly toward them, gauze-wrapped hands a beacon in the dim light of the hall.

She looked like hell. Her hair was fuzzy at the tips, and not rounded out like it usually was. Bell-bottom jeans hung from her hipbones and the black power fist T-shirt she usually filled out floated past her ribs. Carol didn't think Jasmine even noticed.

She'd never seen her friend like this. Not put together. She was clearly in distress, and had been for some time. How had Carol not seen that Jasmine was getting so thin? They had seen each other just a couple of weeks ago.

But Jasmine had been at full power then, on the hilltop

above the California Men's Colony. Her power was part of her glamourie. Jasmine was her own kind of shape-shifter, Carol realized.

Jasmine had the ability to make people see what they wanted to.

But not today.

Carol folded her friend into her arms. She felt the bones of Jasmine's ribs under her hands, and her friend's skin smelled a little sour.

"Thanks for coming," Jasmine mumbled.

"Yeah," Carol whispered in her best friend's ear, then pulled gently away.

Rosalia stepped forward.

"Hechicera, we've come to see if we can help you."

Carol could feel Cecelia then. Feel the anguish in her aura. Where was William? A sound came from the kitchen. Cups rattling on a tray, that was what it was. The scent of coffee hit her then, and Jasmine's father's big shadow filled the hallway.

"Let's sit in here." Cecelia gestured to the living room. "William's bringing coffee. We can talk."

Carol and Ernesto moved toward the navy sofa, and William set the tray down on a teak coffee table.

Rosalia stayed put, staring at Jasmine.

Shit, Carol thought. *This isn't going to be good.* The butterflies in her solar plexus turned to rocks that plummeted to her feet.

Earth. Right. She called on her Element, and coaxed the soles of her feet open to its power. Crenshaw answered, the whole neighborhood reaching out. Strong. Comfortable. Present.

"I think there is no time for talking," Rosalia said. "You

don't look so good, hechicera. But I don't yet know what is wrong."

Cecelia hovered between the open arch leading to the living room and the hallway where the other two sorcerers stood.

Carol smelled loam. That was right. Jasmine's mother was also Earth. Just a slightly different form than Carol.

"Carol, won't you come with me and Jasmine?" Rosalia said. "Ernesto, please, talk with Cecelia and William. We need to share information."

Ernesto stood. "Are you sure?"

Rosalia nodded. "If I need your help, Carol will come get you. You as well, Cecelia."

Jasmine led the way, like a shadow down the hall, bumping the door to her old bedroom open with her shoulder.. It was painted the same old pale blue. Blue flowered bedspread on the twin bed with white painted posts. Carol hadn't been in this room for years. She glanced around. Searching...

There it was. On the shelf of books above the student desk. The photo of the two of them, eating french fries and drinking chocolate shakes. Fifteen years old.

Friends.

Rosalia was laying Jasmine back out on the bed.

"As flat as you can, hechicera. Yes, the pillow is fine."

Carol wanted to cry. Jasmine looked almost hollow. Her skin was usually luminous. Not today.

She looked like a woman being sucked dry from the inside out.

"Carol, come stand on the other side of the bed. I want you to be a second pair of eyes and ears. Anything you feel, hear, or see, you let me know. Entiendes?"

"Yes. Okay."

"Jasmine, I want you to close your eyes, slow your breath down, and just float if you can. Okay?"

Jasmine nodded, then closed her eyes. Carol could feel her trying to relax. To unwind the tension that seemed to be the only thing holding her together.

"She's so depleted," Carol said. But Rosalia could see that better than anyone. Carol re-centered, reached down for Earth, and tried to sense something deeper than the obvious.

Meanwhile, Rosalia was running her hands over Jasmine, around six inches away from her skin and clothes. Carol could sense the energy from Rosalia, but could barely feel Jasmine at all.

Rosalia began humming, low and soft. Then stepped back, scanning with her eyes all the areas her hands had been.

"Do you see it, maga?"

Carol tried to soften her gaze and open her aura out. All she could see around Jasmine was exhaustion, anger, sorrow...and a weird gray area. Like something was blocking the energy and light.

"I can't quite see what it is...but there's something blocking her all up and down her right side, from her hips to her chin."

Rosalia nodded. "Sí. Now. Clear some of the cobwebs out from in front of your eyes."

Carol, following instructions, actually used her fingers to make tugging and brushing motions around her eyes and forehead. There was some static there. Using her sense of touch, she cleared what she could away.

Then looked back at her friend and gasped, hands flying up to her mouth.

"You see it now."

"What is it?" Jasmine's eyes flew open.

Rosalia laid a hand on Jasmine's shoulder.

"Inside your aura, hechicera, is a great big snake."

17

JASMINE

Well damn. I should have known it. I should have known that was why my aura was a raggedy mess. Should have known that was why everything felt like it was draining away.

Should have know why that damn snake kept making it past wards and psychic barriers there was no damn way it should have been able to cross, even after the damn extraction Doreen had done. She clearly hadn't cleared it all out.

That Fed had sent a hook or something into my aura. Must have been back when I went up against him on campus two weeks ago. That was the entry point.

He'd just been biding his time.

Which meant... I wondered how much he knew now. How much the Feds knew. What the FBI had tapped into.

I wanted to vomit. I wanted to cry. I wanted to punch someone. I forced myself to lie still on the bed.

"How long?"

"What, hechicera?" Rosalia had pulled my desk chair up beside the bed. Carol had gone to tell the others what was happening. Make a plan of action, I guessed.

So much confusion swirled through my mind. I was just so *tired.* It was hard to get clear enough to figure out what in all the Powers was going on.

"How long has it been in there?"

The older woman paused. I could almost feel her sensing the air around me. "I am not certain. A thing like this, it is hard to tell. At least one week. Perhaps more."

Perhaps more. Perhaps I had led it into Oakland HQ. Perhaps I had led it to attack Fred Hampton. Perhaps it had been there when we busted Huey Newton out of jail. Perhaps, perhaps, perhaps.

"Well shit."

"Sí. Mierda."

"What are we going to do?"

Rosalia stood again and, leaning over me, put pressure in the hollow where my shoulder met my torso.

"Ah! Shit!" It hurt like fire.

"I think that is the entry point. It is a strange magic, though. And this serpent is not a natural construct, I think."

"What do you mean?" I asked.

She sat back down, frowning, small creases appearing between her black eyebrows. Rosalia's citrine eyes seemed lit from inside. Almost glowing. It was a little spooky, to be honest.

"It isn't Elemental. It isn't an animal ally, the way Las Manos works with them." She looked at me again. Not seeing me, but looking at whatever the fuck was inside me.

"It is almost mathematical."

"Solomonic," I said.

Rosalia's eyes flashed. "Yes. That is it. Solomonic. This is temple magic like I have not seen or felt in decades."

She closed her eyes.

"Cointelpro."

"What's that?" Sounded like some ceremonial magic syllables. They were always chanting something. But I couldn't make out what Rosalia was saying.

"I don't know, hechicera. But that word—if it is a word—is woven into the magic somehow. I am going to take us into la plano astral. We need to find out more."

"Now?" I practically squeaked. "Don't you need some of your, I don't know, candles or something? Shouldn't we call my mother in? Or Carol and Ernesto?"

Rosalia cocked her head to one side, as though she was listening for what was happening in the living room. Frankly, I couldn't hear a thing, except small murmurs.

"No," she said. "They are talking of important things. And we will likely need them later."

She grabbed my hands and ripped me from my room and into the astral. I really almost puked. My head was screaming. The place she'd touched on my shoulder felt like a spearhead dug into it. And that damn snake wrapped and unwrapped itself, moving around me.

I wanted to slice it to bits.

But all I could do was try to hang onto Rosalia's hands.

"Stay with me, hechicera. It is fine."

I didn't have much choice. Even knowing my body was still safe on the bed didn't help. This was freaky. All the colors swirling around us. Technicolor. Like some weird acid trip. If things ever calmed down, I really wanted to learn how Rosalia had access to all of this input on the astral, when for me, it was always just misty white or gray.

"Come. Come. Come." Rosalia said.

A giant bell rang. I felt the vibration inside every cell.

The snake detached itself from me. I slumped down onto my knees, falling down onto some strangely springy surface. Like lush grass.

Rosalia and the serpent faced one another. The serpent stretched up, as if it were a human, standing, but really it was floating in the air in front of the small sorcerer.

She started humming again, rocking slightly back and forth, from the balls of her feet to her heels. Her skirt swayed. Her hands shook. She keened. Crooned.

The snake writhed in front of her, as if it was held there by some magnetism. As if it was charmed by her. Or as if she held it in that space with sheer will.

If I were placing bets, it would be on Rosalia's will, that was for sure.

Then something changed. As if the quality of space and time shifted around us. Not just the usual astral shit. Something...

Started flowing in between them. In between the sorcerer and the snake. A backdrop of royal blue and purple pulsed, and just beyond where my eyes could make out distinct shapes, there were traces of something.

"Oh."

It became clear. Rosalia was pulling information from the serpent. Numbers. Symbols. Cyphers. Codes. They rose from the serpent, spectral gray. She drew them toward her with her hands. Breathed them in.

Her citrine eyes flared bright. The snake writhed and spun, but it seemed as if it was growing weaker.

I was feeling a little better, though. Even on the astral, I could feel the cuts on my hands and mouth start to itch. As if they were healing.

How was she doing this?

I didn't know. But I knew I wanted to learn everything she was possibly willing to teach me.

The flow was slowing down. The bell sounded again.

The snake collapsed.

I stood as Rosalia turned to me.

She was radiant. So bright I could hardly look at her.

"Tonantzin?" Why that name came out of my mouth, I wasn't sure. But it felt right.

She laughed, loud, throwing her head back, teeth flashing.

"I am not she, but some moments, she is more me than other times."

Whatever that meant.

"What do we do now?"

She looked down at the snake, lying quiescent at her feet. She stepped on it, hard, and it shattered into a million pieces of symbols—lines, numbers, dots, dashes—which were sucked into the royal blue and purple with a flash of blinding white. I covered my eyes with my hands.

When I lowered my hands, the snake was gone.

"Is that it, then?" I asked.

Rosalia looked a little sad at that.

"If only sorcery were that easy, hechicera. But no, I am afraid it may only be the beginning."

She took my hand, ready to return us back to my room and our waiting bodies.

"But we have more information now," she said.

18

JASMINE

Rosalia wanted to do another extraction right away. Get that serpent out of my aura so I could start to heal.

I wanted that, too. But I was also scared out of my mind. How in hell had this happened to me?

Lying in my bed, waiting for Rosalia to come back, I kept thinking of that brother in Chicago. Bound and gagged. Chained to a chair in that courtroom, with that hateful judge staring down at him from his bench. What must he have felt? Such a powerful being, trapped like that. Unable to move or speak.

That's how I felt now. A little bit, at least. Something had taken me over without my will. Bound me.

Of course, I knew now that he could have busted free, given enough anger and time. But the cat was protecting the other shifters.

I didn't think any Black Panther would ever be beholden to a racist white man, or a corrupt system, ever again.

Maybe that was it. The Feds couldn't get to the shifters

anymore, and knew it, so they were attacking the next powerful line. The sorcerers. The magic workers.

A sudden chill took me over. I thought of all the people Doreen was training up north. Were they going to be at more risk?

Rosalia came in, followed by my mother and Cecelia, and much to my surprise, the women were followed by Helen.

I'd asked Rosalia to send Carol away. It was bad enough she'd seen me this way. I couldn't afford to be distracted wondering what she was thinking of me. That was my shit, and I owned it, but it was shit that had to be dealt with. Dig?

Carol and I needed to figure out a new dynamic, but that wasn't going to happen today.

My mother bent over and kissed my forehead before stepping back to look at me. As usual, her soft curls were neat around her head, and her clothing was impeccable. She'd put on an orange cardigan over her white, pleat-skirted dress.

The only thing different about my mother was that she looked older all of a sudden. Her face was thinner. I could tell she was worried.

"Hey Mom."

Helen was still hovering near the doorway, her Jackie O bob sleek as a seal. She had her green skirt-suit on, and a chunky chain of gold.

"Helen. I'm surprised to see you here."

I felt my mother's frown at that bit of rudeness, but even laid up, I wasn't prepared to grovel for any Association honchos. Especially when they weren't taking care of things like we'd asked them to. Especially if they were aiding and abetting bullshit.

Rosalia motioned Helen further into the room and shut the door.

Then she spoke.

"Jasmine, Cecelia and Helen are both needed to help ground this energy. They are the sorcerers I picked, because you did not want Ernesto or Carol."

The reprimand was clear. *Behave yourself, Jasmine. Stop acting like a child.*

Well, I wasn't acting like a child, but I was too weak to argue the point.

Too weak to do much of anything.

"Thanks for coming. I appreciate it."

The image of a panther in prison roared in my head. *Yeah, brother. I feel you. But we'll just pretend we aren't in a lot of damn pain, and confused by emotions we can't control.*

"Please..." I said. "Just do what you have to."

Get me back.

"So," Rosalia said, "I need you right where you are, Cecelia. And Helen, come up to the other side of the bed. I'll need you to mirror each other's energies. You are close enough in feel to match."

Helen was a Water sorcerer, but closer to Earth. The flavor of her power was a solid, ice, not liquid like mine was. Of course, my water flowed out from me in what looked to other people like blue fire. All of our energies did that. Once we directed them outward, they looked like colored streams of light, or fire.

"You, hechicera, you just float," Rosalia said. "Try to relax. I do not know exactly what will happen, and can't promise anything, but just try not to fight."

I tensed up at that. Asking a Black Panther not to fight went against all of our training. And asking me, who'd been bristling at authority since I was ten, well, that was a hard order to follow.

But I trusted Rosalia so far. Trusted her power and integrity, even if I didn't exactly understand what her motivations were.

Slowly, I took myself down into the roiling miasma of pain and confusion. Then I willed myself to relax. It was the only way I could get my subconscious to calm down enough to let Rosalia do what she was already—dammit!—doing.

"Fuck."

My mother took in a sharp breath at that.

"Ssh, hechicera. I will try to be more gentle."

Rosalia was down at the foot of my bed, hands hovering just over the soles of my feet. She was drawing something down me. Trying to get it out of me through my feet.

"Not. Going. To. Work." I said.

The snake coiled itself tighter around my chest and neck. Sweat popped out on my forehead. I fought to not black out from lack of air.

"You can breathe, baby girl. Jasmine! Keep breathing!" My mother's voice.

A cool hand on my forehead, smelling of ice cubes and Chanel No 5. Helen.

Opening my mouth, I gasped in, then let myself drop down again, beneath the squeezing and prying and pain.

I felt Rosalia start to scan me from the inside out. It was excruciating. Not painful, but too, too intimate. She was combing through layers I hadn't even let Jimmy into. I doubted even my mother knew me that well.

It took everything in me to not shut down, hard, and shove the sorcerer out of my field.

Helen and my mother did something together, Earth and Ice, and all of a sudden I felt more supported. More clear. Some of the emotions receded. And the squeezing terror of the snake at my solar plexus eased.

How the hell had that thing gotten inside of me? And why hadn't Doreen's extraction worked like we thought it had?

Rosalia started humming, and she must have lit one of my Nag Champa incense sticks, because the scent wreathed around my head and slid down my nostrils.

I breathed it deep. It unclenched my diaphragm, allowing that knot of muscle to calm itself down. That calmed me down.

The humming grew louder. Helen and Cecelia joined in. I was surrounded by sound, and incense, and the soft pillow under my head, and the mattress covered with old quilts, and the power of these women.

"Louder!" Rosalia cried out.

Then I felt the bed shift. Rosalia was crawling on top of it, knees on either side of mine, crouching over me on the mattress, her breath sweet on my face. She began breathing and crooning at the hollow of my shoulder.

My breath came fast and shallow, all the relaxation gone again.

"Aaaaaayyyaaaaaaahhhhhh!" I shouted. The sound ripped itself from my throat, like the howl of a laboring mother.

Rosalia's finger jammed itself into that hollow of flesh between muscle and bone and I screamed until my throat ached.

Helen and my mother hummed louder, clutching at my hands. My body arched, my back bowed, shoulders and heels digging into the mattress as hard as hey could.

Rosalia was up on her knees then, straddling me, tuggingtuggingtugging. My shoulder felt as if it were ripping from my clavicle. Everything was stretched, distended, and on fire.

I screamed and sobbed and shouted and writhed.

Helen fed her ice into my body. My mother stabilized it all with the power of Earth.

Straining, sweating, shrieking, thrashing, I bucked against Rosalia as though it were the end of the world and I had to fight until I died.

Rosalia shouted something.

I heard a window slam up in its frame. And then slam down.

And everything was still.

I could hear Rosalia panting on the floor. And the hiss of something hot plunged in cold water.

The scent of Nag Champa, rich, woody, and sweet.

Helen's icy hands touching my aching shoulder.

And then my mother's face appeared, just above mine.

"It's over, baby. That snake is gone."

19

DOREEN

Doreen opened her door to find three Black Panthers standing there. Jimmy. Leroy. Carlos.

"Please, come in," she said, stepping back into the hallway, almost running into Patrice, who had come out of the sitting room to see what the knocking was about.

As the three of them filed in, three other shapes rushed forward, casting shadows in the dazzling winter sunlight.

Huey P. Newton. And Fred Hampton himself. He was back in Oakland, if he had ever left. Then his girlfriend, Deborah, heavily pregnant, looking ready to deliver any minute.

Every one of them pulsated with wild magic.

Doreen felt a spike of emotion move through her. Those damn ancestors were reminding her of her destiny again. *I know*, she said inside. *I'm paying attention, believe me.*

"Quickly now," she said.

They crowded in the bungalow and she shut and locked the door. Then threw the deadbolt for good measure.

Patrice had already ushered the first wave into the little sitting room and closed the drapes.

"Please," Patrice was saying. "Won't you sit? If there aren't enough chairs, the men can bring some from the kitchen."

Fred spoke. "We don't want to impose. But there are things you need to tell us. And we think there may be some things you need to know."

Patrice had at least gotten Deborah into one of the sturdy armchairs. Good thing she didn't try to lower the woman down onto the couch. She'd never get up again.

"Can I make you coffee? Offer you some water?"

"We need to know more about your magic, ma'am," Huey said. "We heard you all were talking about the revolution and magic down at the church hall. And we shifters haven't been talking like that to the people, so..."

Doreen flashed hot at that. Stung.

"So you decided to come reprimand us, is that it? What exactly does 'All power to the people' mean, young man?"

"It means that the people deserve the power. That it belongs to them," Jimmy quickly said.

Good boy. Doreen knew Jimmy was an ally. The fact that the shifter was sleeping with her niece should have assured her of that, but you never knew.

"You have to understand," Leroy said. "There are security risks as it is. And if you..."

"If we what?" Doreen said. "If we actually *teach* the people how to defend themselves? If we actually *train* people to use the power they have already? Isn't that exactly what you all have been trying to do?"

Deborah cleared her throat. "I think she's right. We apologize, ma'am. And we haven't been properly introduced yet. My name is Deborah. And I'd like that water you offered, if you don't mind."

Doreen looked at the striking young woman with her

sharply groomed eyebrows, full lips, deep-set eyes, face rounded by pregnancy. Her natural was sculpted high on her head. She looked good, despite being in hiding.

Deborah, unbuttoning the brocade coat straining over her stomach, looked up again, a question in her eyes.

Right. Doreen was staring. Her brain was slow. Trying to figure it all out.

"Patrice?"

"I'll get the water," Doreen's lover replied.

The amulet resting on Doreen's breastbone began to warm and quiver. Doreen drew in a breath, feeling the fire already rising inside her.

The scent of musk in the room increased. Doreen looked at the painting of the mountain lion in the golden Southern California hills. Hector.

Fred and Huey were looking at it, too. They both turned to her.

"That's my husband, the year before he was murdered by six LA County sheriffs."

They looked a little startled at that, except for Jimmy, who knew. Fred nodded.

Doreen was stalling for time. What did the ancestors want from her?

Patrice came back with a clear tumbler of water, placing it in Deborah's hand.

Something in that action tickled the back of Doreen's head. Her eyes grew soft. Over Deborah's face, the image of Doreen's Chokwe ancestor smiled.

"I know you all think you came here to talk," Doreen said, "but I need to take you all up to the attic now."

"And why is that, ma'am?" Fred asked.

"Because the ancestors insist upon it. They're battering at my head, telling me they have some things to show you.

Some things that will make all this talk you want to do unnecessary."

Huey had turned back to the portrait of Hector. He spoke now, back turned to the room.

"White America has seen to it that black history has been suppressed in schools and in American history books. The bravery of hundreds of our ancestors who took part in slave rebellions has been lost in the mists of time," he said, then turned and looked straight at Doreen.

Huey looked tired around the eyes, as though prison had taken a toll on him. It had to take a toll on everyone, shifter or not.

He continued in his soft, South-tinged voice, "So whatever messages these ancestors have for us, I'd like to hear."

Fred and Jimmy went to help Deborah up from the chair, but she shook her head.

"I think I'll let all of you climb the stairs. I'll be fine here."

Patrice stepped forward. "I'll stay with Deborah, Doreen."

She could have used her lover's help, but there it was. She walked on through to the kitchen, pausing to get a pitcher of water that she handed off to Jimmy, then out the back door and up the stairs. The four shape-shifting revolutionaries followed as though they were ducklings.

Intimidating ducklings, but ducklings all the same. Doreen smiled at that, and flicked the overhead light on, casting the room in an amber glow. The single window at the far end of the attic was too small to let in much light.

Fred, Huey, and Leroy ducked their heads a bit, then made sure to stand as close to the center beam as they could. Jimmy fit into the attic just fine.

Doreen began lighting candles to warm the space,

ending with the black, red, and gold pillars that lit up the Chokwe mask.

She heard a gasp and turned. The men were all looking at the dark eyes on the elaborate red, black, and white mask, looks of wonder on their faces. Doreen was struck by a fact she often forgot: They were young. Half her age.

Fred was only twenty-one years old. Twenty-one, and already survived an assassination attempt, saving his girlfriend and the child that was due any day.

"Come here." Doreen motioned them toward the altar. "Why don't you kneel down?"

The men did. She could tell they were in awe of the altar. Marxists. Atheists in awe of what they couldn't explain. She just hoped they could all understand. The ancestors meant business. They were working through her, guiding her words, her hands, her thoughts.

The most powerful men in Oakland were in her attic, and the ancestors were going to speak.

"Close your eyes for a moment. Find the root of your strength," she said. "Then open your eyes and look into the eyes of the mask. Listen."

She felt the energy change in the room. Everything settled. Deepened. Her own fire felt light and strong. The big cats inside the men no longer felt restless.

They felt free.

Free like big cats must feel in places where they weren't in constant danger. Where they could live as they chose, according to their nature.

Doreen wanted to live that way, too.

One by one, the young men looked into the mask. To ordinary eyes, the mask didn't change, but in Doreen's sight, a clear beam shone from the eyes, illuminating Fred. Then

Huey. Then Leroy. Then Jimmy. Something got transmitted that was not for her to know.

But this next part was for her.

"Each of you, by way of thanks, pour some water from the pitcher into the ruby glass."

The sound of water pouring and five people breathing softly joined the slight creaking and settling of the attic boards, warming from the candles and their bodies.

Once each man had made his offering, Doreen stepped forward, took the pitcher, and topped up the cut ruby wine glass.

She set the pitcher on one of the low shelves that lined the attic walls.

Closing her eyes, she listened. The ancestors told her clearly what to do.

Dipping her fingertips into the glass, she blessed each man in turn, tracing a line down their foreheads, from scalp to bridge of nose.

"You are blessed," she said. "You are called. My ancestors remind you of your ancestors. You carry the legacy of all freedom fighters throughout time. From Angola. From Burkina Faso. From Kenya. From the Ivory Coast. From South Africa. From Nicaragua. From Bolivia. From Maryland. Louisiana...Oakland."

She looked at their faces, water shining on their foreheads.

"The ancestors are with you. All the way."

The candles flickered. The ancestors prodded. She had to say the words.

"And magic is the birthright of the people."

20

CAROL

Carol and Ernesto were back at the Mansion, walking up the circular driveway, past the fragrant, preternaturally green lawn.

Seeing Jasmine had Carol shook. She didn't want to feel like Jasmine's equal by having her best friend weakened from attack.

Rosalia's theory was that the snake had been easing its way into Jasmine's aura for at least a couple of weeks, widening the tiny puncture hole the initial attack had left.

Doreen must have left a fragment inside during the original extraction, and the sorcery they'd used to bust Huey Newton free had pumped it full of juice again, giving it strength.

"What are we going to do, Ernesto?" she said, walking up the concrete steps, blond hair shining in the winter sun. Her rust knee boots were starting to pinch her pinkie toes. She just wanted to get up to her room and take them off.

He pushed open the heavy, carved wooden front door.

"We need to think, maga. And do more research. There

is something in those sigils you've been seeing. Something that will help us."

He tapped his hand against his pants pocket, jangling the keys inside.

"We just aren't seeing it yet. And we need to."

"Well," Carol said, leading the way down the long hall. "I can meet you in the library or the work room once I get these damn boots off my feet."

"You need to size up, maga."

"Who knew my feet hadn't stopped growing yet?" she complained.

It hit them like a wall. The wrongness of it. A tingling in the air, as if lightning had just struck, or a cathode tube had blown.

Ernesto held up a hand, as though Carol was going to move blithely along. The hall lights were dark, she noticed then. Dim light came down the hallway from a window set into the end.

"Shit," she said softly. "What's happening?"

Ernesto was quiet. Listening. A slight tapping noise, barely audible, came from their left, just up ahead.

The Mansion felt deserted.

Carol noticed a small slice of light then.

"Terrance," she said. His office door was ajar. Unease prickled all along Carol's skin. She was starting to feel ill, as though she needed to run for the toilet at the end of the hall.

This wasn't good.

"Mierda," Ernesto said. "What do you have on you?"

Carol was confused for a minute, then figured out what he meant.

"Just a crystal in my pocket. And some Minnesota granite."

There was also the string of blue beads from Rosalia that Carol wore around her right wrist. She wasn't sure that would help much.

"I have a pocket knife," he replied. "And a hawk feather."

"Should we get back up? Or more supplies?"

Brow furrowed, he frowned, the lenses of his eyeglasses shining in the dim light.

Carol's nausea worsened. She was torn between wanting to burst into Terrance's office and run away to the safe haven of her bedroom.

"No. I think we need to find out what sort of magia malo is in there."

Okay. Bursting in it was. Granite in one hand, clear quartz crystal in the other, Carol reached beneath the queasiness to find her center. She could barely push her consciousness there, but had to trust the slight connection was all she needed. Then she sent her attention to her feet. Right.

Putting the rocks on the hallway floor, she unzipped the boots and tossed them aside. Her feet felt instantly better. The queasy feeling abated, just a little. Peeling off her thin socks, she dug her feet into the blue carpet. A lot better.

Carol felt as though she could breathe properly for the first time since entering the hallway, and the sense of sickness was now mostly outside of her. Instead of clenching at her stomach, it swirled around them in the air.

Armed with granite and quartz, she was as ready as she could be.

"Good?" Ernesto asked.

"Let's go."

He flung open the door to Terrance Sterling's office and stepped back, slamming into Carol. She barely moved her bare feet out of the way in time.

"What?"

Ernesto was panting. She grabbed his shoulder and shoved him away enough to see the room.

The heavy sapphire drapes were open on the giant windows behind the fancy slab of Terrance's desk, but the room was still dim.

Web after web after web crisscrossed the room, from corner to corner, ceiling to floor. Thick strings in shades of white and gray obscured the furniture, turning everything inside the room to dim shapes, squatting on the blue carpet.

The sick feeling pressed in all around her, leaving the taste of rusting metal in the back of her throat.

"Look," she said, nudging him aside to point at the far corner, where the walls joined above the book and curio shelves, and the bar where Terrance kept his whiskey and soda. Above the bar she could barely make out a new painting. At least, she hadn't seen it before. The space above the heavy walnut sideboard that served as a bar used to be occupied with an old map in a bronze frame.

There was something new there, in shades of blue, black, and cream. She couldn't quite make out what it was. But that wasn't what she had directed Ernesto's gaze toward.

Above the painting, squeezing up against the leather book spines and wooden shelves, two massive spiders battled, darting and receding, lunging and shaking the network of webs.

The whole room vibrated with their magic. And magic it was, filling the room with miasma, sucking all the pure air out.

The spiders were huge, with abdomens the size of dinner plates.

Carol's breath came shallow in her chest. She clutched the granite and quartz, and prayed the blue beads around her wrist would lend extra power to the protective wards set in her aura.

Ernesto clicked open his pocket knife. The three-inch steel blade looked comically small when she looked at the webs.

He held the blade in his right hand, and the hawk feather in his left.

"What do you sense, maga?"

She cast out into the webs, forcing her consciousness open, desperately trying to root her bare feet into the sapphire expanse of carpet, which felt greasy under her toes.

Just do it, Carol. It's now or never, dig?

Holding her hands up, she felt where the granite and quartz met...the sigils. The damn sigils. The temple magic was so obvious to her now. The room was full of the twisted Solomonic stink of it, all frankincense and marble. And something else. Rank sweat. The barest salty, acetone tang of stimulants. Methamphetamines?

Underneath all that, she heard the long, slow beating of a heart.

"I think Terrance is in there!" she said.

Ernesto crouched toward the floor and cut away at the lower layers of webbing. Carol watched the spiders jump back from one another. The white one ran toward the painting. The dark brown one stayed near the ceiling. Waiting.

The brown spider felt familiar to her. Like something she'd seen before. Someone she had met.

Like...Jasmine. Or Doreen. Cecelia.

Carol's head swam and she swayed, hard, knocking her wrists against the door frame to steady herself.

"Don't black out," she said.

Ernesto was halfway to the grouping of couches and chairs.

"He's here, maga!"

She saw the leather sole of one of Terrance's shoes then. The heartbeat was his. But she still couldn't *feel* him.

"Shit," she said. Strange chanting resonated in her head. She caught only snatches of it, as though it, too, was muffled in thick webs. Or coming from far away.

"*Cooooomme... Intelligenssssssse... Cooooeintel...*"

Sweat rolled down her back.

"Shitshitshitshit." The pressure around her built. She fought herself, insisting to her muscles that they stand. And breathe. And that her eyes would focus. Focus!

"He's breathing!" Ernesto called back. She knew that already, because she could still hear the slow, lugubrious beats of Terrance Sterling's heart. Training her eyes on the big brown spider, everything pounding and pressing around her sweaty flesh, Carol let go.

And then she knew. She knew exactly what to do.

The brown spider had told her.

Granite cradled gently in her left hand, Carol raised the piece of quartz and began to trace the sigil in the air. The sigil whose origin she didn't know. The one that had come to her in dreams and visions. The sigil she had scratched onto page after page of white paper in black, black, ink, until it finally tore its way through the pulp.

This sigil, she knew now, was not hers to own. But it was hers to use, for now.

"Co!" she shouted, syllables coming unbidden to her lips.

"In!"

"Tel!"

"Carol, no!" Ernesto screamed.

She traced the sigil, forming it from rainbow light, clearing the webs, causing the room to brighten.

"Pro!" she screamed with all her might. A flash and boom lit up the space. The floor quaked beneath her feet.

Carol drew it all in, filled with power.

She laughed.

And smiled.

21

SNAKES AND SPIDERS

Samuels had grown to hate Los Angeles.

The filthy air. The dirty people. The scraggly palm trees. The Spanish music blasting from the ridiculous low rider cars, with their shining chrome and gaudy paint.

This wasn't a punishment, though it could have been.

For now, Samuels' assignment to Los Angeles was still a sign of the Master's trust.

The Master had been wroth, face red as bull's blood, the vein at this temple throbbing.

Someone had disabled the construct so carefully set up in the heart of that magical Association. It had taken years to infiltrate the organization and begin to corrupt the head. Years to put the thing in place. To get the small codes set. To weave the webs. To make sure the Bureau was controlling the operation.

And the man. That Terrance Sterling. He had been perfect. Too perfect.

It was all shit now. Something had gone wrong.

Someone had split the carapace of the spider and rent the webs.

That brown spider was bad enough, but they'd been fighting it just fine. There was only so much a spirit from the other side could do against a magical operation as tightly run as the Bureau.

But it had help now.

Someone was cracking the code. Someone human. Someone with magic. Someone they had all overlooked somehow.

It wasn't the Panther bitch, that Jasmine Jones, though for some reason she was in Los Angeles now, too.

So, while Samuels had orders to head back to Oakland, to deal with the unrest among the Panthers—and wasn't that all a clusterfuck now?—he was redirected back down to the stinking basin of Los Angeles.

Pacing through the streets of East LA, he sought the infiltrator —the agent provocateur—he still knew was in place, and cursed the one who'd committed suicide by prison guard.

He wanted to spit on the cracked sidewalks under his highly polished shoes. But that would erode his discipline further, and he needed every scrap of it that he could get.

Samuels needed to find and meet with Melvin "Cotton" Smith. The magical tag embedded in the man said he was getting closer. He could almost smell him. The slight tinge of grease and fear, overlaid with the brass of his bravado.

The man really thought he was invincible. The only thing keeping his fear alive was the slight squeeze to his throat that Samuels gave him once a day.

Samuels drew his ring finger toward his thumb and smiled. Let's leave Cotton a little short of breath right now. Let him know we're coming.

Samuels wondered if he should do surveillance on the Mansion. The operatives he had on that case didn't seem to be doing a very good job.

He paused for a moment, looking like a white man trying to catch his bearings. And in a way, he was. There were too many damned threads down here. Too many ways that things could go wrong.

The breach at the Mansion.

The death of that man Lizard and the escape of Huey Newton.

Jasmine Jones leaving Oakland for Los Angeles when he knew how wounded she must be.

And whomever it was down here who'd cracked that code? That was a new menace to be dealt with.

And somewhere in the back of Samuels' mind, there was a tugging to Chicago. Something was going wrong there, too. He just knew it. Not just that damn "revolutionary" shifting into a panther in his cell, though that was bad enough...something else.

Too much to keep track of. But that was his job, wasn't it?

He was going to have to tighten things up down here. Get some better men onto the job. They were stretched thin by the Master's whims. Too many operations. Too many people to spy on. Every situation more delicate than the next.

There weren't enough high-ranked initiates anymore.

The Master had made sure of that. Every time someone slipped up, he was decommissioned—or dead.

Samuels kept walking, smooth leather soles tracing the patterns in the sidewalk, black suit swallowing up the pale Los Angeles sun. He wished some clouds would cover up the sky.

It was too damn bright in LA.

22

———

JASMINE

The snake was gone, but so was a huge chunk of my aura. What should have been the easiest thing in the world, repairing a hole in my energy field, felt impossible. And I wasn't sure I should let anyone know.

Panther leadership had been right to be suspicious, I realized. I was definitely compromised.

I wasn't doing anything more than sitting in my parents' living room, and sweat was rolling down between my shoulder blades. The hollow in front of my shoulder still ached like hell, and I had almost blacked out twice.

The candle on the coffee table guttered, then flared again. I'd been at this for an hour, and nothing was working. The simplest damn baby-step candle-gazing, and I was sweating like a wrestler.

All from doing exercises so basic, a twelve-year-old freshly arrived at the Mansion could master them.

"Damn it."

The water in the wine glass next to the candle was the same level I'd started with. I hadn't even been able to raise the smallest ripple, let alone disperse any of the molecules into another form.

Fury built inside me. Why wasn't this working? My hands lashed out and struck the coffee table. That made the water in the glass move.

Great, Jasmine. Just great.

My emotions were still out of control, even with the damn snake out of my energy field.

So what was I supposed to do now?

My parents were at work. Or at least my dad, William, was. My mother? She worked part time these days. I couldn't recall whether she said she had to go in today or if she was at the Mansion.

She'd been at the Mansion a lot lately, conferring with Helen. I didn't trust what was going on there, but until I had my shit together, there wasn't much I could do about it.

Terrance Sterling was up to something beyond the usual stonewalling and refusing to use the Association resources to do any actual help. Carol and Ernesto said it was bad, but they didn't have enough solid proof to call for a conclave yet.

Terrance was refusing to get help, too, which was going to become an even bigger problem soon, if I had any say in the matter.

Or maybe it was finally time to walk away from the Association of Magical Arts and Sorcery. I was done with those honkies anyway. Who needed them?

Disgust and loathing roiled in my belly, rising into my chest. I swallowed the bile.

And went cold with fear, sweat clammy on my skin.

Were my emotions not just out of control? Were they—was I—still being manipulated somehow?

I ran my hands over my sweaty face, then wiped them off on my jeans.

Not sure how to tell the difference, I really needed help. But where was that going to come from? There wasn't anyone I knew I could trust. Even Jimmy was siding with Panther leadership now. He had to. His loyalty was to the Party. I got that, but I didn't appreciate it.

And thinking all that wasn't really fair. Jimmy wasn't siding with anyone. Not really.

Except that meant he wasn't siding with me, either. And that felt like a betrayal.

I hadn't called Carol since she was here at my parent's house. She'd called once, and I wouldn't talk to her.

It was funny. I'd wanted Carol to recognize her power for years. I used to get so irritated at her for giving it away to that pompous ass, Terrance. And for undermining herself all the time.

But now she was powerful and I was some weak-ass motherfucker.

That made me grin a little at least. When had I become so foul-mouthed? I'd better keep that in my thoughts, man, or my parents would flip.

Getting up, I shook my hands out and paced the living room from the navy sofa to the white brick fireplace. I needed to move, but was scared to go outside until the gaping hole in my field was repaired. It didn't even feel one-hundred-percent safe in here, behind my mother's wards.

I shook my head. My ears felt funny all of a sudden. It wasn't quite like someone had stuffed cotton into them. It was as if they were filled with the static white noise that happened when the news went off the air on Doreen's television. A nothing filled with not quite something.

Feeling like I was about to puke, I sat on one of the chairs, putting my head between my knees.

The static resolved into a long, low hiss. Some babbled syllables. Then hissing again.

Shitshitshitshit.

"Oh. Powers. Help me. Help me." I was practically moaning into the knees of my jeans.

Then the whole world tilted. The syllables poked and jabbed, the hissing...I could almost feel it prodding at the hole above my shoulder. It was the strangest thing, as though something was both outside Cecelia's wards and in. As though it was in two places at once.

But it wanted to be inside me. I knew it. Could feel it reaching, slithering, squirming.

"Help me!" I cried out.

Rocking back and forth, I pushed with all my might. The Powers were there. They had to be. The Powers were always there. Accessible to anyone who needed them. My mother told me that when I was five years old, and every day of my childhood. But I couldn't reach them.

I pulled then, trying to access the ocean. It was right there, damn it. Crenshaw wasn't far from the coast at all. Not for a Water sorcerer like me.

Not for a Water sorcerer like I used to be.

This was worseworseworseworse. Worse than the damn snake. Worse.

I collapsed on my knees as the poking, prodding, jabbing, hissing ripped into my skin and made my ears ache from the echoes.

Through all this noise, barely, there was the sound of the front door opening and closing. The shush of low heels on carpet.

Arms around my shaking shoulders. The scent of loam and butterflies. Cecelia. Mother.

"Jasmine? Jasmine, baby? Shhhh. Shhhh."

"Mom?"

"It's me. Jasmine. What do you need? What's happening?"

"It's still here, Mom." I was shaking. Couldn't manage to sit up straight.

"The snake?"

"No. Yes. Maybe." I managed to raise my head enough, but didn't see anything but the white bricks of the fireplace. One of them was chipped at the corner. Someone had painted over the chip.

"It's something trying to get at me, Mom. Maybe I'm going crazy."

"Sshhh." She held me. Tugged at me until I uncurled, then pulled me to her chest.

"Mom? I can't re-set my own protections. I've been trying. I can't make anything happen." My voice was thick, my throat sore. I needed to blow my nose to clear it, but didn't want to leave what felt like safety.

"And my emotions won't let go." I whispered that. Afraid to admit it, even though Rosalia and Doreen both had told me heightened emotions were part of the new phase of my powers.

My powers, which had all been stripped away.

How long had that damn snake been sucking me dry?

I was surrounded by pale, linden-leaf green. It bathed my edges, softening and soothing. My headache receded. The roaring in my ears subsided. And finally, the poking and prodding just...vanished.

Heaving a shuddering sigh, I relaxed against my mother's shoulder.

"You smell like grass," I said.

"Yes. I went out walking. Drove all the way up to Griffith Park. I needed the trees," she said. "And the perspective."

I barked a short laugh at that, wincing as my throat rasped from the strain.

"You can see through the smog today?"

"I can see through the smog every day, when I need to."

"Wish I could."

23

JASMINE

After a shower and a hot cup of tea, I convinced my mother I was well enough to drive.

That may have been a mistake. For one, I was still shaky. Second, living in Oakland had gotten me out of the driving habit. Navigating Los Angeles to the beach had seemed simple enough setting out, but I hadn't been counting on the disorientation from the sensory overload.

My throat still ached, and my body throbbed with misuse.

But I needed water. Big water.

I'd truly been ripped wide open and my whole being gasped for something familiar. I had to get near the ocean, so I gritted my teeth and made my way through the honking horns, the glare of sun on steel, glass, and concrete, and the acrid taste of smog at the back of my tongue.

The ocean was glorious. Twenty minutes from Crenshaw, the pale yellow sand of Santa Monica stretched right and left. The breezes cleared the coastal sky to a pale and vivid blue.

I wanted to start sobbing, and almost let myself go, but

there were still people around. My people. Black people. Nostalgia or some homing sense had taken me directly to the Bay Street Beach, also known as the Inkwell.

Though supposedly we could go anywhere now, black folks still liked to gather here, even on this mid-December weekday.

The beach wasn't crowded, like it would be come spring and summer, but clearly others needed the taste of salt and the scent of brine. Not just me.

An older couple walked near the water's edge, his pants cuffs rolled, her legs bare under a plain skirt. Shoes dangled from their hands. I wondered for a moment if I would ever have someone like that, Jimmy or someone else.

If I would ever grow old.

Bending down, I took off my boots. I needed to feel the sand.

Fred said "I believe I will die a revolutionary..." and he almost did. The assassination attempt was real. If they weren't shifters, he and Deborah would both likely be dead now.

I was a sorcerer, but no shifter. Sure, I had special powers, but was in no way bulletproof. And now? I wasn't even magic-proof. Tears rolled down my cheeks and I dashed them away with my hands.

On a shuddering breath, I sank my heels into the cool, grainy sand. Then I opened my heart and reached for the ocean.

It was right there. Waiting for me. Boots clutched in my right hand, I made my way toward water's edge. The breeze rifled through my tight curls. And then the water lapped at my toes. All the tension holding me together broke then, and I began to cry in earnest.

"Help me," I said softly to the waves. Drawing on the

water of the ocean and the Elemental Water that had claimed me at my birth, I began to fill with as much ocean as my battered body and psyche could take. There was still a small tear in my aura, I could feel it, though my mother had temporarily patched it.

No way was I at full power, but *you've gotta rebuild somehow, Jasmine.* The chant I'd learned when I was five, and just learning to work with Elemental Water, came back to me then. I hadn't even thought of it in years.

Rocking back and forth, gently, toes, then feet, then calves being splashed and surrounded by the tide, I let the words come out to greet the water. Softly. Surely. I began to sing.

"Water wash me. Water claim me. Water lend me power.

Water flowing, water shining, water fill me now!"

Then the hissing started in my ears again. Clamping down the edges of my aura, I felt the flare in my energy field just as the magic hit.

I whirled and there he was.

The snake. The man in the black suit. The Fed. The man who had entered my aura and staked a damn claim, like the Imperialist pig that he was. Crenshaw upbringing be damned. I was calling the man what he was.

He walked slowly toward me down the beach, backlit by the sun. One hand was raised casually, as if he was about to wave at an old friend.

Power was pouring from that hand, spiraling toward me, hunting me down.

The patch in my aura began to crumble. I whispered a word of power and drew more ocean to me, filling myself with the roaring depths and covering myself with the lightness of foam.

The blue-tinged fire built inside me. I waited. Let him come to me. Let the ocean build inside me.

He was so foolish to meet me here. To track me down to the place where endless water crashed onto the shore.

And the waves were crashing now. I could hear them. I could feel them. The bottom of my skirt grew wet. The next wave might splash me to my shoulders. Let it.

That was the thing about being a sorcerer. The things that will knock another person down, or lay a different magic worker to waste? If they are tied to our Element, they will only make us strong.

Mr. Black Suit Federal Agent couldn't have picked a worse spot, even as compromised as his Solomonic bullshit had made me.

He was close enough now that I could see the small slice of grin across his white face. The damn beach had cleared. It was just him, me, and the seagulls crying overhead.

No one wanted to be around a white man in a black suit on a Southern California beach.

I had enough ocean in me now to send off a blast, and began forming the blue fire inside my hands.

Every once in awhile, one of his attempts glanced off my aura edges, causing flares and sparks. But so far, the ocean had my back. Nothing was getting through.

Breathing in more ocean power, I tried to ignore the fact that despite all the water moving through me, my mouth was dry with fear. Drawing on all the swagger and sorcery bequeathed to me, I sank my heels a little deeper in the sand and water, feeling the slight sucking as the sand opened to me. Good. That was good.

Fear be damned.

"By all the Powers, my sorcery is in the service of the

people," I said to the breeze whipping sand around my thighs.

Then I blasted that Fed with a calculated shot, blue energy aimed right at his head.

The man tried to duck, but I had aimed low enough that it smacked him in the eyes, rocking him back for a moment, arms windmilling to regain equilibrium.

"Take that, honky."

Crouching low, he blasted back.

His next blast tore the patch right off my aura. I think I screamed. Or maybe it was the gulls.

No time to patch it, I focused on pulling out whatever damn magical hook was trying to root itself into me. It hurt like crazy.

A low whine started up in the base of my throat. I let the power of the ocean roll on through, not trying to control it anymore, while I tugged at his barb with one hand and lobbed energy at the man with the other.

He was still coming, though I had clearly slowed him down.

Tears poured down my face. Anger threatened to throttle me. I breathed deep and let the ocean rush, stronger, faster, louder, deeper.

I became the ocean. I was nothing now but water. Not woman. Not sorcerer. Not Black Panther. Not Jasmine.

"Waaaaaatttteeeeerrrrrrr!" I screamed into the sky.

Pulling both arms back, then punching forward with all my might, I let the liquid energy of blue fire move through my fingertips.

I hit him with the whole ocean.

He disappeared. One minute, we were battling, and then, somehow, in the maelstrom of my sorcery, the man was just gone.

I didn't see how that was even possible. He had more magic than I thought, and a lot of power to back it up.

Because the cops in that alley? They'd been knocked out and down by my sorcery. We'd left them unconscious in the alley.

But the man in black? He was just gone.

Not even a footprint left on the sand.

I stood there, breath heaving, the power of Elemental Water still moving through my veins, and wondered what in all the Powers I'd gotten myself into.

24

DOREEN

Doreen held Patrice's hand across the kitchen table. The remains of a late lunch littered the red Formica. Sandwich crusts. Half of a Red Delicious apple.

The coffee was cold in their cups.

Doreen's body was filled with a sense of deep satisfaction and power. She also knew that if Patrice hadn't seemed to need to talk right now, she would have dragged her lover into bed.

"The ancestors blessed them?" Patrice said.

Doreen started to rise, wanting to work off some of the excess energy by clearing up. Patrice tugged her back down.

"Stay, baby."

"What's wrong, Patrice?" Doreen asked.

"I don't know, exactly. I just wish I could have been there. It was interesting talking with Deborah, don't get me wrong. These young people are so *powerful*, it amazes me. And so *clear* about everything."

Doreen agreed. The intelligence of Panther leadership was one thing. But their insight and strength were even more impressive. She didn't think she'd known so much at their age.

In her early twenties, Doreen had been too busy falling in love with Hector and practicing magic. And sure, she had been involved with the Association and all, but she surely hadn't been taking on the world.

Not like the Black Panthers.

The way they walked through the world—even when the world was gunning for their heads, doing its best to tear them apart—was an inspiration. The Panthers walked tall, heads high. With purpose. Like they knew just what they were about, racist world be damned.

She looked at her lover, lipstick faded from their lunch. Patrice was beautiful. Doreen was so lucky to have found her, here, in the middle of her life, with bullets and magic falling from the sky.

But her lover wanted something from her. Or was trying to tell her something. Doreen needed to draw herself back from the young people who'd snuck out through her yard to a waiting car that took them who knew where. Someplace safe, she hoped.

"Don't you feel clear, Patrice?"

"I'm getting clear. I'm clear that I've led a comfortable life, and it's been good. I'm also getting clear that I need more."

Doreen shoved one of the empty plates aside and leaned in.

"More what?"

"Everything!" Patrice said, then put a hand to her mouth as if she'd said too much.

She shook her head, jostling her perfect curls.

"Those kids, I know they're not kids, those Panthers... they *know* things. And they *do* things."

"You do things, too."

"Not like that," Patrice replied. "Not like you and Jasmine, and those Panthers."

Patrice stood up then, and started clearing dishes, scraping bread crusts into the garbage can. Clattering the plates together in the sink.

"Patrice. What's going on?" Doreen said, rising, putting her arms around her lover, who had her back turned to the kitchen, head down, arms braced on the sink. Doreen smelled the cocoa butter, Aqua Net, Patrice scent at her neck.

"Tell me, baby."

"Is there some sort of blessing *I* can have? Some, I don't know, initiation or something? Some way of being more than what I am?"

Doreen gently squeezed her lover's belly, feeling the softness give beneath her hands.

"You're more than enough for me, Patrice. And you are helping those Panthers, and this community. And me."

Patrice turned in Doreen's arms, but still wouldn't look her in the face.

"That's not what I mean. I want to be like you."

"I can't turn you into a sorcerer," Doreen said. "But there *is* something I can do."

She could give her lover more magic.

She could initiate her into the mysteries so ancient, they had no name. She could breathe life into her lover, and speak the secret names that would act as a shield and a source of endless power.

Not quite endless enough to keep a dying person alive, but endless enough to help a person through what they were facing.

And it could feel like enough to carry them both. To

protect them against whatever evil stalked these streets and invaded her niece's mind. There was evil walking in sharp black suits, evil that flew through the sky and crouched in corners.

And Patrice was right. She'd thrown in her lot with Doreen, and Jasmine, and the Panthers, with little more knowledge than something needed to be done, and little more protection than a spell bag and her skin.

"Come with me," Doreen said. And she led her lover to the bedroom after all.

Standing in front of the dresser-top altar, she breathed in, wriggling her toes in her crocheted slippers, then pulled them off her feet. She'd be naked soon enough anyway. Only one way to do this, whether standing up or lying down, and that was skin to skin.

"Doreen." Patrice put a hand on her arm, pausing her. "What I was trying to say there, in the kitchen..." Her eyes searched Doreen's, looking for something.

"I want to be a real partner to you," she continued. "Not just your lover. Not just someone who helps you with your magic. I want to be able to really *be* with you. Share the power you and Jasmine have. Be more."

"Then that's what we'll do," Doreen replied.

Lighting the white tapers in their silver holders, she picked up a silver-backed mirror from the wooden chest of drawers.

Beckoning to Patrice, she held the mirror up. It reflected the two women's face, side by side.

"Look," she said.

"What am I looking at?" Patrice asked.

Doreen moved out of the frame. "Look at yourself."

The only sound in the room was the slight hiss of flame eating wick, and two women breathing. Sure, there were cars in the distance, and the shouts of children coming home from school, but in that bedroom?

Just the two of them.

The two of them and the ancestors already gathering around.

The two of them and the ancient Gods and Goddesses, ancestors, and Elemental forces Doreen was already touching with her mind. The things they called the Powers.

The Association liked to act like the Powers only worked for and with the sorcerers. But Doreen knew that wasn't true. That just made Association members feel special. And as though they could lord it over people who were just trying to get through their own lives.

Well. That stopped here and now. Jasmine and the Panthers had one form of revolution, and Doreen would die supporting that if necessary, she knew that now.

But here in her bedroom, with her lover's breath filling up the room?

Doreen was about to start her own revolution.

She lowered the mirror.

Looked in her lover's eyes.

Patrice was quivering inside, Doreen could tell, but her lover kept herself steady all the same.

"This is an old rite. And there are other ways we could do it, but really, the best way, and the way I know best, is through some form of touch. And since we're lovers already, the easiest form of touch is what we already do."

"Sex."

"Yes."

Patrice started to remove her clothing, folding them up and laying them neatly on a chair beside the bed.

"Should I lie down?" she asked.

Doreen paused for a moment, drinking in the lush,

curved hips, the sagging, heavy breasts, the slight bronze shimmer of stretch marks around the belly.

"You are so beautiful," she said.

Patrice just smiled. Waiting.

"Stand for now. Here. In front of the altar. They want to see you."

Doreen stripped her own clothing off in record time. Then found her center. Raised her Fire. She let it flow down to her toes, up through her thighs. It lit up her hands. Her shoulders. Her sex. Fire filled her throat, her cheeks, her eyes. It shot out the top of her head and showered in a rain of sparks back down to bless the earth.

Doreen kissed her lover's lips. Slowly. Patrice breathed in, and kissed her back.

Doreen turned her lover around, so they stood, front to back, one of Doreen's arms pressing Patrice's body close to her own.

She touched Patrice's skin, soft as a butterfly. Smooth. Patrice's breath quickened.

Doreen's hands roamed over knob of collarbone, the heaviness of breast, the fullness of hip, taking her time, building the magic, stoking the Fire.

Until she touched her favorite place. The place of mystery. Her fingers knew exactly where to go, filling her lover with her Fire.

Then Doreen leaned her mouth toward Patrice's ear.

And she began to speak the ancient names aloud.

25

———

CAROL

The library was quiet. Carol could hear some small thumps and murmurs from the second floor, but that was all. The quiet felt good. She needed a little quiet.

She should have been freaked out, but didn't feel that way at all.

Carol tasted the power on her lips. She felt it in her feet and hands. This was what everyone talked about. Sorcery. This was sorcery.

This must be what Jasmine felt like all the time.

Except Jasmine didn't feel like this right now. Carol hoped her best friend was okay. She wished she could tell Jasmine about the spiders taking over Terrance's office, and what she and Ernesto had just done.

That she, Carol, had fought the big white spider. That she had connected it to the sigils.

That Ernesto was convinced it was the government. Just like Jasmine's snake. The US government. Doing magic. Old Temple magic. Or as Jasmine would put it, "Solomonic shit."

Well, geometry could be busted open with more geometry, couldn't it?

At least, that was the plan.

Carol was waiting for Ernesto in the library. He had run and gotten two of the other teachers to help and they had dragged Terrance to his bedroom. An Association healer was with him now. He was barely breathing. Held in some suspended state.

She swirled the amber liquid in a heavy cut glass tumbler. Terrance's whiskey.

"Brandy would be better, but this is what we have," Ernesto had said before leaving her. "Drink as much of it as you can. I'll be back soon."

And then he had kissed her.

The liquor burned, but that felt good. Carol thought she'd be drunk by now, but the sorcery seemed to be eating up the alcohol as quickly as she sipped it down.

It felt groovy. Yeah. In the groove.

As if she was finally part of everything. Of all the magic swirling in all of the worlds.

The four worlds with their twelve spheres. And Terrance was missing from this one, the sphere of Earth. The world of matter.

Maybe he was up in the sphere of the Moon, ready to be re-formed. Getting a new blueprint. Or maybe, she thought—taking another sip of whiskey as she scanned the library shelves, barely taking in dusky leather spines —maybe he was caught in the Qlippoth. The shadow Tree of Life. The place every magician feared to go. Because a person never knew if they would or could return.

The stakes felt too high all of a sudden. Or maybe Carol was finally coming down from the magic.

All she knew was when Ernesto walked back into the library and shut the door, she moved toward him and kissed him hard. Clutching the back of his neck with her left hand, still gripping the whiskey tumbler in her right.

He moaned into her mouth and all she wanted then was what she had wanted since she was fifteen. For Ernesto to make love to her, here, on the library floor.

She let herself grow heavy, trying to drag him down with her.

"Maga! Carol!" he growled into her cheek. "We can't."

"Why can't we?" she asked.

"Terrance…"

She tugged at him, left hand on his belt now, reaching for a shelf with her right, wanting to set the whiskey down.

"Oh. By the Powers…" he moaned.

"By the Powers," she whispered.

What was happening to her? She was becoming the person she'd always been meant to become.

They hit the floor, and she rolled on top of him. They kissed as if they were sinking into Earth. She wrapped their bodies in her Element. Her bones sought out his bones. His muscle sought her muscle.

They kissed. And kissed. And kissed.

And then she grew lighter. He was pushing on her Earth with Air. And everything inside her became clear.

Looking down at his eyes through the glasses she must have smudged with her forehead or her nose, she knew. Like the crystal whiskey glass. Faceted, yet clear.

"I love you," she said.

Raising his head to look at her better, he said, "I know. I love you, too."

Then Ernesto groaned again, letting his head flop to the Turkish rug.

"But we have work to do," she said.

"We have so much work to do."

One more kiss, and then they were helping each other off the floor and into the chintz barrel chairs set near the big flagstone fireplace.

This time they both had whiskey in their hands.

"We really need to eat something," Ernesto said.

"We really need to have sex." Carol grinned. He shook his head at that, smiling.

She was bold now. That felt good, too.

But really? He was right. Now that the sorcery wasn't propping her up, Carol realized she was ravenous.

"But we should talk first, before food or anything else," she said, regretfully. Being an adult had its good points, but talking before sex or eating wasn't what she really wanted.

She took a deep breath.

"That white spider..."

"Did you get a sense of what it was?"

Nodding rapidly, she raised the tumbler to her nose and breathed in the scent.

"It's a construct. Made of magic and geometry. It seems fueled by ideas, which is strange, rather than by blood, or breath, or energy. I mean..." By the Powers, it was hard to explain what she had sensed.

"I mean, there were traces of blood and sweat, and something thick and salty." She blushed as she realized what she must have just described. She'd read about it enough, late at night.

Ernesto's face was slightly more ruddy than usual, so yeah, that must have been it.

"But mostly it was just numbers. Not numbers. Formulae. Shapes. And those sigils."

"Any idea how to take it down?"

"Not yet," she said, getting up to pace again. The energy had receded, but she was still full enough of the sorcery to feel the need to move. And to distract herself from running her fingers down the dark hairs of his arms. She almost told Ernesto to roll his sleeves back down.

"But that brown spider? That's an ally, like we thought. And it has some connection to Jasmine's family."

Ernesto's gaze grew sharp. The silver wolf ring glinted on the hand wrapped around his whiskey glass.

"In what way?" he asked.

Carol stopped pacing the edges of the rug and looked up at the timbered ceiling, to where the whitewashed walls met wood. The library was much closer to the original state of the Spanish-style mansion than Terrance's office was. He must have asked for his room to look more English or something. Which was weird.

Marring the nature of a thing in order to make it more your own. All sorcerers did a little of that, but the best sorcerers followed the original shape or nature of their materials. Working in harmony with the world made the world stronger. It meant everything could do its best work, from its place. And grow.

Everything stopped inside her then.

That was it. The thing that was wrong. How many years had Terrance Sterling been working against the nature of things, in order to increase his power and authority?

Was that why she had always felt so small and cowed? As if she'd never be more than a nanny to the *real* sorcerer's kids when they came? As if she'd always stand in Jasmine's shadow?

And how, by all the Powers, had Jasmine escaped this? And what was happening to her friend now?

"What is it, maga?" Ernesto asked.

"Terrance. He's been growing things out of season." She cast about for a good way to explain it. "He's been forcing things into shapes they shouldn't take. Something finally went really wrong."

Ernesto nodded, slowly, then took another sip of whiskey.

"He must have lost his own bargain with the Procrustean Bed," Ernesto said. "Chopping off his own soul in order to make it fit."

Carol found her chair again and sat, suddenly heavy.

"The Solomonic magic, Ernesto. He's been working that. Somehow. He must have been."

Ernesto didn't say anything. Just drank some whiskey. But his knuckles were yellow against the brown of his skin, as if he was straining, clutching at the glass.

"Maga, those sounds. The syllables you were shouting..."

"I don't know what they were, Ernesto. But they're connected to the sigils and the spiders somehow."

He sighed. Tapped his wolf ring against the glass until it rang.

"Do you think Terrance let that white spider into the Mansion?" Carol asked.

"I think that was his plan all along, maga. And I think the spider is now eating him for lunch."

He set his whiskey on the coffee table then, and stood.

"I just hope it doesn't try to eat us all."

26

JASMINE

"You can't *protect* me anymore! I'm grown!"

I was pacing my parent's kitchen. It was all blond wood cabinets, with blue dish towels and curtains to match the blue linoleum floor.

Blue like an ocean layer.

The aftermath of blasting the Fed on the beach still hummed through me, though I was freaked out about the fact that he'd disappeared. At least I had the power of Water, filling me up, easing the aches in my muscles and bones.

It wasn't calming my emotions down. Yet. But when I scanned the hole in my auric field, it seemed to be shrinking, so I was grateful for that at least.

But I wasn't grateful for the reaction from my mother when I'd walked back through her door.

She had felt the blast, with me a twenty-minute drive away, which meant I wasn't healed. We both knew it. So my mother was talking some bull about needing more healing before I was fit to go back out to the streets.

To my work.

By all the Powers, if it were up to her, I'd be locked away

in a UC Berkeley dorm for the next two years, not allowed to leave the campus.

As if campus was safe. I shook my head.

My father sautéed mushrooms at the old white hulk of a stove. Slices of beef sat ready to be added to the pan when the mushrooms had cooked down to his liking. My stomach growled at the scent, but my throat was still so raw and tight I wasn't sure if I'd be able to swallow dinner.

"Jasmine." Oh, the patience in my mother's voice made me want to scream. "You clearly need help."

She was ripping iceberg leaves for salad into a big yellow bowl.

"It's okay to need help, baby. Happens to us all," my father said. William, the rock of our family. The one who kept my mother and I steady and on course.

"*You* don't need this kind of help," I said. "No one looks at *you* like you're a screaming child."

I was being petulant and knew it, but I couldn't stop myself. The emotions still roiled inside me, even though I was doing my best to center and calm down.

"Jasmine girl," my mother said, "we aren't looking at you like you're a screaming child. We just know what it's like when the Powers take us over and everything goes on high alert. We all need help to get back on track. Not just you."

"Daddy doesn't know what it's like."

He sighed at that, and started layering the beef strips into the pan. They sizzled when they hit the cast iron. My stomach growled louder.

Shut up, stomach. Whose side are you on, anyway?

"Your father put up with my changes, girl." Mother's voice was sharper than before. She was losing patience. Good.

"Jasmine," my dad said, turning the heat down on the

pan a notch before turning around to face me. "I know you think I don't have any magic. And it's true, as far as it goes. I'm no sorcerer. But I've helped your mother do her magic all these years."

I watched Cecelia's hands grow still, then start ripping at the leaves again, the crunch of lettuce and the sizzle of searing beef loud in my ears.

"I would have lost it without him, Jasmine," she said quietly, still rending the pale green leaves. "Your father saved me. That's some kind of magic of its own."

"I don't want to be saved," I spat out.

"Well, I don't care!"

My mother whirled on me then and stepped two inches from my face.

"You will get help whether you like it or not!" she said, then began to clap her hands and stomp her right foot on the ground. "If Terrance had gotten help by now, you think we'd be in the mess we're in? What if something like that happens to you? You think it won't, *but you don't know!*"

The clapping and stomping freaked me out. The blue linoleum shuddered beneath my feet. The wind of my mother's hands, smacking palm to palm, wafted across my cheeks. Her hands were too close to me.

Her Earth built beneath me. Around me. Closing me in. Making a dam to hold my Water.

Barely aware of it, I heard the scrape of cast iron being moved from the hot burner, and the click of a knob as my father turned off the stove.

Shit.

"Come to us now!" My mother's voice.

My father's hands on my shoulders from behind, steadying me.

"Ancestors, see your child!"

My father's warmth, steering my suddenly wobbling legs into a kitchen chair.

Clapping. Stomping. The bell-like melody of fingers pressing on the metal keys of a kissanje gourd. Angola. Chokwe. Where had that sound come from? Not from within this room.

The air grew thick. The spirits pressed in on me, tingling on my skin. I was grateful for the sensation of my father's hands through the gauze fabric of my shirt.

I needed the anchor.

My mother's voice grew louder in my ears. She was chanting some nonsense language that I'd never heard before. Not a magical language. None of the European languages I knew of. But it didn't sound like the snippets of Kiswahili I'd heard before, either. I'd never heard any other African languages spoken, but I didn't think it was any of them.

My mother was speaking in tongues.

Her body shook and rattled. Her movements grew looser as her hands snapped themselves together, first on the right side of my face, then the left. Then above my crown. Then below my chin. She was clapping out an equal-armed cross around my head.

I vibrated with her power. Her Earth crashed up against the shores of my Water.

My father, William, was steady through it all.

The bottom dropped out of my stomach and warmth spread on the chair. One sliver of my mind sent out a prayer that I hadn't just wet myself, but there was no time to worry.

My back ground against the wooden chair slats. The balls of my feet strained against the linoleum. The fluorescent lights above the stove and sink hummed, splitting through my mind like a serrated knife.

"Water! Water! Ocean! Be with me!" I cried out, and heaved against my father's hands. My mother's Earth was still too strong around me. Ocean couldn't get through. I was left with what was inside me.

Biting the inside of my cheeks, I felt water and salty blood flood my mouth. I drew on that, as hard as I could, pressing out against the surrounding clay and the tingling ghost hands flickering around my skin.

Then the snap and burn of a slap across my face broke the spell. I sank over my knees, sobbing. Felt my father's hands stroke my back. My mother bent her knees and wrapped her arms around me.

Mother and Father rocked me.

My mother's voice whispered those strange syllables into my left ear, then my right. The whispers slid all the way down my ear canals and into my heart. I could feel the ancestors following, repeating my name.

My father gently sat me up again.

My mother spoke out loud, her voice rough with effort.

"Ancestors, be with our daughter, Jasmine, as she walks her path. Surround her with protection. Let her know your love is as real as her fingers and the tip of her precious nose. Teach her the ways of our people."

My breath heaved in and out of my chest. Even though the press of Earth had receded, it still felt hard to breathe, with all the ancestors crowded inside and out.

"Please help me," I whispered.

A calm settled inside me then. I was able to take in a full breath. Then another.

My mother spoke again. "Ancestors, I apologize for ever doubting your power. I will honor you from this day on. I will learn. I will make offerings. I will speak your names."

Looking at my mother, I saw a firmness to her face that

hadn't been there before. There was steel in her eyes, but not directed at me.

It was directed at whatever, whoever, had done this to me.

I knew that now.

She reached out and grasped my hand. My father put his hand on top of ours.

We were together. I got that now. I dug the power of my family for the first time in my life.

And I knew what needed to be done.

But I was damned if I'd do anything before I took a shower and ate my father's beef and mushroom sauté.

27

JASMINE

I needed to be around radicals again.

I needed to see the Panthers, to get my grounding in LA, but with 41st and Central shot up and shut down, I wasn't sure where to even find them. I'd heard they were working on a free medical clinic named for Bunchy Carter, whose death was coming up on a year ago, but as far as I knew, it wasn't open yet.

Bunchy Carter and John Huggins, it turned out, were stalwart Panther leaders, but not shape-shifters. People said they were killed by some black nationalists from the US organization. The more I found out about it, the more suspicious I became.

There was a bad taste in my mouth about *all* of the recent events down here. The killing of Bunchy and John. The raid at 41st and Central...when I tuned into them down here, I sensed snake. Everywhere.

Yeah. That Fed was around. Despite the fact that I'd blasted him on the beach, since I didn't see where he went, I had no idea where he *was*. That got under my skin, too. What kind of magic made a man able to disappear in the middle of a firefight? I'd have to ask my mother about that. Or maybe Ernesto would know.

I steered my father's car down to the old HQ, figuring there might still be folks clearing through the rubble. Driving past the gas station advertising Coca Cola, and small shops selling odds and ends. A barber shop. People were out and about, pulling on small, two-wheeled metal shopping carts, or standing on the sidewalk, talking and smoking.

And there it was. Next to the shop whose metal grate was pulled shut under a battered Used Clothing sign with a white Impala parked in front, was what looked like just another storefront. But this one had Panther Party posters taped up in the windows.

A sign stuck out from the building, like a metal banner over the sidewalk, ready to greet anyone who walked by. "Feed Hungry Children Breakfast" it read. And in the corner, under the words "Free Huey" was a small painting of his face.

Well, Huey was free now. We'd seen to that. But HQ looked pretty empty this particular afternoon.

I'd been told there might be a rally starting at Los Angeles City Hall, so I turned the car that direction and glanced at the small silver watch around my wrist. I had about forty minutes to get there and figure out where to park. What should have been a twenty minute drive took me half an hour because of Friday traffic.

I drove past Little Tokyo, ignoring the honking cars and the acrid taste of smog, until I saw the big, white stone WPA building that dominated the neighborhood.

Scraggly palm trees reached toward the brown-tinged sky. Los Angeles almost never looked like the photos. The blue sky only appeared when the wind was blowing just right, or you were closer to the ocean than I was right then.

A gold Buick pulled out in front of me, and I decided I was close enough to walk, and took the spot.

After stuffing some coins into the meter, I began walking toward the corner, toward the front of the building. As I turned the corner, on the cascade of front steps leading to the vast portico that opened onto a courtyard in front of the tall main building, I saw hundreds were already gathered, with more arriving by the minute.

Like when I first saw the Panthers massing on the Oakland courthouse steps when I first arrived up north, the sight brought the sharp pricking of tears in my eyes.

I pushed my way into a spot across the street, because the steps and sidewalk were already filling, corner to corner, and I wanted to be able to see. I just hoped the sound system set up at the top of the concrete steps had strong speakers.

"Protest Panther Genocide" read a sign carried by a young man. I gave him the fist salute. He raised his right fist in acknowledgement.

"Power to the people! Power to the people! Power to the people!" everyone shouted.

Middle-aged women in flowered blouses and blue skirt suits held signs that read "We will remember 41st and Central." There were young men in denim jackets and berets. Men in starched shirts and ties. The mingled scents of cologne, cigarettes, and marijuana.

The crowd roared like the ocean. I turned and saw that the civic center park behind me was jammed full with young sisters and brothers, and middle-aged black folks, with a sprinkling of white faces here and there.

"Because the power is yours!" a young woman in a long

leather coat stepped toward the mic and said. I was glad for my own leather coat and wool beret. The breeze was cool.

I thought the woman at the microphone was Ericka Huggins, John's widow, but I couldn't be sure. She started to explain the new paramilitary squad in charge of the shoot-out. Something called SWAT. I'd seen the photos in the paper, black canvas pants tucked into military boots. Tan flak jackets. Apparently since the raid, they had been patrolling the neighborhoods, intimidating the community.

And then the breath left my lungs. Pushing her way toward the microphone was Angela Davis. I'd never met her, but she loomed large in my mind.

"There is a conspiracy in the land and that conspiracy is headed by Nixon," she said. "It's directed by Attorney General Mitchell. Agreed to by Ronald Reagan. And Chief of Police Davis is carrying that conspiracy out. Now what is this conspiracy? We have to call it by its name. It's genocide."

Angela Davis, huge natural blowing in the LA breeze, commanded the microphone and the massive crowd.

There were thousands of us out here now. The cops I could see on the side streets must have been terrified. I wondered if any shifters were in the crowd, cursing myself for not working harder to contact the local party after I arrived.

Then I took a breath and remembered: I hadn't been myself these past few days. Tracing the edge of my aura with my mind, I exhaled. Good. Whatever my mother and the ancestors had done seemed to be holding for now. I just hoped I'd be able to get back in better shape soon.

Jimmy and leadership were right to be nervous around me. My sorcery was a loose cannon since we busted Huey free. Tears pooled in my eyes again. Oh Jasmine.

Revolutionaries got no time to feel sorry for ourselves.

"We just need to get free," I murmured.

"Excuse me?" a young white woman, brown hair shining down the back of her green corduroy coat, looked at me expectantly.

"I'm sorry." I gave a little smile. "I was just thinking. Didn't mean to speak aloud."

She turned her attention back to the ersatz stage. A man was on the microphone now, calling on the crowd to march across the street to the Hall of Justice.

People started moving, en masse, walking calmly, some chanting, some trying to cross when there were breaks in traffic. There was no way for me to escape even if I wanted to. I was fairly near the big white stone building hulking on the corner. People jostled me from the sides. I opened out my senses and began to help steer myself and those closest to me safely toward the doors. The light changed and we crossed. I looked up at the bronze metal dividing the windows over the heavy glass doors.

"Hall of Justice" read bronze letters inlayed into stone just above. What did that even mean? There was no justice in those halls for the likes of us.

The marble entryway was already crammed full. People began to climb the sweep of stairs.

A chant started up, voices rumbling and rising, filling the space all the way to the inset medallions on the ceiling, and bouncing back to us from the chandeliers, creating a constant cascade of vibration and sound.

"Power to the people!" the voices cried. "Power to the people."

My bones shook with it. My mind expanded to take it all in. The water inside my mouth coated the words before I shoved them past my lips.

"Power to the people!" I shouted, fist raised.

And then, I smelled something I shouldn't have. Felt a tugging and looked up.

At the top of the stairs. Black suit. Starched white shirt. Glasses dark as night.

That damn snake of a man was staring down at me.

How in all the Powers was he here?

And how had he known I'd be here?

28

DOREEN

The flower shop felt like an alien landscape after all that had been going on.

It had been Doreen's haven and grounding cord for so many years. Now it just felt strange. The sorcery had drawn her fully in again, making anything that didn't have to do with magic begin to feel like a simulacrum.

How people lived without their magic, Doreen didn't know, though Powers know, she had certainly tried.

Patrice wanting more magic made sense to Doreen on a deep level. And the ancestors and Powers felt...pleased. Doreen hadn't had cause to do an initiation in what felt like more years than she could count, but it turned out that juice was juice, and yes indeed, she and Patrice were juicy.

Doreen smiled and breathed in the scent of flowers. Spicy marigolds. The earthy scent of pansies. The spring field whiff of daisies. All of it was dampened by the cold. Flowers wilted in the heat once they were picked.

She hung her navy overcoat on a hook in the back and tied a green apron on over her striped navy dress.

But even though it was a little strange, part of her was happy to be back in the shop, doing ordinary things.

Doreen dragged the big buckets of less expensive bouquets, plus a variety of carnations and baby's breath, out to the sidewalk, arranging them in front of the shop window.

The streets outside seemed ordinary today. The barber shop was opening. Folks were shopping. Mothers or grandparents with toddlers in buggies, getting them out of the house.

Of course, life went on, even when magical forces were at war, and police were patrolling and could shoot your cousin or friend down at any moment.

People needed normal, even though things weren't normal anymore.

Drake's encounter with the police had galvanized the boy. She'd never seen someone step into his power so quick. No wonder Patrice wanted more, too. Everyone was feeling the need to step it up.

Back inside the shop, Doreen went through the orders and began pulling some long ferns out to make an arrangement. Someone's retirement party. That was nice.

The bells over the shop door jangled. Doreen looked up to see Tanya, looking pinched and half afraid, standing just inside the door.

The woman's hair was still pressed smooth. Her makeup was still subtle and well done. Neatly dressed in boots and a slim coat, she looked every inch the professional.

But that meant she should be at her bank job. What in the world was she doing here?

"Tanya? It's good to see you." Doreen walked out from around the big table where she was was working on the flowers, past the counter toward the customer area of the shop. "Is everything all right? Do you need to sit down?"

Tanya played with the straps of her patchwork leather purse.

"That would be good," she said. "Thank you."

Doreen brought her back and got her settled on a stool.

"Coffee?" she asked.

"No thank you, ma'am. I'm fine. I can't stay long. I called in late to work," she admitted. "Told them I had a doctor's appointment."

Doreen went back to going through the ferns, battling the urge to sit down, grab the woman's hands, and force her to say whatever was on her mind.

She felt Tanya relax a little. At least, she relaxed enough to set that crazy purse down on the table and stop fiddling with the strap.

"So," Doreen asked, beginning to pull out deep orange lilies and purple iris, setting them on the counter in heaps next to the ferns. "What's on your mind?"

Tanya took a breath. "I'm not sure I even know, you dig? But truth is, I'm scared. I'm scared for my kids. Scared for everyone at their school. Scared for my family."

She paused then.

"May I have a cup of water?"

"Of course."

Doreen set an iris down and went to fill a cup at the deep shop sink.

Setting it down next to Tanya's hand, she was surprised when the young woman looked up at her, and then clutched her hand.

"Doreen, I'm scared of the pigs, you know? They're getting worse. I swear they've been following me to work.

I'm scared they're gonna start following my children home from school."

"Won't the Panthers escort you?"

Tanya sipped some water, then made an impatient sound in her throat.

"There aren't enough of them, ma'am. Too much is goin' on. You know that. I need some more protection. I need to know if you can help."

Doreen brought out a large, clear vase and poured some small rocks into the bottom. She began to lay a base of fern, layering in the lilies and iris as she went.

"What kind of help do you want? We have the magic classes. You know that you and the children are always welcome to join in. Drake is very good with the little ones."

"Thing is, Doreen, I'm scared of the magic, too. When Jasmine told me about it, I kind of freaked, you dig? She wanted me to watch for white spiders and...I don't like feeling like I gotta be on guard like that at the kitchen."

Doreen poked an iris stem into the stones, then stepped back to look at the shape of the arrangement. It needed another lily in the back to set the pattern. A couple more fern fronds at the base.

She knew she needed to move carefully around Tanya. The woman was strong—had to be to raise two kids, work full time, and fulfill her duties with the Panthers. But even strong people could become brittle if they were under enough stress for long enough.

And everyone in this neighborhood was under stress. The increased police patrols and harassment of people on the street only cranked up the dial. Pretty soon the boiler was going to blow again.

They're testing us. Doreen thought. *Seeing if they can get folks agitated enough that we'll explode. Wouldn't they just love another excuse to crack down.*

And she knew the magic was behind it all, goading, prodding, priming the police toward suspicion and violence, whether they knew it or not. Things always seemed like they couldn't get any worse.

Until they did.

Not just the fact of the magic they were using in the community. The magic that was attacking them all, insinuating itself in their heads, infiltrating everything. Temple magic. Snake magic. Spider magic.

Looking at Tanya, a worried young mother, just trying to live her life, Doreen was struck. She wondered when she herself had crossed over. Become more like Jasmine. She knew she'd made commitments to the people, but these thoughts? Huh. They were new.

She guessed anyone could learn and change if there was enough proof.

But she still hadn't answered Tanya, who worried her purse strap again.

"Tanya, wouldn't you do anything to protect your children?"

"Of course I would!" she replied.

"You teach them to look both ways crossing the street. You teach them to avoid the police, and to say 'yes sir' if stopped, no matter what they didn't do. You teach them to be home before dark."

Tanya nodded, a little warily, Doreen thought. She knew what was coming.

"Magic is no different, Tanya. There are things in the world that can help your children. Forces that can look out for them and help them look out for themselves."

"Like angels? I don't believe in all that."

Doreen shrugged, and went back to slotting blooms into the empty spaces in the vase, filling out the arrangement. Purple and orange, with a green backdrop.

"You don't have to believe in angels. Or white spiders. You don't even have to believe in magic. Your children just have to believe that there is something that can help them defend themselves, no matter what gets thrown at them."

"What do you mean?"

"Think of magic as a form of confidence, Tanya. It helps you in any situation, as long as you know how to apply it."

The young woman nodded, then took a sip of water.

"I guess that's okay, then. At least...it's enough for now."

Then her face hardened, and she stood.

"But I swear to you, Doreen, if this magic gets my children hurt, I'll come after you."

Doreen fought down a smile.

"I wouldn't expect anything else."

Tanya gathered up her purse and started walking toward the door.

"Tanya." Doreen stopped her.

Tanya swung her dark hair over her shoulder as she turned back to look at Doreen.

"Catch," Doreen said, lobbing a ball of red fire at the woman's head.

Tanya reached up and caught it with her right hand. The ball flared and disappeared as soon as it touched her palm.

Tanya just stood there, eyes wide, hand still in the air.

"You and your children? You're going to have as much magic as you need. I just wanted you to feel that."

Doreen truly hoped it was enough.

29

CAROL

osalia's shop felt soothing, despite the bustle in the air.

"The Brown Berets need protection, maga," Rosalia said. Stiff brown patches, machine embroidered with cream sigils, were laid out on the long glass countertop. A pile of the same patches were in a heap at the Guadalupe statue's feet.

Candles burned everywhere, filling the shop with the scent of beeswax, paraffin, and smoke. The only thing missing was copal. Carol was sure it was coming soon.

"How in the world did you get these made?"

"There's a small embroidery shop in Pico Rivera. They know the Brown Berets. And they know me." Rosalia wouldn't say anything more than that, but the implications were clear.

Ernesto just looked distracted, his orange paisley shirt rumpled around the collar, its color jarring in the dim shop. Carol knew he was more disturbed by what they'd found in Terrance's office than he was letting on.

She just hoped he wasn't also disturbed by her. Whatever power had poured into her had clicked together some pieces of her sorcery—and her self—that felt like they'd been floating far too long.

But teasing all of that apart was going to need to wait. They had to figure out what to do about Terrance, and figure out the implications of all of this for the Association.

They'd come to Rosalia for help, but she was so busy, Carol wasn't sure the sorcerer was going to be much help.

"If you are going to be here, you are going have to work," Rosalia had said when they arrived.

"Can't we just charge these up all at once?" Carol asked.

Ernesto snorted at that, which irritated her. He was really acting weird and she hoped they'd be cool again soon.

"Well?" she asked again.

He finally looked at her, and she saw through the illusion he'd pasted over the edges of his aura. Her former teacher and hopeful lover was afraid. And confused.

No wonder he'd pushed her away.

Ernesto saw the change in her face. He must have. He looked down at the row of patches on the counter, and ran a hand over the thick dark wave of his hair.

Rosalia was making preparations around the Guadalupe statue. Sure enough, there was the scent of copal, and a cloud of smoke rising from the abalone shell.

"Tell her, Ernesto," Rosalia said, back turned to them as she lit still more candles and fussed at two small round vases filled with roses.

Offerings.

He cleared his throat, looking at her again. Then Carol felt him reach for his primary Element, Air. The candle flames wavered and then stood straight again. Ernesto's face cleared.

"For a working such as this, when warriors may need to

go into battle against an enemy whose strength is unknown, the magic on the sigils must be precise. If these were hand-stitched, it might be more possible to charge many of them at once, because the stitches would already hold our prayers."

"But the machine stitching means they need more juice?"

"Yes. You could say that. What these patches need is extra care. Focus. They are the only shields our warriors have, maga."

She still didn't quite get it, but helped lay the patches out in groupings of five. She and Ernesto would bless each grouping with the power of all the Elements—"Since you are here," Rosalia had said, "may as well make use of your sorcery"—and then Rosalia would lay them at the feet of Guadalupe/Tonantzin for whatever extra blessing she saw fit.

"Can we ask you questions while you work, hechicera?" Carol asked.

Rosalia turned then, her citrine eyes bright and distant. As if she wasn't quite focusing on Carol's face. The sorcerer was clearly walking in between the planes. Carol hoped she could learn to do that herself someday.

Though that ability hadn't seemed to do Jasmine any good. And look at the mess Terrance had brought to their door.

"Ask," Rosalia said, then went behind the counter and started looking through the jars on the row of shelves.

"Ernesto, bring out two oranges from the back room, please," Rosalia said.

Carol's fingers played across the patches, tracing the silken, raised cream-colored threads of the sigils. She could tell the sigils had power by looking at them, but Ernesto was right. There wasn't any magic reaching out to touch her fingers. Not yet.

"Ask your question, maga."

"Terrance...we all know he's lost. His soul. But we found something even more disturbing..."

"He's given himself to the spider." Rosalia said, shaking some seed pods from one of the stuffed jars out into her fingers, separating the ones she wanted, then dropping the remainder back into the jar. The brown pods were star-shaped, and smelled like licorice. Star anise.

The seeds were used for luck, but also to ward off the evil eye, Carol remembered. Some people also used the scent to induce dreams or visions. She supposed Rosalia was working with them to boost the protections around the Brown Berets. But any of the other associations could be equally true.

Rosalia had her ways, and Carol could still barely fathom what her motivations might be.

Or how the older woman knew half the things she knew.

"How did you know that?" Carol asked. "About the spider? And what does it mean, that he gave himself to it?"

Rosalia fixed her citrine eyes on Carol, focusing on her this time. Carol fought to keep her own gaze steady.

"How did I know the pendejo had given his soul over to danger?" Rosalia harrumphed and snorted. "It does not take a very keen eye to see the direction he was heading, maga. Everything in the cosmos adds together, if you care to look."

"But we didn't..."

"You are too used to seeing him as a leader." Rosalia began placing one star anise pod on top of each pile of patches. "And perhaps you and Ernesto are too close to everything, spending so much time in that Mansion, entiendes?"

Carol nodded. Ernesto came out with the oranges and set them on the counter—what had taken him so long? Carol looked at him, and his brown eyes finally held hers. He must have done something to get himself together back there. Good.

"Put those on either side of Tonantzin. She needs all of the ofrendas we can give her today."

"Rosalia is right, Carol," Ernesto said, as he carefully set the oranges on either side of the statue, next to the small vases filled with roses. "It took us far too long to notice what was happening with Terrance. Helen and I are to blame."

"Well, we've figured out now that Helen has been protecting him," Carol said. "It makes sense to me now, that she went and saw Doreen. Cecelia would have seen right through her. They've worked together too closely, I think. But Doreen was out of the loop for years."

Ernesto paused and nodded. "I think you may be right. I also know what it's like to feel conflicted between what you think is right, and what you've been upholding all along."

Carol didn't get that. Not at all.

Ernesto came back and started pouring slim rings of salt around each pile of patches. Nothing would get past that salt. They would have to focus their energies precisely.

That must be what the anise was for. Not just added protection, Carol realized, but a point of focus for their sorcery. All of the elements would pass through the center of the little brown stars, into the patches below, tracing each sigil in its turn, forming as strong a seal of protection as was possible without tracing a sphere around each Chicano warrior's aura, one at a time.

"So what do we do now?"

"We use our sorcery on these sigils, maga," Rosalia said. "And then Ernesto makes us lavender tea and we talk about how Las Manos can help those of you in the Association who haven't gone completely crazy with your power."

Rosalia threw some more copal onto the charcoal and fanned the smoke out over the small piles of patches.

"Things are not so good in this world right now. Evil stalks our dreams and walks down these streets. But our sorcery is strong, maga." The citrine eyes sought out Carol again, boring into her, holding her fixed to the floor. "Our sorcery is strong."

30

SNAKES AND SPIDERS

The roaring of agitated voices hurt his ears, booming and crashing up the slick, gray-veined stairs.

At least the light inside the marble edifice was dim enough to be comfortable to Samuels' eyes under the dark glasses that wrapped his face whenever he left his home, night or day. Without the glasses, the reflections of light on marble would have damaged his retinas.

The roar and stink of the crowd were almost overwhelming, though, a sign that whatever it was that Panther bitch had thrown at him on the beach had done some damage.

More damage than he wanted to admit. At least he'd managed to throw up a strong enough illusion that she thought he had disappeared. A useful technique, and one he hoped he didn't need to use for a long while.

It took too much out of him. Especially now.

He'd taken too many hits in the past week. Listen to him, whining. Samuels' body ached from it all. He would need another round with the flail to keep his mind in line.

"Power to the people!"

As though they had any power at all. Puppets, every last one *of them. Slaves to emotion and chance. Run by whims and booze and sex.*

So easy to manipulate.

Samuels allowed a small grin to pierce his pale face.

The crowd was thick below. The brass banister warmed beneath his palms as his eyes searched the teeming throng below.

He knew she was here. She had to be.

Samuels traced a small sigil on the banister, then breathed a silent word toward the traces left by his fingertips. It was a word he'd used many times, imbuing it with power every time it left his lips. The syllables had built up so much charge, connected to his personal signature, that he no longer needed to speak the word aloud.

It did his bidding. Like so many things.

Like she would.

Like the Master would some day.

Below him, the top of the soft cloud of her hair lit up, illumined for a moment by the reflection of light off marble, and the power of the spell he'd sent to find her. She raised one delicate fist, brown and firm, into the air.

Her face tilted upward, shouting the words they all were shouting. The words that had no magic and no power of their own.

If only these people knew...

But then his job would become too difficult. It was not for the people to walk the halls of power. It was for the people to listen and obey.

And, barring that, it was for the people to think they had the will to do what they wished, when really, they were being controlled by wiser forces all along.

Forces that wanted what was best for the world. Order. Not chaos and chance.

People could flourish under order. Just like he did.

Sending a little push out toward his nemesis, Samuels smiled again.

She looked at him, shock moving across her face so rapidly he would have missed it if his gaze were less than careful.

But he was being careful now.

And Samuels would be careful from now on.

"I'll get you," he mouthed at her upturned face.

She stood stock still, in the midst of the moving, chanting crowd.

31

JASMINE

The Powers had made certain I got to the Hall of Justice, hadn't they?

Here I thought I just needed to be back among some comrades, but really, I'd been steered straight into the viper's den.

I could feel his magic now. How had I missed it? Over the push and flesh and sound. Over the scent of Brut, cocoa butter, patchouli, marijuana, and warm skin. Over the anger and excitement...

Over it all was the calm, cool, marble of the Temple. Over it all was the dry, papery scent of snake. And the tingling of the Solomonic shit that it was seeming I'd need to get used to.

I put my hand on a woman's shoulder, the same white woman in the corduroy coat from outside.

"Excuse me," I said.

She frowned a little, then nodded, angling her torso, making a small space for me to squeeze on by.

"Thanks."

I tapped a burly man in a denim jacket and deep red afro.

"Excuse me, brother. Let me through?"

He tapped the two people ahead of him. They angled out another wedge.

I nodded my thanks and moved on through, then looked up at the crowd that filled the stairs.

This was going to take forever. I sent a rivulet of my energy ahead of me. It insinuated itself in between the bodies, causing them to open. The slimmest path appeared and I took it.

By the time I reached the stairs themselves, though, and started climbing, something in the room felt different. The crowd was growing angrier, more restive. They needed leadership. A way to direct their power.

I couldn't bother with that right now. I had to get to him.

How exactly I was going to confront him in a jam-packed government building, I didn't know yet.

Angling through the crowded stairs, I gripped the brass rail and searched for his pale face. Too many people in the way.

The Temple magic was receding. And the snaky smell was faint, growing harder to trace.

Damn.

Sure enough, Mr. Feeb was gone. The Man had left the building.

It was just as well. It meant I didn't need to risk a lot of people getting hurt.

I did one last scan, just to be sure. He wasn't in the vaulted entryway. Must have found a back door out. Or he was hiding in an office behind some magical smoke screen for awhile.

I exhaled. At any rate, someone needed to deal with this crowd now.

Looking up and down the stairs, I sought someone I recognized. Anyone. Angela? Ericka? Geronimo? Elaine? Huey? Though I doubted he would show up at such an open space. Not this soon.

There may have been local leadership here, but none I knew well enough to pick up by sight alone.

Guess it was up to me.

Before I began, a quick scan of my aura was in order. Probing my own edges, like a tongue seeking out gaps in teeth, I felt around, making sure that gaping hole left by the snake was truly closed.

It was. For now. There was still some mushiness to the front of my shoulder, but I'd have to deal with that later, maybe with my mother's help. *Or Carol's*, a little voice inside my head replied. I'd deal with *that* situation later, too.

Good to go. I remembered the feel of ocean from yesterday. Recalled the taste of salty brine on my lips and the feel of it on my skin. Then I tuned in to every drop of spit and sweat in that overcrowded, booming foyer.

And I pulled, feeling the air exiting the crowd for one bare moment, then I slowly, gently, eased the water back into them all.

They were so wide open, all of them, a few exceptions scattered here and there. It would be so easy to abuse this. But I wouldn't.

This was power for the people. Because, as Ericka had said, the people were the power.

I was just focusing their power for a moment. Showing it a slightly different route. Once they felt it too, they could choose, yes or no. I wasn't reaching into their souls to turn them, all I was doing was offering a suggestion.

Here's one way, my sorcery said to that room. *Take it if you want to. It might work.*

The water rolled through the room, buoying the energy, brightening it, like sea foam, deepening it, like the currents six miles down.

The chanting changed. The stomping became syncopated.

We were all uplifted.

"Power, power, power to the peo-*ple!*" a swell of voices said.

"Ju. *Stice!*" came the answer to the call.

"Power, power, power to the peo-*ple!*"

"Ju. *Stice!*"

The stomping, chanting, rolling filled the room and made me smile. This was power. This was magic. This was what we wanted. For the people to feel in their bones that the words they spoke were true.

That was more powerful than any of the twisted up Solomonic Temple shit the Man could throw our way.

Near the door, I saw the crowd begin to part like a mighty wave was pushing through it, like a river spilling toward the ocean, pushing out, and being welcomed by the tide.

Head and shoulders above the crowd, proud face gleaming, musky scent dominating the other smells in the room... there he was. I almost started laughing.

It was Roland Freeman. Shifter. Leader.

The damn cops were going to lose their minds.

Following on his heels was Geronimo Pratt, the discipline of his years of training evident in the way he held his head. Captains of the revolution.

Black Panthers, all the way.

Angela, Ericka, and Elaine entered in their wake, determined looks on their faces, just as proud.

My heart almost burst in my chest. The power of ocean swelled around me.

Angela snapped her face around and looked straight at me. Then Roland, Ericka, and Geronimo did, too.

Angela smiled at me then, hugely, her slightly crooked teeth so beautiful in that wide mouth. She raised her right fist.

I raised mine back.

Then Roland nodded at me, giving me some sort of permission. To do something.

Anything.

To show them what it was that I could do.

Taking a deep breath, I called on the deepest part of Ocean I could find.

Then raised both of my arms, palms up, like a conductor. Then, palms open, I felt the waves of sorcery up above me, and down below. I blew upon the waters, and they calmed.

The chanting and stomping came to a sudden halt.

Then Roland spoke, voice deep and smooth as honey, just a little terrifying in its gentleness. It calmed something at my core.

"Attend to our sister, Jasmine, up on the stairs. She has some things to say."

How did he know my name? Then I remembered, he was in the building the night we met to discuss busting Huey free. He had looked into the meeting room, and waved a hand, but hadn't stopped in. Someone must have told him who I was.

And what I could do.

So. I needed to get my sorcery together and show these people something.

"Hold up your fists!" I said. All I could hear now, in the echo of the booming voices suddenly gone, was the breath of several hundred people, and the murmuring of voices of those packed against the outside doors. Someone shifted. Another person coughed.

But every fist slowly rose into the air.

I called on the Powers to help me. And asked the ancestors to give me the right words.

Then I took another breath, all the way down below my navel, feeling the oxygen entering me, and the exhalation that pushed breath all the way out to my toes.

"Feel the power of the blood pumping in your veins. Feel the blood of your ancestors, all of those people who survived. You carry that. And you carry that here. To this battle. To this place."

I could feel their faces turned toward me, expectant. Waiting. I had the sense that the leadership gathered here were testing me.

That was okay. So far, things were cool.

"Now open up your palms. Hold your palms out, toward me."

Fists unfurled, exposing the paler skin beneath.

I sent a wave of my Water Power around the room. Just a touch of the blue fire, kissing the center of each upraised palm.

Gasps and small curses moved in a ripple around the space.

I smiled again, and looked at leadership. They were all smiling, too.

"I'm here to tell you all, that not only do the people have *power*, but that power is magic. You all have magic, singing in your blood, carried on your breath, hidden in your bones."

Silence, except for some shifting of bodies crammed too close together, trying to make a little more room.

"What the hell that mean?" a man's voice came from behind me.

I turned my head and looked up the stairs. It was an older man, maybe sixty, neatly dressed in a brown-striped shirt, hair white and cut close on his round head.

"It means that there is more you can do, that we *all* can do, to protect ourselves and our communities. And I'm going to show you how. And then I'm going to introduce you to other people who can help you."

I looked down at Roland, Angela, Geronimo, Ericka, and Elaine, scanning their faces, one by one.

"The magic cell of the Black Panther Party has officially opened an LA chapter. We have a lot to teach you. Let's get to work," I said.

Then, with a smile that practically split my face, I shouted, "All power to the people!"

The crowd roared in return.

32

JASMINE

I paced the edge of the giant Turkish carpet that cost more than most people in Oakland made in two months.

It was beautiful, I gave it that, but these days, the studied opulence of the Mansion left a bitter taste on the back of my tongue. I'd driven straight there from the civic center, after spending close to an hour in the park across from the the Hall of Justice getting folks paired up and teaching them the basics of shielding themselves and throwing energy like basketballs from hand to hand.

Leadership seemed impressed. That was good. Maybe they'd put in a good word for me up in Oakland, where everyone was still a little skittish. Even Jimmy's voice still sounded strained when we last spoke on the phone. And it wasn't just the stress of increased harassment and police raids.

Angela left early, after shaking my hand. She wasn't officially a member of the Party, just a strong supporter, and a radical in her own right. One righteous sister, she headed up the Che-Lumumba Club, which had gotten her in trouble with her teaching job at UCLA.

The others had stayed, picking up on what I was doing pretty quickly, and walking through the crowd, helping pass on to groups of four or six, what I'd been trying to teach en masse.

My skin still hummed with exhilaration, but it was quickly giving way to impatience. The fact that I was ravenous wasn't helping.

Carol sat in one of the brocade, stuffed chairs grouped with a couple of couches near the library fireplace. Too warm for a fire today, but I still admired the long stone lines of it, and loved the smell of the old books on the shelves set in rows at a safe distance from the seating and the fire.

"Do you think any of these moldy people here will help?" I asked.

Carol laughed at that, but it didn't have much humor in it. She was dour today.

Oh, she looked the same as always, thin and blond, maybe a bit more curvy in her purple maxi skirt and white gauze top with purple threads smocking the yoke, and her hair fell in its usual straight sheet around her shoulders.

But something was wrong. I could smell it on her, could hear it in her voice and see it in the way she tried to hard to make me think everything was all right.

Huh. That made me pause in my pacing for a moment. Maybe what was wrong with Carol was *me*.

"I think we have our hands full, Jasmine." She lowered her voice then. "There are things we need to tell you. New stuff about Terrance, dig? But I wanted to wait until Ernesto was done teaching his class."

"Have you been keeping things from me?" I asked,

finally sitting down on the second chair flanking the couches.

Carol flushed at that, anger or embarrassment, I couldn't tell.

"You haven't exactly been available to talk to, Jasmine."

Well, well, well. She finally *had* grown a spine.

Carol cleared her throat and kept going. "We've been too worried about you, and frankly you've been too out of it, for us to want to put this on you, too."

I noticed my fingers tapping on the tufted edges of the chair arm and willed them to be still. Screaming at the person who used to be my best friend wasn't going to help our relationship any. But the anger was there. *Right* there. Close enough to taste the copper penny of it in my mouth. I swallowed hard.

Found my center. Found the pool of water always resting there. Breathed.

My stomach growled.

"How long 'til Ernesto's done? I really need to eat." Maybe that would help my mood.

Carol stood, smoothing her long skirt down with pale, tapered hands.

"Let's go to the kitchen. There's always cheese and stuff in the fridge. Ernesto will find us there."

He would, huh? That was another surprise. Carol and Ernesto, linking mind to mind? And what else was going on?

"There something else you want to tell me?" I asked, as she led the way out the door.

She blushed for real this time.

"I'm not going to talk about it in the hallway," she said.

"But you'll tell me in the kitchen?"

"I guess I have to, now."

The hallway took a couple of turns, leading us toward the back of the Mansion. I hadn't been this way in years. Everything still looked the same. Blue carpet on the floors. Paintings on the walls. Heavy wooden beams.

But it felt different. Less solid. Like the air was stuck.

The place was spotless, but there were patches here and there that felt like they needed to be cleaned anyway.

Carol didn't seem to notice, just forged on ahead until we came to a swinging wooden door leading to the kitchen, terra-cotta tiles on the floors, counters white ceramic tile with a backsplash of bright blue and orange and red Mexican tiles dotted through the white.

A big, tiled prep counter stood in the center of the room. Carol opened the fridge and started bringing out wrapped packets of yellow and white cheeses, and a hard salami.

I reached past her and grabbed some olives, too. I was really hungry.

"Bread?" I asked.

"In the metal box on the counter. Mustard?" she asked.

"Yeah. Sounds good."

I started slathering the bright yellow stuff on the wheat bread while Carol sliced some cheese.

"So. Ernesto."

She blushed again.

"We're kind of seeing each other. I think. Not that there's been any time for an actual date."

It took us two minutes to put the sandwiches together. I sat on one of the stools at the central counter, picked up my sandwich, and did a rolling wave of my hand in her direction.

"Go on."

She sat down herself, and picked up her sandwich. I

took a huge bite of mine. Cheddar, Swiss, salami, and mustard. Wow. So good.

And then the door swung open and Ernesto walked in the room, wearing pressed dark brown slacks and starched gold shirt.

Damn. He couldn't have waited ten more minutes?

Okay. I'd ask some other questions then, but I gave Carol one of those "we're talking about this later" looks. She gave me a grin.

"Want some cheese?" she asked.

Ernesto popped an olive in his mouth and pulled out another stool.

"We having a meeting?" he asked.

"I need to know what in all the Powers is actually going on with Terrance, despite being a pompous honky who likely needs a soul retrieval," I said, pitching my voice low.

Ernesto sighed.

"What has Carol told you?"

"Nothing yet."

"We think his soul got eaten by the white spider," Carol blurted out then.

That sent a jolt of ice down my back. I put my sandwich down.

"I don't understand. How?"

"That's what we've been trying to figure out," Ernesto said, dark eyes looking worried behind his tortoiseshell frames. "But it must have been going on slowly, over time."

Then it hit me.

"You think he let that thing in here."

Ernesto and Carol just nodded, mouths tight. Carol had a crease between her brows.

"And what are we gonna do about this? Why hasn't he been replaced? Why isn't he on magical lockdown?"

It was hard to keep my voice from rising, from opening every faucet with my mind and flooding the whole damn bourgie place.

Ernesto put a hand up, as though to stop me.

"He is currently incapable of doing anything, hechicera. He's delirious in his bed. The doctor doesn't know when his fever will break, if ever."

I didn't care.

"Don't you feel how messed up the energies in this place are?" I hissed through my teeth. "He poisoned this Mansion. He's poisoned the Association. What happens to our sorcery now?"

Carol went white as a sheet. I guess she hadn't thought of that.

"You haven't told her? You and Helen working something out between you, Ernesto?"

His skin grew red at that. Good. Let him be angry. I was angry.

"Ernesto?" Carol asked.

He looked at her.

"No, maga. I haven't done anything behind your back. You know that."

"Well," I said, picking up my sandwich again. "We'd better call Helen in here now. We have a lot of shit to discuss."

33

DOREEN

Out on the cracking blacktop, underneath the chain basketball hoops, a group of twenty gathered, all bundled up on what was looking to be a sunny December morning. The temperature was in the mid-forties, and folks had knit caps and fedoras pulled down over their ears. Topcoats and peacoats and gloves.

They'd be taking the gloves off soon, which would cause some grumbling, Doreen was sure, but it was hard to do magic in gloves, unless a person had been training for years and was born to it.

Breath streamed white from people's mouths as they talked, waiting. Some of the women had thermoses of coffee and hot chocolate set up on the side benches. Patrice was one of those women. She'd smiled at Doreen as she handed her a cardboard cup.

"Dark and sweet," she'd said. Doreen still tingled with it. That was still a bit strange, but nice, after so many years.

"Look at them," Doreen said. "This just might work, baby."

Patrice squeezed her arm, then let go. They weren't quite

open with the whole community yet. People were assimilating new information enough right now.

"It just might," Patrice replied. "You don't have to have sex with all of them, do you?"

Doreen practically spit her coffee on the asphalt.

Patrice just laughed.

People stood on the cracked playground, clutching the cardboard cups as though they were a lifeline. They were, Doreen supposed.

It was a Saturday afternoon, but the folks gathered here worked hard. She knew some of them were on a lunch break, and others had slacked off on all the chores that didn't get done during the week. And the night-shift workers should have been asleep right now.

"Okay, friends. Let's get started!" Doreen called out.

Doreen and Jasmine had made a deal with leadership to teach protective and defensive magic only. Anything else would take too much time.

Doreen huffed, her own breath puffing white into the air. "And fighting with the damn Association over something as basic as all this," she muttered.

But the ancestors had also given her the charge to awaken the magic nascent in each person. That was more important than even the basic spellwork and castings.

Doreen wasn't yet sure how exactly she was supposed to do that. She hoped working with folks would help her figure it out.

Doreen and Jasmine had bandied about the idea of breaking away and form their own magical alliance. The Cooperative, they were think of of calling it, dreaming it all up around the kitchen table on exhausted night.

They pretended they were only half serious and just speaking out of anger. But Doreen wondered if they weren't also harboring real plans. A someday operation that would bring more magic back into the world.

More magic, and more justice.

"Let's all gather over here," Patrice said.

The group moved toward them, some still holding their cardboard cups of coffee, others trailing off the ends of whatever conversations they'd been having. Twenty serious sets of eyes all looked at her. Waiting.

Taking a deep breath, like she would for any magical operation, Doreen centered herself, getting ready to speak. This, she wasn't used to yet. Jasmine told her she had to be.

Drake stepped up next to her, looking chilly in his scuffed brown jacket and red plaid shirt. He looked the same as when she'd met him, button nose and tight natural, with the round cheeks of the young. But he looked different, too. His eyes were more serious than they used to be, and he carried himself a little taller.

Doreen pulled her wool coat tighter and adjusted the cranberry scarf around her neck.

"I hope you all hung up the blessing charms we handed out last Saturday. Any front window, or above the front doorway of your apartments or houses will do. Are there any questions you have about that, before we get to today's lesson?"

A man near the front—a bus driver just off shift, from the looks of it—raised a tentative hand. What was his name? Frank.

"Yes, Frank?"

He cleared his throat and shoved his hands back in the pockets of his dark blue jacket.

"Mizz Doreen, you told us we would do well to clean our space before we hung up the charms, but I got a question about that."

Doreen nodded.

"I did all the regular cleaning, like you said we should, but I wasn't too sure about the other kind of cleaning you talked about. Can you go over that stuff a bit again?"

Closing her eyes for a moment, she tapped the fire at the center of the earth and drew the energy up through her toes. Wishing she didn't get nervous when talking in front of a group wouldn't help. Jasmine wasn't there, and she needed to help these people.

"Yes. There are different ways a magic person uses to clean the space spiritually. You can either bless each room with salt water, or by burning incense, or ringing bells. Those are common ways to do it. Just walk through every room, touching the walls with the salt water, or ringing the bells, for example, and imagine the room getting brighter and cleaner."

Frank got a strange look on his face at that.

"Was there a problem you had?"

"Well, no, I guess. I did all that with some salt water, but it just felt strange to me, like it wasn't doing much. I wanted to make sure I hadn't missed something, is all."

"You hung the charm up afterward?"

He nodded, as did several others.

"And how have you been sleeping at night? Or in the morning, I should say. You work night shift, right?"

He looked thoughtful at that. "I've been sleeping more peaceful, now that you say it."

"That's one sign the protection charm is working. Any other questions?"

Jasmine and Doreen had both decided not to stress the protection element too strongly. It wouldn't do to have people getting so nervous about doing magic that they stayed away. A lot of these were church folks. Good Baptists.

African Methodists. Anything that smacked of dealing with the devil would scare them off too badly.

Even though there was some sort of devil involved. It wore a black suit and dark glasses, and smelled a lot like snake.

A chill walked across her spine.

It was time to train these people to protect their own.

That was the least she could do. To prepare them for whatever battle was coming.

Because bad as things seemed?

They were going to get much worse.

Show them. Make them feel there's something more, the ancestors whispered at the base of her skull.

And she knew one thing she could do. A thing so second nature now, she'd almost forgotten it was there.

"Okay," she said, brightening up her face. "If there aren't more questions, I'd like to start with some meditation."

People looked at each other, a little uncomfortable.

"Just close your eyes. Patrice will keep watch over the playground, I promise."

"How 'bout me, Mrs. Doreen?" Drake asked.

"You, too. Close your eyes."

They all did.

"Now, slow your breathing down. Then I want you to think of your favorite thing. It could be a moment. It could be the way you feel around a certain person, or at church, or walking in the park. It could be something from your childhood. Doesn't matter. Call to mind your favorite thing."

The faces in front of her changed, relaxing, slackening, growing more smooth. For some of them, likely for the first time in years.

So much had been stolen from these people. It was time to take it back.

"As you breathe, I want you to imagine filling up with as much of your sense of that thing as you can."

Drake's face started to shine.

A police car cruised past the park, slowing down, white face staring at the people gathered there.

Patrice looked at Doreen, tense now, a question on her face.

Doreen shook her head no, and send a little *push* to the protections they'd set up around the cyclone fence. Let the police move right on by.

"Now, imagine you can push that feeling out around you every time you exhale. Imagine it can create a bubble of goodness around you. Then feel what that does to your own sense of power. Of strength."

"What now, Mrs. Doreen?" Drake asked, eyes still closed.

"Then tell yourself, '*I have magic inside of me. And I can share this magic with the world.*'"

She saw lips begin to move, mouthing the words.

That was good.

The thing the ancestors had reminded her of? Magic starts with imagination, and imagination feeds belief.

That was something Fred and Huey knew, she realized. Along with feeding hungry people, the Black Panther Party had captured their imaginations.

And that was were every kind of revolution had to start, magical or otherwise.

There might be evil in the air, but there was magic right here in this playground, too. And she was teaching people the Association would say had no magic at all.

She was going to prove that they did.

34

CAROL

Jasmine was angry, and Carol couldn't blame her.

Helen was angry, too.

She hadn't liked being summoned, and Carol had been foolish enough to do it. She should have sent Ernesto. He would have smoothed things over somehow. Ernesto could be so charming; placating, even. No matter how difficult the situation was, he always seemed able to talk people toward reason.

At least with Ernesto, Helen might have at least felt less threatened by someone who was closer to a peer.

Carol just pissed Helen off.

As Terrance Sterling's second-in-command, Helen still lorded it over them all a bit, even with things so obviously crumbling around their ears.

What did the woman think was happening? Did she actually think Carol and Ernesto were going to pretend they hadn't dragged Terrance Sterling unconscious from his office?

Carol sighed. Old habits were hard to break. And Carol didn't much care how Helen felt. Something had to change.

So she had simply stood there, in the doorway of Helen's office, and insisted there were things that needed discussion, and that discussion needed to happen now.

And then she said Ernesto had asked for Helen to come. That paved the way for grudging acceptance.

Even so, it had taken all of Carol's Earth sorcery to give her the strength to face down Helen's displeasure. Carol was kind of glad Jasmine was the locus for it now.

Even recovering from that thing sucking on her aura, Jasmine was still strong.

"Did you know about all of this, Helen?" Jasmine asked, voice brittle with rage. The Water pressure in the kitchen was rising already. Carol, glad she hadn't sat back down when she came back with Helen, rooted her feet a little more deeply, making sure she was well connected to Earth.

She stifled a gasp as she felt Ernesto reach out and caress her with a puff of Air. She looked at him then, and saw his slight smile. He was trying to reassure her. That was nice. Maybe he'd reassure her some more, later.

"What I know and don't know about the business of the Association is none of your business, Jasmine Jones."

Oh, that was so not good.

"The *business of the Association* is the business of all members. Or have you forgotten that, high up on the hill in this fancy place?"

Jasmine's hand whipped out, gesturing to the kitchen, to top-of-the line appliances and the expensive, hand-set tiles.

The scent of ice filled the room. Helen's sorcery. The smell of brine increased to match it. Carol fought to control the urge to push more Earth energy forward. The space just didn't need it. She looked at Ernesto again.

He nodded and took one step forward.

"Please," he said, holding up his hands, "this isn't getting us anywhere. Jasmine, if you'll back off for just one moment..."

"And who are *you* to tell me to back down?"

"I am nobody. But there is something I want to say to Mrs. Price, if I may?"

Jasmine scowled and crossed her arms under her breasts, afro practically bristling with the power she was pumping out.

"Helen, as you know, Carol and I found Terrance unconscious, wrapped in silk thread, with spiderwebs filling his office, and two spiders battling each other in the room." His voice was calm. Carol was amazed. But Helen, her own arms crossed over her cream Chanel suit, seemed to be listening, though her head was tilted to one side, telegraphing annoyance.

"Do you really think you can keep anything from us any longer?" he continued.

"And do you really think you *should*?" Carol asked. "Really, Helen, you think we haven't noticed that Terrance has been in the middle of a lot of weird shit happening here lately? You think we've been too distracted to notice that along with the head of the Association foaming at the mouth, that outside forces have clearly broken through what are supposed to be impermeable wards?" Carol stopped then to take a breath, a little startled she'd found the words.

She straightened up her spine. She was an Earth sorcerer, and Ernesto and Jasmine were right, Carol was as much an Association member as Helen Price.

The sense of Water and ice pushing toward one another slightly receded.

Jasmine spoke again. "Helen. We need this information. Too much is going down outside these walls right now. I'd been trying to get the Association involved to help, but frankly, right now I'm worried the Association is a damn liability."

"We can't protect Terrance anymore, Helen. Membership needs to know," Carol said.

Helen's lips were pursed together.

"You're *all* against us now?" she asked.

"Oh for the Power's sake!" Jasmine spat out. "This isn't about *you!* This isn't about *Terrance,* though you know it could be. This isn't about our little *club* here! This is about people being shot down in the streets and this is about our little *Association* not even being able to protect its own people, let alone anyone outside these walls! Don't you see how dangerous this is, Helen?"

Jasmine was still angry, but Carol could also see that she was also pleading with Helen. It was all over her face, and pooling from her eyes. That was something new. Something since whatever this change or initiation Jasmine was going through had started.

"Jasmine, we should show you the office," Ernesto broke in. "Maybe you'll catch something there that Carol and I missed."

"Helen?" Carol asked.

Helen nodded. Once. Twice. Then turned on her heel and walked through the door. Ernesto followed.

Carol reached out to Jasmine, and grasped her arm for a moment.

"Hey," she said. "You okay? Do you need something before we go in there?"

She held her best friend's brown eyes with her own blue ones. Yes. Jasmine was still her best friend, whether Jasmine knew it or not.

"I'm cool. Well, not really, but I'm getting there. Okay?"

For the first time in years, Carol saw a softness in Jasmine's eyes. A sense of...she wasn't sure yet.

So she just nodded and turned to follow Ernesto and Helen out the swinging kitchen door.

"Hey, Carol." Jasmine stopped her.

Carol turned.

"I appreciate it."

"Anytime."

"And I want you to know, I see your Power now. You did good with busting Huey out of prison. I was too messed up before to tell you that."

Jasmine walked toward her friend and put a hand on her shoulder, face breaking into a grin.

"And I think whatever's cooking between you and Ernesto is groovy, too."

Carol smiled, and whacked Jasmine on the arm.

"You aren't the only one around here who can get a handsome man."

They laughed.

It felt good to laugh.

There hadn't been much laughter for awhile.

35

———

JASMINE

Terrance's office was intense.

Despite an obvious attempt at cleanup, spider silk was still hanging from the corners and wrapping half the furniture. This shit was going to take time to unravel. And the Mansion couldn't just call in a cleaning service to take care of the mess.

I made my way carefully across the blue carpet, sending my senses out on multiple levels, the way Rosalia had shown me. This world. The astral plane. And several layers of the æthers in between.

I was pretty convinced by now that the hechicera, as Ernesto and Carol called her, could walk through as many damn planes of existence as she wanted. Not there yet, I could at least do three at a time. Maybe more, once I was fully healed.

The sparkle of the astral around me, I gazed at the far corner, above Terrance's cut crystal whiskey decanter and the fancy wire-wrapped soda syphon. There. Something pinged my attention.

Something off, but not unfriendly. As if something had

tried its best to repair the gaping hole into the shadow worlds, to keep nasty forces from getting in.

And it was pretty clear that the other magic traces in this room? Came from a nasty thing.

But what was this...?

I closed my eyes, trying to tune in deeper. To catch the thread.

And a familiar image lit up in my brain. Momma Beatrice's crystal ball. Warm hands on my shoulders. The scent of...licorice?

I'd never met my grandmother, but Doreen and my mother talked about her with awe. Said she was the most powerful sorcerer they'd ever known. And if she was busting through the æthers like this, impacting the physical world after death? Yeah. I'd say she deserved my respect.

"You the brown spider then, Momma Beatrice?" I used her honorific. She was Momma Beatrice to a whole generation of my Crenshaw neighborhood.

The scent of licorice increased, as did a tugging in my solar plexus.

"What do you want me to see?"

I could feel Carol and Ernesto, waiting quietly behind me. Helen cleared her throat. Tapped her foot.

Well, I was just gonna ignore that, wasn't I?

Opening my eyes, I looked in the direction Momma Beatrice seemed to be pointing me toward. It was a spot where the art and book-filled cases met the corner above the sideboard that held the crystal decanter and glasses.

All I saw was a ripped-up tangle of webs. I stepped closer. There. A dark patch, here, on the physical plane. I reached my hand out, but before I touched anything, I closed my eyes again.

There. On the astral.

"Powers be damned," I said.

"What do you see?" Helen's voice cracked out across the room.

"Something you aren't going to like at all."

In the floating gray-cloud space before me, I saw a clear image of Terrance's blue faience scarab ring. His sign of office. I always thought it was a bit pretentious, but he insisted it showed that his sorcery went all the way back to Egypt.

Maybe it did, but sometimes it sounded like a lot of white man's posturing to me.

But that wasn't the worst thing, his badge of office, separated from the man like that.

What was worse were the running bands of sigils moving in arcs around the ring, like electrons orbiting an atomic nucleus. They moved too fast for me to make out exact shapes, but I could tell it was a repeating stream of the same glyph, over and over again.

"Carol?" I asked, keeping my eyes closed. I really wished I had Rosalia's powers, man, so I could see all these planes of existence with my physical eyes, too.

"What do you need?" She was standing next to me all of a sudden.

"Tell me what is going on!" Helen said.

"Let Jasmine work." I heard Ernesto reply.

"Carol, those sigils you've been seeing, you have drawings of them?"

"Yes," she said.

"Can you describe them?"

Her breath huffed out.

"Come on, Carol. I need this."

"I'm trying to figure out how to describe it! Give me a minute."

I needed to hold the vision a little longer, and I needed to slow the sigils down.

Sweat popped out on my forehead. There was something else going on here. But I couldn't untangle it yet. *Come on, Jasmine. You can bend walls with Jimmy, you can slow the damn sigil molecules down.*

"Come. On." I whispered. With a lurch of my intestines, my muscles started to quiver, but I did it. The arcs slowed enough for me to see the individual sigils making up the streaming flow that wrapped the blue scarab, imprisoning it.

"It's kind of like the Greek letter Phi. You know, a big capital "I" with a circle in the middle. But the top and bottom bars are long, like a real capital I. And four squiggly lines radiate out from the O, like rays of a sun."

My gut clenched. That was exactly what I was seeing.

"Or like the legs of a spider?" I asked her.

"Oh shit," she replied.

I took a breath and stepped my astral body back down to the physical, away from the astral plane. Then I opened my eyes, and ran for the fancy metal trash can I knew was next to Terrance Sterling's desk.

That salami and cheese sandwich came right back up.

I retched and heaved over the metal can, hoping it would be big enough.

Once the heaving slowed, I felt a hand on my shoulder.

"Sip this," Ernesto said. He helped me sit back, leaning against the desk, and pressed a cut glass tumbler in my hand.

I sipped. Soda water. With whiskey. I sipped some more.

"You sure I should?"

"You need to shut it down, Jasmine. Whiskey is easy."

Yeah. The combination was doing its trick, the soda

settling my stomach a bit, and the whiskey shutting down my psychic centers, one by one. Taking the edge off.

"That's never happened to me before," I said.

"You've been injured and you've overtaxed yourself too often in the last two weeks, so I'm not surprised," Ernesto replied.

"Can you tell us what you *saw?*" Helen asked again.

I handed the tumbler back to Ernesto and gestured for him to help me up.

"Carol, would you look at the spiderweb in the corner? Middle of the seam?"

She walked over, hands clasped behind her back so she wouldn't touch anything. That was smart. She leaned toward the corner, until her eyes were a foot away from the wall. And she gasped.

"What *is* it?" Helen again. She was seriously getting annoying. The older woman grabbed Carol's shoulders and practically shoved her out of the way.

"Hey!" Carol said, grabbing Helen's arm.

"What is it, maga?" Ernesto asked quietly. But it was Helen who turned toward us first.

"A dead white spider."

Carol spoke then, "That isn't all. Tell them, Helen."

"The little tiger eye bead," Helen said. "From Terrance's tie tack."

The sphere of Earth. His connection to the physical plane, trapped in a spider web as surely as his essence and authority was trapped up on the astral.

"And what did you see, Jasmine?" Ernesto asked.

"Terrance's blue scarab."

I felt so heavy all of a sudden. All the energy drained out of me, as though I could sleep for a year. My mouth was foul and I needed a bath.

But we weren't done here yet. Leaning on Terrance's big slab of a desk, I cleared my throat, trying to speak the words that needed to be said.

"Terrance's blue scarab. Enclosed in a jail of sigils. Sigils shaped like a column from a temple, with a spider in the middle, where the rising sun should be."

I hoped Momma Beatrice's spirit had some insight about that.

All I knew was, this was turning into one bad trip.

36

JASMINE

"Terrance Sterling!" My voice reverberated in the long hallway upstairs, and my boot heels stomped down the polished wooden floors.

"Shh!" Helen grabbed at my arm. I shook her off. My stomach was still queasy, but the power of ocean was growing inside of me again, increasing my power.

Two young faces—one black, one Chinese, both around twelve years old—poked out from a classroom, an adult head just over them, dyed blond hair around a white face. Mrs. Chisolm.

Wasn't it late in the afternoon for class? Ernesto paused to talk to them.

I heard the classroom door snick shut behind me and whipped my head toward Helen.

"Will he be in his bedroom suite or in the Temple room?"

"His bedroom," she replied, lips practically white against her pale skin, her usual lipstick eaten off from stress, I guessed. That Jackie O bob of hair was still perfect, though. "You can't disturb him, Jasmine! He's ill!"

I reversed course then, and shoved past Helen Price. Back toward the staircase to the third floor.

"Oh, I know he's sick all right," I said. "And I think we know what the cause of that illness is, now don't we?"

Cutting my eyes at Helen for a moment, I saw a look of terror cross her face before she shut it down.

Ernesto waited patiently at the curved staircase, a grim look on his face.

Carol caught my wrist as I went by. "Jasmine. What are you going to do?"

"Talk to Terrance," I said, innocent lilt to my voice, then gave her a little push to keep walking. "Seriously, girl, don't you think this has gone on long enough?"

Great. More stairs. My queasiness, coupled with the climb, gave me vertigo. Clutching at the rails, I breathed as deep into my belly as I could, willing myself upward, calling on Elemental Water to buoy me up.

Seems like I should be calling on the ancestors, too.

Ancestors to bring "the fire next time," as the Christians would have it. Ancestors to bring judgment on the inner planes, as the magicians would say.

Ancestors to hold his ass accountable. That's how *I* would have it.

Momma Beatrice? What do you have to say about this right now? I asked inside my mind. The scent of licorice grew stronger, so I took it as a sign, gripped the wrought iron Spanish-style stair railing, and kept climbing. Almost there.

The top floor of the Mansion held a couple of small single bedrooms like Carol's and suites for the teachers, Terrance, and Helen. There were more bedrooms on the second floor, shared by under the half dozen out-of-state students in residence at any time. Two classrooms flanked the second floor.

I had never been up here, having lived at my parent's home the whole time I was training.

The light was glorious. There was a large arched window at the end of the hallway and a skylight in the middle.

"Which room?" I asked Helen, still walking.

She didn't respond. I stopped.

"Helen, do you really want me to start shouting again? Or using my sorcery?"

"At the end," she ground out between her teeth.

"Thank you."

The hall felt pleasant enough, but something weird was going on all the same. It seemed to be stretching. Like some shit was affecting space and time. My head started pounding and my stomach threatened to erupt again. That was the last thing I needed.

I breathed in deep, imagining the calmest pool of water in my center, rippling out to reinforce my aura with blue, watery flame. I needed to be calm. To focus. Not let my overuse of magic mess things up.

And not let my anger do too much damage before I got more information.

The walnut door at the end of the bright hallway confronted me. Solid. Heavy.

Well, so was I.

I breathed the power of Ocean down my arms and into both hands.

Queasy stomach and vertigo or not, I was ready.

Bang! Bang! Bang! My right fist practically bounced off the hard wood.

"Come!" Terrance's voice sounded strong even behind the thick wood.

I turned the brass knob and entered, Helen crowding right behind me.

And there he stood in the sitting area of his two room suite, adjusting silver cufflinks on a snowy white shirt, purple-paisley-print tie knotted firmly under his chiseled chin.

I swear, the man matched his surroundings. The tasteful Egyptian-style paintings in heavy gold frames. The statues on built-in book cases. The chairs set, so cozy, ready for conversation.

Except, Terrance Sterling wasn't cozy. He stood there, sharp as a tack. Silver hair perfect. Black shoes shining under tastefully striped navy trousers.

Terrance Sterling didn't look sick at all. His sapphire eyes glinted from behind his glasses.

"Terrance?" Helen asked.

I could feel Ernesto and Carol's distress and confusion behind me. None of us had expected…this. This vision of the arrogant head of the Association, un-cowed. Strong, even.

"Yes, Helen? Is something wrong, that you all trooped up the stairs to barge in on me in my private demesne?"

"You aren't in bed!" Helen sputtered.

"Yes, Terrance. You aren't in bed." I said, staring at those blue eyes. What in all the Powers was going on with his eyes?

His pupils were dilated. That was it. There was barely any blue around the black holes in the center of his eyes.

Was Terrance high?

Carol moved up beside me, and took a breath, like she was about to speak. Good for her. I could smell the grassy Earth scent of her. But it was darker, deeper than it used to be.

"Terrance," Carol said. "Your tie tack."

He smoothed the purple silk of his tie down before peering at the silver Tree of Life. The Tree of Life with every gem in place.

I looked at Carol, confused. She had told me the tiger eye for Earth was gone.

She was holding out the small, brown-and-gold swirled bead in one white hand.

"That's where it went," Terrance said, hand darting out to grab it.

Carol closed her fist and drew it to her chest.

"Carol? That's my property," he said.

I looked more closely at the tie tack. Sure enough, the tiger eye had been replaced by a gunmetal gray stone. Hematite. Designed to drag the wearer back into their body.

Someone was doing some pretty heavy magic to keep Terrance here on the physical plane.

"You aren't getting anything until you tell us what the fuck is going on," I said.

That rocked him back for a moment. Then a cruel sneer smeared itself across his patrician face.

"You think I care about you, girl? You think your *fucking* sorcery can match mine?"

"Terrance!" Helen said. "What is happening?"

He tore his eyes from mine and looked toward her. The person who'd been his advocate and right hand for as long as I'd been aware of the political machinations of the Association of Magical Arts and Sorcery.

"Nothing, Helen. Just had a little experiment go awry. You all have been so worried about me, but really, there's no need."

"You said you would go to a healer." Ernesto spoke

quietly from the back of the sitting room. Was he guarding the door? Humph. Good idea.

"No," Terrance replied. "You all strongly suggested I see a healer. Some ultimatums were issued, I believe. Well. I'm still head of the Association, aren't I?"

Then I saw something I'd missed before. Yes, the sigils were tracing around his auric egg, just like I'd seen them on the astral.

He was wearing the blue faience scarab ring.

But he was also wearing something new.

A silver pentagon shape winked from his right lapel.

Now, Elemental sorcerers can work with any shape, and any tool. But we don't need to. We don't need wands, or crystals, cups, or plates, or cubes, or pentagrams.

Sometimes, on occasion, we let them help us, to boost our natural magic, the stuff we all were born with.

But a pentagon? That was some Solomonic shit if ever I saw it.

Terrance was still looking at Ernesto, waiting for him to speak again.

Say something, Ernesto.

"We choose whether or not you are Association head, Señor," Ernesto said.

I tapped Carol's arm and jerked my head, just a little, toward Terrance's suit.

"So, now you are challenging me? After all I've done for you?"

Terrance had the gall to sit down in one of the leather club chairs. As though all of us standing there didn't have any power over him at all.

"I know about your seditious activities, Mr. Alvarez. The time you've been spending with the Brown Berets? The

Association might not look to kindly upon a man like you teaching their children."

Carol squeezed my arm, letting me know she'd seen the silver pentagon. She leaned in to whisper in my ear, "I think I've figured something out. Let's get out of here."

I nodded.

"You don't have to take this from him, Ernesto," I spoke aloud. "Now that we know Terrance is well enough to face an Association Quorum, I think we should get on that."

I turned to leave the room.

"If you challenge me again, Jasmine Jones, it will not go well for you," Terrance said to my back.

And then I saw one more thing.

Above the deep walnut lintel, on the whitewashed wall, there was that Powers-be-damned sigil. The fool had actually inscribed it over the door.

A temple column, with a spidery shape where there should have been a shining sun.

"Let's go," I said, and pulled open the door.

Yeah. Terrance Sterling was compromised, all right. But what were we going to do about it?

37

CAROL

Helen wasn't too happy to have Jasmine acting like she was in charge, and Carol couldn't blame her.

But she couldn't blame Jasmine, either. Really, how long had Helen known? She was the closest person to Terrance in the whole Association. How long had Helen thought she could keep it a secret?

Once Jasmine had pointed out the weird patches in the Mansion's protective field, Carol felt so stupid to not have noticed them before. They'd been so busy with everything else. The jailbreak. Trying to protect the Brown Berets. The whole *coming upon Terrance wrapped in spiderwebs* thing.

Carol just hadn't thought to do an overall assessment of the place. She wondered if Association members who didn't live nearby were noticing yet.

And how in the world had Terrance recovered like that? Jasmine insisted she'd seen some weirdness in his eyes.

It had to be magic, and not his own sorcery. There was no way he could have recovered that quickly.

So here they were, meeting in a union hall of all places, because they needed to talk to Rosalia again, but she said she was too busy to meet at her shop. If the group wanted to talk, they had to come to her.

So Carol, Ernesto, and Jasmine had practically forced Helen into her car and instructed her to drive them to the union hall.

The union hall was in a neighborhood squashed between downtown and Westlake, with Pico to the south. Carol hoped there'd be time to go to Koreatown after the meeting for dinner. She hadn't tried that kind of food before. Jasmine said it would be too spicy for her Minnesota tongue, but Carol didn't care.

She was busting out, and it was cool.

The union hall was a long, nondescript building on West 8th. A big, two-story rectangle, one of the rare brick buildings in LA. The bricks were painted white, with big squares of goldenrod under the windows. It stood across four lanes of traffic from a couple of crumbling houses. There was some sort of Mexican Pentecostal church on the corner.

Inside the building was no more interesting than out. The long meeting room had a drop ceiling, and fluorescent lights cast a white pallor over the stackable orange formed chairs and the skin of all the people gathered in the room, whether they were brown, black, or white.

Rosalia sat near the front, with two of the union leaders. Also in the room were several Brown Berets, and a few Black Panthers. That person Jasmine had mentioned, Geronimo Pratt. A couple of women. And a man with a high forehead who had introduced himself to Carol as Cotton.

He seemed a little off to her. Trying too hard. A little greasy. Strange. But she couldn't exactly place why. Carol just assumed there was some *weird black man talking to a white woman* trip going on, and tried to drop it.

Besides, Cotton wasn't the only strange thing. It seemed as if the whole gathering must be strange for a union meeting, but what did Carol know? The Association didn't mix with *any* of these people, and her dad's union in Minnesota was mostly white, and not very political. At least, not that he'd ever mentioned.

The room smelled like old chalk, rubber shoes, and cigarette smoke. It made her so glad no one was allowed to smoke inside the Mansion. The official story was that it interrupted the vibrations, but really it was that Terrance was allergic. Thank the Powers for that, Carol guessed.

"You all know that the contract from our last strike is being challenged." A bushy-haired white man in a plaid shirt was speaking.

"How long do we have to stand here?" Helen whispered in Carol's ear. They were standing to the side of the room, leaning against one of the long walls. Carol looked down. Helen's feet must have been killing her in those pumps. Or, more likely, the woman just wasn't used to standing when people below her station were sitting down. Carol grinned inside.

She was starting to sound like Jasmine. And she wasn't one-hundred-percent sure Helen should have been with them anyway. It was still freaky to not trust the people you'd been trained to trust above all others.

"As long as it takes," Carol replied. Helen drew in a sharp breath. Carol had never talked to her that way before.

Well, Carol was getting as tired of the Association as was Jasmine, and frankly, she and Ernesto still needed a long talk.

And hopefully some more kissing.

Ernesto's warm fingers sought out her own. She laced her fingertips with his and smiled. Then hurriedly locked down her mind again. Shit. She hoped she wasn't actually broadcasting, and that it was just their personal connection.

And, perhaps, that he just liked the way she felt, standing next to him.

The way she liked feeling the slight pressure of his shoulder and hip against her. The overcrowded room was good for that, at least.

Carol turned her attention back to what the union leader was saying.

"The police haven't treated us well. They busted a few heads in '66, and we're not happy about it. We're not happy they're busting *your* heads, either, or trying to shoot you to death in your sleep."

The Panthers and Brown Berets were nodding.

"So our union has voted to support you, full stop. We passed a resolution to voice our protest of the attacks on Panthers across the country. We are also demanding the release of all political prisoners." He paused for a moment, lowered his head, and then looked up at them from beneath his bushy salt-and-pepper eyebrows. "Whether they're actual panthers or the ordinary human kind."

That got a laugh from everyone in the room. Carol felt Jasmine's aura relax on the other side of Ernesto, while Helen tensed up, growing more spiky.

Afraid.

"We plan to march and hope that you all will join us. Okay, I think I've said enough for now."

Carol was fascinated. Her life had been so sheltered, first in Minnesota and then behind the Mansion walls. Who *were* these people? And how were they so casual about the fact that there were likely shape-shifters in the room? And that they were sitting calmly with known revolutionaries?

Was everyone in Los Angeles a revolutionary now?

Well, not Helen, that was for sure, but Carol even had suspicions about that. Jasmine had mentioned some things about Helen coming up to visit, and the car getting shot up, and meeting Helen and Doreen outside Panther headquarters in Oakland.

All things Helen never mentioned when she came back home.

"I just wanted a visit with Doreen," she had said.

Carol wondered now if Helen hadn't been up in Oakland asking for help with Terrance Sterling. Or spying for him.

Rosalia was on her feet now. The room quieted down.

"The Chicano community thanks you for your help. I know that there are many of us in your union, but I also know that unions don't always care about those of us on the darker end of the spectrum."

No laughter greeted that statement, Carol noticed, but she saw a few grimaces and some uneasy shifting in chairs.

"My name is Rosalia, and I am here not only as someone interested in helping our brothers and sisters in the Brown Berets and the Black Panthers, but to offer help from my organization to you, the union."

"Is she going to out herself?" Carol whispered in Ernesto's ear. "Is that okay?"

Ernesto leaned in closer, murmuring, "Rosalia does what she will, but never moves without assessing the will of the people first. That is why they trust her. Las Manos will support her in this."

Okay. Wow.

"...we are sorcerers," Rosalia was saying. "Our magic is different from the Panthers, here. It is very old, traced all the way back to before the white men invaded this land. It comes from las poblaciones indígenas, our ancestors. As you have offered your assistance to our people, we are proud to offer the assistance of our magic to you."

It was on, Carol realized. Whatever she still felt about Jasmine's revolution, and whatever was happening with the implosion of the Association, it was all of one piece. She could feel it in her bones.

The revolution had come to her, a skinny white girl from Minnesota.

She just needed to figure out her part.

38

DOREEN

Fred Hampton lay on the attic floor. Every candle in the room was lit. They'd gotten Deborah up the back stairs for this, because "There's no way you're doing this kind of magic on my man without me there to help him," she'd said.

The heavily pregnant woman had to be due any moment. Patrice got her settled in a living room chair Fred had humped up the stairs. No way could she sit on the floor, or even in a folding chair for too long.

After Jasmine had called, telling her about Terrance's recovery, and what Momma had done...and about the spiders...Doreen had gotten a vision from Momma herself.

Momma was clear that to get to the root of what was happening, they needed to go through a Panther. Jasmine's boyfriend, Jimmy, had offered, but Doreen had the sense someone else was going to be necessary.

Someone more central to the operation. Fred had pretty quickly volunteered. It should have been Huey, but he was back in hiding for a while. Besides, Fred had already been a target, whether that was on purpose, or because opportunity arose.

And Doreen was scared out of her mind.

She was going to have to put that damn Chokwe mask over her face. She was going to have to look through its white-ringed eyes, and feel the black-and-red crown surround her own head like a halo.

Doreen had never done this kind of magic before.

Oh, she'd heard of it, sure, but it wasn't a thing sorcerers had much truck with. This was shaman territory. Or serious seer territory.

Of course, Momma was a serious seer, and a sorcerer, too. That rare combination drew people to her, and had them treating her like a queen. It was simple: Momma Beatrice ruled over the community just by being who she was. Nothing and no one else was like her, now or then.

Doreen certainly wasn't. But Momma had set her this challenge all the same. Doreen sighed. Who knew that this long after her death, the woman would still wield so much power?

"Do I need to do anything?" Fred Hampton's voice shocked Doreen from her reverie.

"Just stay open," Doreen replied. "And if you need anything, say something, or raise a hand. Patrice is here to help you."

"Doreen?" Patrice asked. "Do *you* need anything?"

"I'm fine, baby. Take care of Fred and Deborah. If I need you, I'll holler."

Right. If a spider didn't drag Doreen off somewhere, or the ancestors didn't crack her skull and make her crazy.

Doreen was delaying now. Hoping Momma would offer some reprieve.

"Okay," Doreen said. "Fred, we're doing this to try and find the connection between the Panthers and whatever this malevolent magic is. Since the snake attacked you, you're a target. What we need to figure out is how and why."

He chuckled at that, dry and sarcastic. "I can tell you why I'm a target, Mrs. Doreen. Deborah and I have a shot-up apartment as proof."

He looked at her then, eyes dark with anger, and some small amount of pride. "We're dangerous to the Man. And that's how it ought to be."

"That's right, baby," Deborah murmured.

Strong woman. Stronger than Doreen.

"Patrice, pour out the water, please. And light the ancestor candles."

Doreen's lover moved toward the big altar under the sharp peak of the attic ceiling. The only lights came from candles, casting shadows on her rounded cheeks and lush lips.

Doreen hoped they'd make it through this magical operation well enough that she could kiss those lips tonight.

"Fred," Doreen said, "I'm going to enter the realm of the ancestors and get some information, and hopefully a blessing, to bring back to you. You just lie here and keep your breathing slow. I'm going to link us together, so your energy can ride with me, okay?"

The young man nodded. Doreen closed her eyes, dropped her attention deep below her solar plexus, and reached. There he was. Warm. Glowing. Steady. Strong. With a hint of anger at the core, wrapped around a deep, abiding love.

Doreen drew a strand of etheric energy from around the young man's body, anchoring it into her hands.

Then she sent out a prayer to the Powers that the operation would work. This was seriously uncharted territory.

The sound of water pouring into Momma's red glass chalice soothed Doreen's soul. The snick of a match brought the whiff of sulfur that flared her nostrils.

Fire. She inhaled deeply: the sulfur, the beeswax, the oily burn of paraffin. It all fed the Elemental Fire inside her. She opened the energy centers in the soles of her feet and in her hands. Her head was wide open already. Part of her was champing at the bit to let the ancestors come through. The part that wasn't terrified.

Red, green, and black candles lit, Patrice picked up the heavy mask and held it toward Doreen.

It was weighty in Doreen's hands. She peered into the black-painted concave face, looking out through the eyeholes. The candles wavered. She drew it to her face, nose to nose, chin to chin, eyes to eyes.

Patrice tied the heavy cords behind her head.

And Doreen's head was on fire.

Vision after vision after vision. Light flickering into light. Stampeding ibex. Small, red-shouldered birds in flight. Moon on a pool of water. Women walking in the sun, proud heads erect, red ochre mud drying on their coils of hair.

And there she was. The woman with the missing left incisor. Doreen's ancestor, staring at her. Staring into the eyes of the Chokwe mask.

A brown spider crawled across the woman's cheek.

Doreen flinched at the sight of it.

The ancestor nodded, then held up her right hand, which gripped a black snake. She looked from the snake to Doreen, to the snake again.

The brown spider reached the woman's heavy coils of

ochre-smeared hair, turned itself around, and, lifting its abdomen, shot a strand of sticky white webbing from a spinneret. Straight toward the mask. Doreen felt it hit the center of the forehead.

Right where her third eye would be.

Doreen's ancestor lifted the snake to her mouth and, baring her teeth, that gap with the missing incisor glowing black, she bit that snake's back.

It writhed and slapped its tail against the woman's belly.

Doreen panted behind the mask. She gripped her body, pressing her arms around her breasts as though she were her own mother, and that would keep her safe somehow.

Her body burned with Elemental Fire and the dryness of the landscape where they stood.

The woman chewed all the way through that snake's body, dropping the head to the dry ground, blood streaming down her chin.

Then she bit off a piece of that snake's belly and held it out to Doreen, pushing it through the mouth hole, until bloody snake touched Doreen's lips.

It tasted like power. It tasted like death. It tasted like bad magic. It tasted like a strong desire twisted in on itself.

Doreen almost retched with the foul taste of it. Forced herself to chew the rubbery snake. And swallow it down.

And then she knew. She saw.

The knowledge raced through her bloodstream.

"Fred!"

Dimly, Doreen heard Patrice's voice call out from the other place. Saying a name.

She looked down to the dry ground and saw a young man writhing there, trying to change his shape, trapped. He roared into the air.

Doreen hadn't meant to bring him here, into this place. Clearly the ancestors had other ideas.

The ancestor straddled him, bent over his torso, smearing his face with the blood of the snake. Fred fought it, body arching up against her, screaming at the sky.

"Co! INnnn! Teeeelllll! Tell me! Tell me! Tell me what I should know!" he screamed and shouted until the ancestor bit off another chunk of snake and spat it into his open, roaring mouth.

His face a shocked rictus, Fred swallowed. And his dark eyes rolled back up into his head.

Doreen lifted her arms to the sky, calling on the fire of the harsh sun. She traced a benediction over the ancestor's head, then lower, over the body of the young man on the ground.

She passed them both a taste of her Fire.

This was the way of sorcery and magic. The Elements taught all they knew. The animals passed on their wisdom through the blood.

The ancestors were always inside. Waiting for a chance to speak.

"Speak to me," Doreen said to the golden air.

The ancestor looked at her, blood-smeared chin and steady black eyes.

Her lips opened and formed words in a language Doreen did not know, but their meaning rang clear inside her head.

"*You must stop the white spider, by means you already know.*"

"What means are those?" Doreen asked.

"The means of revolution." Fred Hampton's voice rang out in both worlds.

Doreen bowed to the ancestor. Bowed to the brown spider on her baked ochre head. Bowed to the land, and the tiny, red-shouldered birds. Then she took in a great, shuddering breath, and brought herself back home, dragging the young panther shifter with her.

39

JASMINE

We walked down the sidewalk toward my parent's house. I had to get out of that damned Mansion. No way was I having this conversation within those walls.

Who knew how much surveillance equipment—magical or otherwise—was planted in every room?

The sun was bright and the day had grown warm. It must have climbed to seventy-five degrees. Typical Los Angeles weather: nice enough to sit out in my mother's garden, under the jacaranda tree.

"Will Cecelia be home?" Ernesto asked, coming up the driveway behind me. I'd told him to just park in the driveway, but he insisted along the sidewalk was just fine.

"I can never remember her work schedule," I replied. "I hope so, though; we need a meeting right away."

Helen's heels clattered on the concrete. I swear, that woman always dressed like some corporate wife. She looked good, though, I had to admit that. She and my mother were two of a kind in that way, though not in others, I was glad to say.

The front door was unlocked.

"Mother?"

I stepped into the entryway and glanced into the living room. It was empty, sun shining off the white bricks of the fireplace. Turning to the others, I saw Ernesto shut the door behind him. Carol looked at me expectantly.

Even though she was put together, Helen actually looked a little ill.

"She has to be around somewhere. She wouldn't have left the house unlocked," I said.

Carol cocked her head for a moment. "I think she's out back. I can feel something going on with the plants."

Hmph. Handy having an Earth Sorcerer around.

We trooped on down the hallway through the kitchen, and out the back door, which stuck a little in its frame, into the little laundry room on a screened-in porch.

Sure enough, there was my mother, wearing tan slacks and a white shirt under a flowered apron, kneeling on a gardening mat in front of a lavender bush, garden sheers in her gloved hands.

There was a pile of jacaranda branches in the corner. She must have been pruning. That was usually my father's job, unless mom really needed to recharge. The way things had been going lately? I didn't blame her.

I banged the screen door open and stepped out into the yard.

"Hello, Mother."

She nodded and smiled, then held up a hand to give her a moment.

She took a spray of lavender and some sage and, bowing, laid them on the altar stone at the back of the garden. There was already a lemon on the stone, and some flowers.

Taking off her gloves, she held her hands out, palm

down, over the herbs and the big California granite slab. We all stood respectfully, waiting for her to be done.

My mother pushed herself up off the mat and turned to greet us.

Her smiled pretty quickly turned to a frown.

"Helen?" she said. "Are you all right?"

I snapped my head toward Helen. Her face was almost ghostly now under her dark bob of hair. Lips tight, she shook her head.

My mother walked across the grass in the canvas sneakers she wore only for gardening, straight for her Helen, whose Chanel suit was incongruous in the Crenshaw garden. Then she folded her friend into her arms.

Helen started shaking.

I looked at Ernesto and Carol. They both just shrugged.

Okay. Up to me, then. I rubbed at the aching spot in front of my shoulder, rolled my head on my neck, and then straightened my spine. I needed an Elemental boost if I was going to take charge.

I cast out toward the coastline, seeking Ocean. Dropping my attention deeper, I sought the water underneath the grass. I got an answer from both, and drew a little bit extra into my bloodstream and my cells, feeding my sorcery the Water it was made of.

Better.

"We need to have a meeting," I said then. "And I'm sorry, but we need to have that meeting now."

My mother, still hugging Helen, turned her head toward me and asked, "What in all the Powers just happened? I was out here in the garden and felt a shift in the Elemental forces, and started gathering supplies to make an offering."

She patted Helen's back and stepped away, looking at her friend.

"But before we meet, let me go get some iced tea for everyone. Jasmine and Carol? Please arrange the garden chairs under the tree. And when you're done, you may want to spend a minute at the offering stone yourselves."

My mother turned toward the house. "Ernesto, will you help me with the glasses?"

I huffed out a breath. Okay. Not in charge then. Carol and I wrestled the old metal chairs with thick beige cushions into a square under the tree. There were only four of them.

"There's a folding chair by the side of the house," I said to Carol. "You get that and I'll grab the table."

Helen was still standing where my mother had left her.

"Helen?" I asked. "Why don't you sit down?"

She nodded and made her way over to the chairs under the green leaves.

By the time my mother and Ernesto came back with water glasses imprinted with yellow lemon slices on the sides, and a pitcher of tea, Carol and I had five chairs set up around a small, round, glass-topped table.

"So, tell me what happened," my mother said.

"Short story? Terrance went from wrapped up in spider webs, practically in a coma, to fully dressed, sharp as a tack, with eyes that look like he's on some sort of drugs," I said. "Oh, and with a damn sigil that shouldn't be there is drawn in black paint over his door."

"We need to do the soul retrieval..." Helen murmured.

"Excuse me, but I think it's too late for that," I snapped.

"Jasmine," my mother said.

"I hate to say this, Helen, but Jasmine is correct," Ernesto said. "What I saw in Terrance's face terrified me."

Ernesto set down his tea, ice cubes rattling in the glass.

He continued. "And he's refused all help, even after you decreed it, Cecelia."

"Damn," my mother said. She looked up at Ernesto. "Do we need to involve membership yet?"

He shrugged.

"We're going to need to tell them soon, because the man has to be displaced. Frankly, I'm surprised they don't already know, considering the mess that's going on. And the fact that some of them *were* called early on, only to have Terrance send them away. Which means you and he must have been pulling some elaborate bluff on who knows how many Association members." His voice was like steel.

"We're talking a coup now?" Helen's voice was shrill and brittle, ice cubes banging against the glass gripped in her right hand.

"What do you think, Helen? You think Terrance is fit to lead the Association? You think everything's still groovy? Wake *up!*" I said.

My mother put a cool hand on my arm, and spoke.

"I'm also afraid Jasmine is correct. We've let this go on far too long, and now the whole Association is in danger. And it sounds as if you've been complicit in this, Helen. For how long?"

The silky hairs at the base of my neck stood at attention and the edges of my aura flared. Shoving my chair back, I stood and turned right as the back gate opened with a *snick*.

Ernesto and my mother stood with me, staring as the pale man in the black suit and glasses, with his movie-star wave of hair, slinked onto the cropped grass.

"Who are you?" my mother said.

"He's the snake."

A slick, tight grin flashed over his face. A baring of teeth, then the pale lips were closed once more.

He walked toward us, hand outstretched toward my mother.

"I'm just a man, looking for answers, ma'am. And it seems like I can find some here."

"And how exactly did you get past my wards?" My mother's voice was like granite.

I could feel Ernesto and Carol linking, ready to combine Ernesto's two elements—Air and Fire—with Carol's Earth if needed. I breathed out, sending a wave of sorcery their way. Carol caught it, and began to weave it into the structure they were building.

The Fed shrugged, tilting his chin slightly my way.

Damn it. They said they'd gotten rid of the tag. Why in all the Powers could he still find me?

Then I felt my mother's magic join us. Two types of Earth, then Air, Fire and Water. All four Elements combined. I wasn't letting Helen's magic anywhere near this weaving. Who knew what she had done?

"You can throw my magic away, but once a snake—as you call me—catches the scent of its prey, it's hard for the prey to mask itself again. Just a tiny chink in your very good magical systems."

He had reached the table by now, and picked up my lemon-embossed glass of iced tea. Taking a long drink, he looked at me.

"And my magic is better, of course."

I drew on the power of our combined sorcery and threw Water with all my might.

The tea shot out of the glass and blasted his face. Every single glass of tea released its liquid seconds later, drenching the man and pelting him with ice. A large cube connected with his left temple and he staggered slightly with the blow, lifting his arms and muttering some incantation that made my stomach twist.

Then my mother's magic hit him with a jacaranda branch, knocking him cold. He crashed against the glass-topped table as he fell. I heard his nose snap and caught the scent of fresh blood.

My mother dropped the branch.

"He didn't find you because of that tag, though we should make sure when we have time," my mother said, barely breathing hard. "I think someone sent him here."

She turned to Helen, who was the only one who hadn't linked with us. Hadn't even tried to use her sorcery.

"What the *hell* is your involvement here? What have you brought into my *home*?"

Helen's lips went white.

"I was only trying to help. It's the government...and Terrance said it would make him strong again..."

She straightened up a little. "You said you wanted to heal his soul."

"Stupid white woman," I said, shaking my head in disgust. "You've been trusting all the wrong people. And unfortunately, we've been trusting you. Giving you too many chances. Too many Powers-damned times!"

My mother didn't even rebuke me for my disrespect.

40

———

SNAKES AND SPIDERS

*D*amn her. *Damn them all.*

How dare they?

It was humiliating. The Panther bitch had bested him twice. He knew she was weak. There was no way she should still wield that kind of power.

They had bound him, but not tightly enough. With the power of the sigils on his side, there was no magical cage simple sorcery could weave that would hold him for long.

They'd left him alone, trussed up and gagged in a corner of that damn, sun-infected garden. It didn't take much to extricate himself, once he'd finally come to.

He'd thought about blasting into that tidy little home, obliterating everyone inside it. But that would interfere with the plan.

So Samuels paced the streets of Los Angeles, head pounding, practically blind with migraine. He needed dark. Quiet. But he also needed to keep moving.

The Master would be looking for him. Wanting a report. Wanting to mete out punishment for his failures. There would be agents at his hotel, waiting. And operatives watching his car.

He had botched this all. Too badly. He needed more time.

So Samuels walked, leather soles smacking concrete, jarring his head with every step.

Dimly, he realized the neighborhood looked familiar. It was half a mile away from 41st and Central. He must be near...

There it was. The curved, fake stone wall with a window set into stucco above it, leading to a shadowy entryway. Behind the scarred wood door was the place he had found his man, Lizard.

The one who didn't do as he was told. The one who got himself killed before Samuels could deal with him.

Maybe Samuels needed to hide out for a while. Gather his strength. He supposed he should find a restaurant. He didn't know when the last time was he'd given his body some fuel.

But something about the bar drew him. He could sit in a corner. Drink a whiskey.

Chase out the locals. No way they would want to sit with the likes of him.

He grimaced and lurched forward. He didn't care what the locals thought. He was the Man. And that had to have its compensations.

The heavy door shushed open. All conversation stopped. Just the jukebox, playing some song about sex. All jukebox songs were about sex.

Samuels heard a muttered curse from behind the bar and smiled as he approached. It was dimmer in here. That was good for his eyes. And his head.

Glancing at the bottles lit up with golden light behind the scratched-up wooden bar with its red Naugahyde bumper, he saw one he could deign to drink. Sandwiched between the glaring yellow label of Cutty Sark and a bottle of Ancient Age was Hiram Walker's eight-year-old bourbon. It would do.

"Walker's, neat, side of water," he said. The bartender slid the glasses across the wood.

"Five dollars," the bartender said.

Samuels looked at the man's slim face, the dark skin and flared nose, and grunted. "A little high, don't you think?"

"Not for an eight year old," the man replied.

And not for a white man in a black suit who's scaring all my customers out the door, *was left unsaid.*

Exchange done, Samuels turned. The room had emptied, except for one man in the back corner.

The reason something in the back of Samuel's brain had led him here.

Cotton. His most loyal plant in the Black Panther Party, Los Angeles Chapter, since Lizard had turned traitor and then died.

Samuels grinned.

41

CAROL

The library was quiet, with the exception of Jasmine's pacing and Ernesto's sighs.

And pages being turned as they all looked for some clues.

Carol looked out at the green lawn and the small circle of manzanita near her favorite bench.

She felt weird being here, not knowing where Terrance was, or whether the place was wired, like Jasmine said.

But Ernesto insisted that the library was the next step, and these books were the best they were going to find.

Sighing, she went back to her book, barely seeing the words on the page.

One thing bothered Carol.

Well, a lot of things bugged her. Terrified her, even.

But the thing she kept coming back to was Terrance's jewelry. First, the altered Tree of Life tie tack.

Then, the scarab Jasmine saw on the astral plane, surrounded by the nasty sigils, which meant his ring was compromised.

And now, that new lapel pin.

A pentagon-shaped piece of silver.

Not something any sorcerer would need. Even the Tree of Life was a bit too ceremonial for the likes of an Association member, though they studied all magical systems, and the correspondences to the other worlds was useful.

But a pentagon? Not a shape associated with any of the elements. Sure, it appeared sometimes in nature, like in morning glories, or okra, if she recalled correctly. But mostly it was a shape for building things.

Or big military complexes that fueled the war machine and sent boys off to kill in Vietnam.

The book in front of her, an old grimoire written two hundred years ago, revealed nothing. She carefully shut the heavy, blue-bound cover.

Everyone used pent*agrams*, but hardly anyone used pent*agons*.

Except the U.S. Government.

Speaking of which, the agent escaped.

They'd taped his mouth, put tight bags over his hands before binding them behind his back, blindfolded him, and dragged him to the corner of the garden. Ernesto and Cecelia had also put magical bindings over the physical ones.

He'd gotten free anyway, before they could figure out how to deal with him.

The Feds and military clearly had stronger magic than they'd figured on.

Then it hit her.

The Pentagon. Of course. Those weird hippies had tried to levitate the Pentagon and been arrested for it, even though nothing had happened.

Seventy-thousand hippies and "yippies," as they called themselves, had tried to do an exorcism on the place.

"Ernesto," she said. He shut his book and stretched his arms above his head.

"Yes, maga?"

"Those hippies that tried to levitate the Pentagon…"

He sat up straight at that. And Jasmine stopped her pacing.

"That's it!" Jasmine said. "That's what we've been missing. It *has* to be."

"And we cannot talk about this here," Ernesto said.

Carol grabbed her coat and bag.

"What are we waiting for?"

42

———

DOREEN

"We need to get more bold," Doreen said.

She paced her living room, past the television cabinet flanked by two chairs, under the watchful eye of the golden mountain lion painting and the photograph of Dr. King.

Turning near the doorway, she faced the chairs and sofa and the people gathered there. Some sat on the floor. A couple of the red kitchen chairs were shoved into the corners of the room.

Every face was thoughtful, though the emotions ranged from surprise to something a bit more grim.

Jimmy was there. And Tarika, whom Doreen didn't really know. Fred Hampton. Huey Newton. Deborah. Patrice. Leroy. Drake. Tanya couldn't make it that night. Her kids needed her.

Drake worried a small hole in the knee of his jeans, dark eyes flashing with a combination of excitement and fear. He was the youngest person in the room, and Doreen and Patrice had both insisted he be there. This was his fight as much as anybody's.

And after Jasmine and Carol's report on what was going on with Terrance Sterling, it was clear the fight needed leadership *now*. She and Jasmine couldn't wait any longer.

The Ancestor had confirmed it all, as had Fred's shout that the means were the revolution.

The means were magic.

She, Hector, the Association—they had all been wrong. They all had thought hiding their magic, or pretending it was something small, was going to help the people. Keep them safe.

All it really was? Was giving up the responsibility they should have taken in this world and in all the worlds.

The Ancestor was right. They had the means. They knew the ways. They just had done things one way for so long, they'd failed to see that way was wrong.

"We've been going about this all wrong," Doreen said.

"What do you mean by *that*?" Leroy challenged.

"Cool it, man," Jimmy replied.

Doreen held up her hands to stop the bickering. They'd had too many rounds of that already.

"What I mean," she said, holding Leroy's gaze. His jaw was clenched, and his musk was rising. "What I mean is, a few panther shifters showing up now and then isn't enough. What I mean is, a few sorcerers teaching a few people basic magic isn't enough. We aren't risking enough. We aren't being *proud* enough!" Her voice broke on that, and she fell silent, recalling the Ancestor's face. That brown spider whose web hit Doreen through the mask, opening up a portal in her mind.

She understood now.

Sorcery and shifters' magic were both ancient and strong. They were built upon the bloodlines, true, but more importantly, the imaginations, of the people. The Ancestors knew this, and walked in the world as whole beings, always sharing knowledge, not hoarding it.

The Association worked in secret. For the sorcerers to have sequestered themselves like they had was to diminish people's ability to vision the worlds to come. It had trapped them in endless cycles of war and birth and destruction.

Some of them knew there must be a different way, and sought it eagerly, but that way was always just beyond their grasp.

Because the Animal People—the shifters—and the sorcerers, and the witches who still hid in forests and the warehouses of abandoned cities, occasionally offering healing or protection...they had all kept the knowledge from the people who needed it most, calling themselves their guardians.

Treating the people as though they were children with no magic of their own.

By not giving them a chance, they had ensured those children could never create the very cities that would nourish them the most.

It was a risk to awaken nascent magic. It was a wild card of massive proportions.

But thousands of years of doing the opposite had brought them to this endless war.

It was time.

"Doreen?" Patrice asked.

Doreen cleared her throat. Realized the air around her smelled of cinnamon. Her sorcery was moving on its own right now.

"You need some water?" Patrice said, rising smoothly to pour some from the pitcher on the coffee table. "How about you, Deborah?"

"Yes, thank you, but not too much." The younger woman gestured to her rounded belly. "I'll just need to pee."

"Can we please get back to this supposed mistake we've all been making? The ways in which we aren't doing enough?" Leroy huffed.

Doreen sipped at the water.

"I could reassure you all that you're doing plenty. But I need us to be honest with ourselves. Feeding children and opening clinics isn't enough. The Ancestor told me we could fight the white spider with the means we already had. I asked what those were and Fred here shouted that the means were revolution."

"And what is that supposed to mean?" Tarika asked.

"I think you know," Doreen said. "I think everyone in this room knows. It's time to stop hiding. It's time for the Black Panther Party to roam the streets in panther form, patrolling, letting the people *and the cops* see the full power of your magic. Just like your brother in Chicago is doing every single day with those prison guards."

"And what about you, Doreen? What about us?" Patrice asked quietly.

"I'm as much to blame as anyone. I even hid my sorcery from myself for a time. The Association is either going to come out and open its doors, getting with the program of Magic for the People, or it is going down. The world needs to know who we are."

A slow clap started up from one of the kitchen chairs shoved in the corner. Fred Hampton's palms struck against one another. A huge grin split his square face. "Right on."

Then Huey spoke. "Revolution is not an action; it is a process. So what process are you talking about, sister?"

Doreen nodded at that. Yes. Her Fire rose up and shimmered around her, showing the room that she was as powerful as any of the shifters there.

"Magic is a process, too. Sorcery, shape-shifting, they are all processes. We *know* that, but we forgot along the way. And any process can be taught."

"You mean, we can teach people how to be shifters? Come on, now, you know that isn't true," Leroy said.

"No. That's not what I mean at all..."

"She means that even with our natural skills, we've had to train ourselves into our power." Tarika said.

"Yes!" Doreen said. "And the best way to teach them is by showing them who we are. It's time the world knew that there is sick magic happening in the halls of government, and it's being used to keep our communities down. It's time the world knew that shape-shifters aren't rumors, or terrifying legends, but that you all are beings who can help them. And it's time that sorcerers, and witches, and magicians woke up the magic inside every person's soul."

"And used it for revolution," Jimmy replied.

"You still aren't getting what she's saying." Drake sat up a little straighter. "You're all used to this..." He waved his hands around. "You're so used to magic shit, you don't see it anymore."

"So what's she saying, little brother?" Deborah asked.

"She's trying to tell us all that waking up the magic *is* the revolution. And that's what Fred said, too."

Drake continued, "'*All* power to *all* the people.' That's what you all say, right? Well, seems to me you been missing that 'all power' means *all power*. You got power we don't. It's time you learned to share."

Huey laughed at that.

"The revolution has always been in the hands of the young. The young always inherit the revolution," he said.

"Well, you're still pretty young, too," Doreen said.

Jimmy shook his head at that. "We don't feel young, Doreen. And that's the truth. But the young brother is right, we're socialists. What else we gonna do but share?"

"And Doreen is right, too," Drake spoke again. "You all *do* need to show your panther selves more. It would make us all feel safer, knowing there was more than just a couple of you, and that you're not just some exaggeration. We need to see what Black Power really is."

"Black Power is a lot of things," Doreen replied. "But I agree. Sorcery and shape-shifting is part of our inheritance. And if being more public about it is going to help set the people free? So be it."

Leroy rose then, and scratched at his ruddy sideburns.

"All right then, as Brother Malcolm said, 'By any means necessary.'" He crossed his arms over his massive chest. "Guess magic is what's necessary now."

43

JASMINE

People carried brightly colored statues in their arms, or on palanquin-like platforms.

Rose petals of all colors carpeted the sidewalks and the streets. Copal and sage billowed through the air.

In all my years in LA, I'd never seen anything like this. Brown nuts rattled around ankles and a conch shell blew. The dancers twirled and stomped, plumed headdresses waving and dipping. Big mallets thumping out a beat on the stretched skin heads of massive drums helped the dancers to keep time.

Were they Aztec? Or Mayan? I wasn't sure.

I'd need to ask someone who knew. Later, when there was time.

There wasn't any time anymore. Every second ticked like the clock on a bomb and I wasn't sure if we'd be able to defuse it in time.

We'd called my mother. She was going to meet us at Rosalia's shop, but looking at this crowd, I realized there was no guarantee Rosalia would even be there. The hechicera was more likely to be out here with the crowds honoring the Virgin's feast day.

"Ernesto!" I called over the sound of the dancers. He paused in his quest to keep us on track, forging a path through the crowd, and turned his face toward me. "How do we even know she'll be at the shop?"

He smiled at that. The first genuine smile I'd seen in a week. It was like the sun breaking through the lead-filled smog. I could see why Carol had fallen for him.

"She's always at the shop on Guadalupe's Feast Day. You'll see."

Okay then. I forged after, hoping my mother would be able to find parking somewhere closer to the shop than we had.

None of the sights looked familiar to me, with the masses of people in the streets. But then I heard a familiar stomping of boots in formation, rumbling low under the drum beats and the rattling of the hard nut shells around the dancer's ankles.

Were the Panthers here?

My head whipped around, and I saw a mass of Brown Berets, marching behind a phalanx of children strewing rose petals. The patches on their berets sizzled with magical protection. That was good.

I paused and raised my fist as they went by. Several of them raised fists in return.

Turning back, I saw that Carol and Ernesto had disappeared. Shit. I rushed forward, pushing through the tightly packed crowd right as a roar went up.

The dancers had gathered in front of Rosalia's shop. The statue I'd seen inside was now set up on an altar next to the peeling blue door.

Carol and Ernesto stood to one side, along with my mother. They all had roses in their hands.

The hechicera herself held an abalone shell and wafted smoke toward the statue, and then turned to bless the dancers kneeling at her feet. The drums started up again, first a slow bass thump, increasing as the higher tuned drums added their voices to the beat.

One woman stepped forward, receiving the roses from Carol, Ernesto, and my mother. She stepped her feet on the black tarmac in a rhythm syncopated with the drums. Her hands held the flowers to her heart, then to the sky. She danced for the image of the Virgin. The Earth Mother. Known to the ancients as Tonantzin.

The one who crushes the snake.

I almost swooned from the realization. How had I missed this before?

The statue grew larger and larger, practically filling the street, threatening to crush us all under its brown feet.

"Jasmine!" Carol's voice snapped me out of the vision. She grabbed my arm before I fell.

"Ernesto, we have to get her inside the shop!"

My mother was suddenly at my side. "Lean into me. You'll be fine."

I saw Ernesto open the peeling blue door, and stared at the hand in the center of the gold triangle. The hand to ward off evil.

We needed that.

"I'm sorry," I said, once we were inside the cool, dim shop. Jar candles flickered from the long counter. The thump of drums and dancers bounced against the door, but it was much quieter inside than out.

"How are we going to be able to talk to Rosalia with all this going on?" Carol was asking.

Had I just lost some time?

"Once the dancers are ready to move on down the street," Ernesto said. "There are many stations where they honor Tonantzin today. She will bless the dancers and the crowd, then return inside, now that we are here."

"Jasmine?" my mother asked quietly. "Are you okay?"

I nodded, mouth dry. "I'm fine. Just…had a vision or something."

Carol brought me a glass of water. She sipped at one herself.

"Thanks."

Then the door slammed open and Rosalia bustled in the room, bringing a blast of music and chanting from outside, along with her own, inimitable energy.

"What has happened?" she said, carrying the burning sage and copal around the room, wafting it over each of our heads. "You bring a stink of danger with you. I do not like that you come this way!"

I had never seen Rosalia agitated like this. What in the Powers was going on?

"Hechicera?" Ernesto asked.

"The bad man, he came here. I want to know if you told him where to find me." Her citrine eyes bored into mine.

"No!" I said.

"Good," Rosalia replied. "That is what I told Las Manos, but they insisted that I ask you anyway."

She went and bustled behind the counter. I heard clinking. Five shot glasses and a bottle of amber liquid thunked onto the wood.

"We are having tequila," she announced. "First, because we must honor Tonantzin. Second, because Jasmine is having visions on the street that will call every sorcerer in five miles down on us if we do not shut her down."

Fuck.

"Third," she continued, "because I know what you are here to talk about, and I've decided I need tequila to hear about it on a day that should be reserved for celebration."

"We are sorry, hechicera," Ernesto said.

She snorted at that. "As though I have not had damage brought to my door on holy days before!"

We dragged stools out from the counter and sat down, listening to the procession still going by outside.

The tequila was smooth and burned like fire going down. She was right, it helped my head. Shut down my third eye.

"We need to know about pentagons," Carol said. "We think the FBI is using Temple magic to attack us, and they've gotten to us all by Terrance Sterling. He has weird sigils on his walls, and has a pentagon pin on his lapel."

"Also, he recovered far too quickly, hechicera, from the battle with the spiders. Entiendes?" Ernesto said.

"Entiendo," Rosalia said, taking a small sip of the golden liquid.

"Also," Carol asked more quietly, "I'm wondering what happened to my epiphany in the church. To the realization that Terrance's soul was lost and we could retrieve it. Like the priest said."

"Maga," Rosalia said, and sighed. "That was the truth in that moment. There was a small amount of time when he could still be saved. Then he made another bargain."

She drank more tequila.

"Terrance is gone now. Las Manos has felt this on the æthers. He has joined the Mundo Malo for sure now."

The tequila had dampened down my Sight enough that something in my rational brain clicked in. It was as if alcohol had cut through the psychic noise so I could *hear* again. Huh. I was going to have to remember that.

And find out when to use it...and when to leave well enough alone. There were good reasons sorcerers rarely turned to drink.

But the warmth in my belly and the clarity in my mind showed me one thing. I was furious, as if the whole Pacific lashed and battered my emotions.

"You need to know the snake came to my mother's backyard," I said. "Busted through her wards and we barely even noticed in time. And he got away from us again. You think Terrance Sterling sent him there? Or Helen?"

Rosalia inhaled, long and deeply through her nose. And held the breath inside her. Closed her eyes.

Exhaled, slowly.

"Yes. Yes, I think Terrance Sterling sent the serpiente to your home, Cecelia. And I'm sad to say he may have used Helen to do so. Whether she did so knowingly or not...? We've all seen how sorcery can be manipulated." She turned to Carol then. "And the pentagon is the heart of the five-petaled flower. You have all the Elements among you, and I? I carry Spirit. The Power of the Fifth. We can surround the Pentagon and shake the walls until they crumble. If that is the magic they are using, that is the magic we will surround."

She looked at the rest of us, then held out her glass. We all raised, and clinked. Then the hechicera drew the shot glass to her brown lips and threw back the shot, smacking her empty glass on the counter.

We followed suit.

"But first, we crush this damn snake!"

"So mote it be," my mother said.

So mote it fucking be.

44

——————

JASMINE

To crush the serpent, it was clear I was going to need more help. The Pentagon action...there was definitely something to look at there, but it might need to be put on hold.

We were all excited about taking out evil magicians, but after meeting some more, we all agreed that was going to take a lot of time and preparation.

And we needed to figure out the connection between the twisted version of Solomonic Temple magic used by the FBI and whatever was going on with the Pentagon. Carol was working on it, but there was no way to tell how long it would all take.

There was also a larger pattern playing itself out, and we didn't yet know what it was.

Which was why I was at the Church of the Epiphany in Lincoln Heights, along with Carol, my mother, and Rosalia.

Rosalia and Las Manos were taking the Brown Berets through their paces. The boots stomped, the arms slashed out, and every fist was filled with magic.

Almost. Occasional yelps showed where things were

backfiring on the casters. But I was impressed. They'd come far, pretty quickly. Las Manos sorcerers walked among the rows, making subtle energetic adjustments to people's auras, and correcting posture on a few.

Posture mattered when casting magic. No magic worker can cast properly hunched over, without access to breath. Doesn't matter if you're a hereditary sorcerer, a Temple magic user, or a hedge witch.

Or a radical Chicano learning how to use the magic that flows through everything for the first time in your life.

Rosalia and Carol had showed me how the patches on the berets were infused with protection magic. The sigils were all charged up.

I was waiting on some of the people I'd started working with in the park. Leadership down here promised they'd get word out that folks were meeting in the church.

My insides were keyed up with tension, and I was missing Jimmy something fierce. I needed to get back home to Oakland but I had so much work to do down here.

The fact that the Fed kept coming back, even after being blasted, meant he really needed to be dealt with now, and much as I hated to admit it, that was going to take more people than just me.

Besides, Doreen, Patrice, and Drake were still teaching folks in Oakland. Doreen said the Panthers up there had agreed to be more visible. And she had, too.

That meant we needed to work on folks down here.

We had to get everyone together. The Panthers. The Brown Berets. Las Manos. And those of us ready to say fuck you to the Association of Magical Arts and Sorcery.

Ernesto had to teach the three students he was mentoring. I didn't see how he could possibly focus on anything to do with the Association right now, but he insisted that the teens still needed training, no matter what.

He was right. But it still left a bitter taste in my mouth.

"Jasmine Jones?" A woman's voice cut through the marching boots and blasts of magic.

I turned. It was a white woman. The woman in the green corduroy coat with the cascade of thick brown hair. She held out a hand.

It was cold. She smelled like patchouli.

"My name's Tessa. I think what you're doing is pretty groovy and I want to help."

"Okay. Cool."

"The others are outside." She waved a hand through the jam-packed church hall. "We poked our heads in and saw how crowded it was. Where do you want us to meet?"

"We can meet in the church."

Her eyes grew wide. "In the church?"

"Father John's down with the cause. He just made himself scarce today, you know?" I winked, shocking a laugh from her throat.

I was going to like Tessa.

Waving a hand to get Carol's attention, I jerked my head to the door connecting the meeting hall to the church. She came over, inching her way past the practicing Brown Berets.

"Ready?"

"Yeah. They're here."

We got everyone gathered in the pews. Before we started blasting folks, they needed to tap into the deeper magics.

And this was something I'd never done before. Not with folks who weren't already sorcerers. Doreen insisted it could be done, and I'd seen a little of it, but had never tried to lead it.

A few of the local Panthers were in the back. One of them, a thin man in a pale blue button-up shirt, had a high forehead under his receding hairline, and apple cheeks and a dark mustache. He looked like a salesman, not a radical. But the Party needed everyone, I reminded myself.

He noticed me looking at him and came forward.

"Name's Cotton, sister. I'm part of security for this meeting. Glad you're here to help us."

I sniffed the air. No musk, so he wasn't a shifter. Just an ordinary man, trying to help the people. Then I remembered...his name had come up in relation to 41st and Central shootout. And I'd seen him in the union hall. Seen him introduce himself to Carol.

"I'm glad to be here, Cotton. My name is Jasmine."

"Oh, I know who you are!" He laughed, showing his long teeth under the dark bushy mustache.

"Well, we're going to get started here. You joining in?"

"I'll be on the doors," he said. "Keeping guard. But I'll be watching."

Watching his back, I tried to place what had unsettled me. I couldn't figure it out. Probably just nerves. Residual discomfort from all the attacks I'd sustained.

I rubbed my shoulder, then turned to the rows of expectant faces before me and smiled.

"All power to the people!" I said.

"All power to the people!" forty voices replied.

The sanctuary felt peaceful even with the sounds of boots and the occasional yell from the church hall. I breathed in the lingering scent of frankincense and the stillness of the space.

"We are the revolution. It starts with us, but it doesn't end with us," I said. "And to support the revolution, we have to reach deep inside ourselves. We can't just fight the Man.

We have to fight every bit of evil that feeds the Man. And to do that?" I paused, looking at the black and brown faces in front of me, a few white and Japanese faces in the mix. They were all waiting. "To do that, we need to activate your magic. We're in this holy place today because we need a space where evil has a harder time walking. Not that it can't get in; evil can get in anywhere."

I wasn't sure where in all the Powers these words were coming from, but I could feel Momma Beatrice at my side. Maybe they were hers.

"Close your eyes for a moment. It's okay. We got brothers at the doors, keeping you safe. Tune in to your breath. Feel it moving in and out of your nostrils. Slow it down. Now imagine a small flame, or a green plant shoot, or a still pool deep in your belly. Imagine you can drop all your attention down there."

As I walked up and down the church aisle, under the high, wood-timbered ceiling, I felt something change inside of me. Maybe this was what I was meant to be. A teacher. A leader. Someone who could help others find their power.

Maybe we could build something together.

"Now, imagine that every breath fans that flame, or deepens that pool, or helps that plant to grow."

Their faces, so trusting, all softened and took on a glow. The magic was building inside them. More subtle than the sorcery I carried, but magic all the same.

The Association had kept this from the people for too long. We needed the people now. I needed the people. No way was I defeating this snake without them.

More snakes would just spring up to take his place.

"That's right. Keep breathing. Keep imagining. Remember that slogan that says *'Be realistic. Demand the impossible.'* That's what we're doing here. We're demanding magic. We're demanding justice. We're demanding food, and shelter, and love, and peace."

The guards stood at attention by the back doors. Four of them. I knew they had guns under their jackets, but they kept them hidden today. Out of respect for the church? I didn't know.

One of the side doors opened and a woman conferred with one of the guards before slipping in. I vaguely recognized her from some of the LA Panther meetings. Her big afro was frayed around the edges, and a black turtleneck framed a delicate face. Elaine, I think her name was.

"So, I told you evil had trouble getting into places like this? That doesn't mean we didn't carry some in ourselves." A few people shifted position at that. Striking home. "But we can clear ourselves. We can clear ourselves and clear our space. And that makes us more powerful against the evil that stalks our streets and rips apart our communities."

I had to take it up a notch. See what these folks could do.

"Keep breathing. Keep that magic in you growing. And let that fire, that water, that growing plant increase until it pushes everything that isn't the magic inside of you out. Imagine it pushing out your pain. Your fear. Your hatred. Imagine it pushing out any regrets you carry, helping you to heal, to move on."

The air was thick with concentration. The air practically trembled with it.

There was a sound to my right. A door shutting. Father John came in from the church hall.

Okay. I took a deeper breath myself. Called on Momma Beatrice to guide me.

"Now, feel that magic inside you, that power. Feel it start to push out of your skin and surround you. Every time you breathe out, I want you to imagine that power of yours pushing all the evil out of this room. Make this space as clear and shining as you can. Feel your power mix with all the folks around you. Share that power. The power of the people to drive out everything that wants to harm the people. Feel it build."

One of the doors at the entrance opened, letting in a rectangle of light. The man with the high forehead and neat button-up shirt...the man named Cotton? He stepped outside.

The door slammed behind him.

45

CAROL

The meeting with the Brown Berets and Las Manos was intense. Carol hadn't felt that much gathered power since the mountaintop, when they'd busted Huey Newton out of the Men's Colony.

If she had only ever listened to the Association, she never would have known sorcery this powerful existed. Or that untrained people could tap into it, and boost the magic, giving the sorcerers more juice to ride.

Maybe they could take down Jasmine's snake and shake up the Pentagon after all. But first, they had to figure out how. And why. And what else was hooked in to the freaky temple magic they were up against.

Carol Johansson, up against the Feds. Never in a hundred years would she have thought this time would come to pass.

Carol was kneeling on the blue-painted floor of Rosalia's shop, bent over the floorboards. The color was new. The broad planks had just been battered and stained before.

"We needed to honor the Virgin," Rosalia had said. "And besides, I like the color."

Carol's knees protested. She was going to have bruises later, she was sure. But a compulsion filled her. This had to be done.

Rosalia, Ernesto, and Cecelia had thrown up extra protections around her working. She should have been doing this in the Mansion's temple room, but there was no way. That place was tainted. She didn't even feel safe sleeping there anymore, but she and Ernesto didn't really have anyplace else to go.

The chalk in her hand felt like a living thing. And as an Earth sorcerer, she supposed it was. Which gave her an idea. She stilled herself inside and dropped her attention down into her center. The painted planks of wood responded beneath her left hand. The chalk was still fairly quiet in her right.

Until she breathed across it, sending her sorcery directly into the white substance. It jumped and started to hum.

Carol drew. And drew. And drew.

She traced a giant pentagon on the center of the floor. She traced the sigil she'd been seeing for the last month in the center. Something *snapped* energetically into place.

Carol looked up at Rosalia, whose citrine eyes stared back.

"This sigil is one of the five columns that uphold the power of the Pentagon. We need to find the others. I think I have one of them in my notebooks, because this isn't the original sigil I saw."

She sat back on her heels, set down the chalk and rubbed at her knees covered in the thin cotton of her bell-bottom jeans.

"I thought I'd been wrong about that first sigil," she said to Ernesto. "Once we got clear on this one, and got confirmation on Terrance's wall, I figured my visions had been wrong."

Ernesto walked over and held out a hand, she grasped his warm brown hand and let him help her up.

Looking down at the pentagon on the floor gave her a chill. She remembered Terrance's weird eyes, with their dilated pupils. And the way he looked more healthy than he should. But brittle-feeling. Off.

"But now you think there are more sigils?" Cecelia asked, thin arms encased in a green ribbed sweater today, crossed over her chest. She wore a dark slacks, and had a paisley scarf tied around her neck.

"Yeah. What I felt from the chalk and the drawing is that every corner of the pentagon shape is actually a column powered by magic. By a sigil. But I don't know what they're connected to, yet."

Rosalia came forward with a broom, and began to sweep the chalk marks into the center.

"They are connected to the five pillars of the Temple of Solomon," the hechicera said.

"I thought there were only two," Ernesto replied.

"In the main temple, the one that people could see, that is true. But there was an inner temple, only spoken of in whispers. And that temple had five walls."

She rested the broom against a wall and went to the statue of the Virgin, bowed, and took one of the small vases of roses.

Then she poured the water from the vase onto the pile of chalk, dissolving it.

"Here," she said, holding out the roses. We each came forward and took one. Carol's was white. Ernesto's red. Cecelia's yellow. Rosalia's was pink.

Rosalia tore the petals from her rose and scattered them

over the area Carol had drawn. Pretty soon, the space was covered with white, red, yellow, and pink petals, and the scent of roses filled the air.

"The Virgin, she will help us." Rosalia looked at Carol. "Lie down on the roses, maga."

"Now?"

"You do not have to do this, but if you do this, it will be of help. You are the only one who has seen visions of these markings. You are the only one who knows the way."

Carol blazed with sudden heat, aura strobing as if she was going to throw up.

"I don't think I can do this."

Ernesto was right beside her all of a sudden, candle flames reflected in his glasses.

"Carol." He held her arms in his hands. "You can do this. You are more powerful than you know, maga. And we need this."

We need this.

"Okay. Okay." She stepped away from him, and turned to look at the rose petals. The faintest chalk lines still traced a pentagon shape on the floor, but the sigil was covered in petals.

She hoped it was safe.

Her body crushed the petals as she lay down, wreathing her head with the scent of them, almost making her gag. She tried to breathe more deeply. To calm down the terror rising inside her...at what?

Rosalia crouched beside her. "Shhh, maga. Shhh. I am with you. And Ernesto and Cecelia are guarding us. Claro?"

Carol just nodded.

The hechicera rose then, and began to shake a rattle over her. Not a rattle. The brown nuts the dancers wore.

They shushed and clacked across her body. They calmed her down.

"Follow the sound, maga. Float upon the roses. Let the Virgin be your guide and your protector. Follow the sigils. Let them take you where you need to be."

And there were the serpents, with eyes of stars and flames. And there was the Temple, floating in darkness. And there were sigils, carved in iron and stone. And there was a fiery sword, and a blooming wand.

And an altar made of black rock. Square and solid.

And on that altar was the bound body of Terrance Sterling, pale and naked on the stone that ate light and cast no shadows.

He had no shadow.

She started keening in the back of her throat, a low whine, like a dog.

"Nonononono..." Carol shook her head.

"Walk forward, maga. Tell us what you see."

"I see the sigils. I see five columns. I see...swords and wands. But...nononono."

"Breathe, Carol!" Ernesto's voice cut through the awful visions.

"It's Terrance! He...he's tied up on a black altar!"

"Move away from that for now, maga. Try to see the sigils." Rosalia's voice again.

Okay. She could do that. Okay.

Carol walked toward the pillars. There was the first sigil. The one she had drawn over and over again. A plinth, or a column. An I with a circle in the center, crossed by a massive N canted to the side. And there was the I with the spider shape. She pushed on, the air growing thick around her. Rounding toward the third pillar, she stopped. The columnar I again, with the same circle, and a crescent C topping the I.

Carol was confused. She didn't see what any of these symbols had to do with... She pushed on.

Trying to walk toward the fourth pillar was almost impossible. Grunting, panting, heaving, she threw her shoulders forward and pushed out with her hands.

Boom! Her body flew backward, smacking her skull against a pillar.

"Ouch!"

"Maga! I am with you!"

"Okayokayokay," Carol mumbled.

"We need to get her out of there!" Ernesto's voice again?

Then a cool hand on her forehead. In which world? The astral? Or on earth?

"Maga. You've done well. I need you to look at the altar one more time. What is there?"

Carol groaned, but got up again. She stumbled. Righted herself.

Walked through the increasing billows of mist, lit by the fiery sword. Toward the altar. Toward Terrance's bound-up body.

Then she saw it. The sigils painted all over his white skin. Black. Red. Pulsing.

And then she saw...

And came to, rolling on the rose petals, gagging. She rolled to her right side and puked on the blue-painted floor. Heaving and sobbing, retching until there was no more inside.

Ernesto's arms, gathering her toward his chest.

Rosalia's cool hands on her head.

Cecelia, bringing the scent of mint and lavender tea, holding a thick mug out to her hands.

Carol's teeth chattered in her skull.

"Sip the tea, maga. It will help."

She did. It did. Warmth. Soothing. Washing the taste of vomit from her lips. Replacing it with mint.

Carol leaned back against Ernesto's solid warmth.

"Maga," Rosalia said. "What did you see?"

Carol took another sip of tea, then looked up, searching out Cecelia's deep brown eyes and Rosalia's citrine gaze.

"They took his eyes."

46

DOREEN

oreen and Drake had a whole cadre of magical apprentices going through their paces now.

Since the meeting with the Panthers, they'd decided to step things up and get deeper with the training.

It astonished Doreen that this many folks would be interested in learning.

"Of course they're interested," Drake said, slipping his ratty old red sweater over his head and hanging it over the worn brown jacket he'd already draped on the back of a folding chair. Despite the cold outside, the attic was warm from the little space heater he'd dragged up the back stairs.

He was on Christmas break from school, and his parents were happy he had a place to stay out of trouble. Not that he wasn't in harm's way everywhere he went, but they'd come to trust Doreen with their son's life.

Even though working with Doreen had almost gotten him beaten up by the police.

Well, she was doing her best to protect Drake now, and all the other children in Oakland.

"If you offer them a way to protect themselves? Their

families? 'Specially if it isn't with a gun? People gonna take it."

Doreen just nodded and continued getting jars out from the low bookcases that lined the knee walls of the attic. Another thing Drake had helped with. Patrice, too, though she'd be coming later. Between the three of them, they'd made this old attic a real working space, complete with the huge ancestor altar at the far end, with Momma's crystal ball, now shrouded in black velvet, and the black, red, and white mask from the Chokwe in Angola. Her family's people. Or so the spirits told her.

Doreen knew Drake was right. She shouldn't even have to be reminded. But the ways of the Association were still ingrained in her thoughts. Sorcery and spellwork were both considered rarified activities. Reserved only for a few.

"Bullshit," she muttered.

"What's that, ma'am?" Drake asked. He was rooting through a wooden box, taking out cloth for spell bags.

Doreen shook her head and went back to the jars of roots, seeds, herbs, and shells.

"Nothing, Drake. Nothing. You're right about that, though," she said. Then paused, hand inside a jar of star anise. She took a deep breath of the fragrant seed pods. "Of course people want to defend themselves. As soon as they know its possible."

"It's like Frederick Douglass said," Doreen continued, "'The limits of tyrants are prescribed by the endurance of those whom they oppress.'"

Drake laid the cloths out on a long table set in the middle of the wide Douglas fir plank floor. Blue. Black. White. Green. And several spools of heavy red thread.

"Have you learned about Frederick Douglass?" Doreen asked.

Drake rolled his eyes and nodded.

"Don't roll your eyes at me. I don't know what you've learned or haven't learned. What they teach in schools right now is a mystery to me. Besides, it was my parents that taught me about Douglass."

"Mine too," Drake said. "Sorry, Miss Doreen."

"That's all right." Even good kids needed to get sick of adults sometimes.

"Where'd we put the needles?" he asked.

"In the small sewing box, right there." Doreen pointed to the bottom shelf behind him.

"What's that mean, anyway?" the boy finally asked. Thirteen years old, with a button nose and a small afro, a genial nature, and the quickest mind Doreen had seen since Jasmine was his age. The boy was no sorcerer, but he'd taken to magic like a match to a wick. He was part of what made Doreen realize that even people not born to it could learn basic magic. And Drake was proving that they could learn even more.

Damn the Association anyway, for their stupid hierarchies and insistence on only using sorcery, and only teaching those who had been born with an Elemental mark.

Doreen and Jasmine were going to bust all that wide open.

"Douglass was talking about oppression requiring a certain amount of obedience and forbearance on the part of the oppressed. That without our compliance, the people who hold power over us can only go so far."

The boy stopped what he was doing and grew very still. Doreen could almost feel him breathing, and could see the gears turning in his round head.

"That's what the Panthers teach."

"Right," Doreen said. "Are we all set up? Folks should be arriving soon."

And sure enough, there was the ticktock of heels on the stairs outside, leading to the attic from the garden. Doreen smiled. Sounded like Patrice. Her new love, and how about that? What a nice surprise that had been.

Patrice wasn't Hector, but she didn't have to be. She just had to be Patrice.

More footsteps clattered up behind the first, and the attic door opened.

Patrice walked through, bright green coat belted around her trim waist, hair in some fancy updo, with curls that fell down around her dark face. As usual, Patrice's lipstick was a bright beacon outlining full lips. Today's shade was a ruby red.

Three other women from the neighborhood piled in past her, followed by two men. That was about all that could fit into the attic at a time. They could have used the church hall, but despite his generosity, Doreen knew they made Father Neil a bit nervous. No use pushing things. They could work in smaller groups for now.

"Hello Patrice!" Drake said. He loved Patrice. And who could blame him. She slid out of her bright green coat to reveal a burgundy knit dress that skimmed her curvy figure. Um. Hmm. Doreen hoped she could spend the night.

Patrice shot Doreen a smile, but didn't say anything, keeping busy with Drake instead. Just as well. The locals didn't need to know about their relationship just yet. Not that some hadn't guessed already.

Doreen was still having trouble keeping track of everyone's names. So many people were coming to be trained these days. She knew she needed to try.

"T-bone? How are you this evening?" T-bone was a dark-skinned man with round apple cheeks and a plaid wool coat. He always wore a tweed newsboy-style cap on his head.

"I'm fine ma'am. Thank you. Just fine."

Doreen beamed at the rest of the group. The women clearly had come from various types of work. They looked weary, but excited to be there. The men? She knew T-bone would be going to work after this. He worked in one of the local bars, and played music with a jazz combo on his nights off.

The women worked as nurses, nurses' aides, cafeteria staff, and cleaning women. Hard work, all of it. Made Doreen glad of Hector's pension and her part-time job in the florist's shop.

"Hello Loretta, how was work today?" Loretta's hair was in smooth curls around her head, with a slight bouffant in back. She was the best dressed of the women here tonight, besides Patrice. A pink shift dress skimmed her knees, and she had little kitten heels on. Looked like her feet were killing her. She was a restaurant hostess, Doreen recalled.

She hadn't met the other two men before, though she'd seen them at meetings in the church hall. They looked a little nervous, standing near the door, jostling foot to foot. One glanced at the doorknob, as though he hoped he could get away.

Only one remedy for that.

Doreen moved toward them and held out her hand.

"My name is Doreen. You are most welcome here."

"Randy," said one, shifting his watch cap to his left hand and shaking with his right.

"Tyrone," said the other, a skinny little thing for such a big name.

"Don't worry. We'll go slow tonight. You got family?'

Tyrone's face brightened up. "A little girl. Three years old. Name of Khadijah."

"Well, we'll show you how to make a little charm she can wear pinned to her coat. And another one for over her door."

Randy cleared his throat. "Will you give us something to protect our whole place, man? Including my car?"

Drake stepped forward then, and squared his shoulders.

"We can teach you just about anything you need to know," he said. "Including how to use the magic inside you." The pride in his voice made Doreen's eyes grow hot with tears.

Damn Terrance and the Association anyway.

These people deserved magic. Every bit that she could give them.

The Association was going to change, or could be damned.

"Let's get started," she said.

47

JASMINE

The union hall was bursting at the the seams. There wasn't even room for chairs. Everyone stood or crowded on the floor, except for around a dozen people—some elders and disabled folks—who absolutely needed the orange chairs.

Everyone was present. Black Panthers, including two who'd already shifted. I thought it was Elaine and Ericka, but I couldn't tell. Brown Berets. Union members. And Las Manos. Plus our small cadre of Association folks. Doreen had insisted she was coming down—she, Patrice, and Drake were going to drive—but hadn't arrived yet.

Panther musk mixed with cologne, sweat, and cigarettes. The air was already thick with gray, adding soot to the yellow-tinged walls.

Carol, Ernesto, my mother, and I held up a wall again, just like last time.

I recognized a few of the dancers from the procession, too. They looked different out of their traditional clothing, wearing jeans and shirts today.

People were angry, nervous, excited. Another group of high school students had gotten their heads bashed in, and we'd heard they'd shackled our Panther brother in his cell in Chicago using silver chains. How that was going to work when he should still be able to shift in and out of form, I wasn't sure. Speculation was they'd drugged him.

Chicago Panthers wanted our help to get him out, too. I had a feeling that if we could get to the bottom of this shit with the snakes, the FBI, and whatever the Pentagon connection was, that all of our political prisoners would be free.

"Silencio por favor!"

Rosalia's voice snapped across the hall. The conversations slowed to a murmur, and then stopped, leaving the sound of breathing, people shifting to more comfortable positions on the crowded floor, and the distant whoosh of traffic from the freeway.

She stood, so small and powerful at the head of the room, flanked by standing Las Manos sorcerers, silver bangles up and down her arms, heavy pendant at her throat. Purple velvet skirts. Black jersey long-sleeved shirt. Her uniform.

There was a small cleared space around her, as though people were afraid to get too close.

"Thank you all for gathering here today. Our union brothers have pledged their help to the Black Panthers and the Brown Berets. It is now time that we all pledge to help each other."

She slid her citrine eyes over the whole crowd, gathering them to her with the sheer force of her will.

"What is the phrase you Panthers say?" she asked.

"All power to all the people!" I shouted. One of the

shifters roared. By all the Powers, I missed my Jimmy. He was going to try to make it down, too, but needed to make sure the patrols were all in place in Berkeley and Oakland.

"*All* power to *all* the people," Rosalia repeated, giving me a nod. "This means we all must share the power we have, to serve and protect our communities. What la policía say they aim to do, we must *actually* do."

"What does that mean?" asked one of the union leaders, a portly white man with thick blond sideburns and a union cap on his head.

"It means that we need your help. We think the FBI is behind the attacks on the Panthers, the Brown Berets, our students, and the unions. We want to battle one snake in particular, who seems to be everywhere, up and down the coast, and in Chicago, Baltimore, and New York, too."

That startled me. I didn't realize reports had come in from that far away. I wondered what Rosalia knew. Good thing I trusted her.

"What we want to do today is get a pledge from you all, that you will join your power with our magic and combat the magic of the FBI."

"Come on! You expect us to believe this?" the same union man said. Some people shushed him, but others grumbled their agreement.

The two shifters roared again, startling the room into silence, then padded silently toward the head of the room where Rosalia stood, winding their large, black-furred bodies between the seated crowd.

I could hear small gasps as they passed. But what was funny was that I wasn't feeling fear. What I felt from the people in the room was a sense of awe. Wonder.

"Jasmine, will you come forward, please?"

I grabbed Carol's hand and we wound and stepped our own way over the seated bodies.

"Please," Rosalia said, gesturing to the cleared space.

I squeezed Carol's hand and dropped it, stepping into Rosalia's force field. Then I took a breath and faced the length of the room, two panther shifters at my side. The one on my right bumped my hand. I looked down. Its head was tilted up, staring at me with golden eyes. Then it yawned.

Okay. Don't know what that was about. Telling me to chill? I said a quick prayer to Momma Beatrice and felt her steady hands upon my shoulders.

"My name is Jasmine Jones. I'm a member of the Black Panther Party up in Oakland. I'm also a sorcerer, a member of the Association of Magical Arts and Sorcery. You've never heard of us."

I knew exactly what I needed to say.

"But all of that is about to change. There's a new world being born around us. All the violence we're seeing? That's just the birthing pangs. The old world? It needs to die, though. Or it needs to change. And we know that's all the same, dig? So I'm standing here with these panthers"—I gestured to the shifters—"and with Las Manos, and the honored Rosalia." I bowed to the hechicera then, guided by Momma Beatrice.

Every face was rapt. Paying close attention now.

"And we offer our magic to you, full stop. There's been a serpent attacking the Panthers and it is gnawing at the root of my Association, too. We think it's only a matter of time before it attacks all of you, too. So we need your help, to defeat it."

A Chicana near the front wept, tears streaming down her light brown cheeks.

"What's the matter, sister?"

"El serpiente, I think he took my cousin." She collapsed into the woman next to her, who held her close as she cried.

"So, it is already begun." Rosalia stepped forward. "We will train you. Jasmine and Carol have already begun this. Some of you here have been to Iglesia de Epifania and begun the work of awakening your magic. This is good."

There was some restlessness in the room again. Rosalia held up her hands.

"Not all of you need your magic awakened, though anyone who wants it? We will help. What we *do* need from everyone is your power. Your commitment. Your willingness to help stamp out the evil that sends our children to war in the jungle, and shoots them down in our streets."

The hechicera raised her arms then, silver bangles chiming against each other, as though to call upon some ancient power.

"Will you help us?" she asked.

The room was filled with silence.

"Will you help us?" I asked.

The door near the back of the room opened.

"Will you help us?" Huey Newton spoke. Every head turned his way.

Slowly, one by one, then in groups, speaking over each other, every voice in the room said, "Yes."

"Lift your heads for a blessing," Rosalia said, once the chorus had died down.

She stretched her palms out, sending waves of sorcery out into the room. I could feel it tingling at the crown of my head, and the center of my forehead burned, as though it had been kissed with the cold fire of the stars.

"Ancestors, we call on you. Bless your people. Keep us strong. Guide us toward truth. Help us defeat evil."

"So mote it be," I heard my mother say.

"So mote it be," I murmured back.
"All power to the people!" Fred shouted out.
"All power to the people!" we replied.

48

SNAKES AND SPIDERS

I t wasn't enough. It was never going to be enough. But it was all Samuels had.

He waited in the Master's office. Six other agents ringed the room, providing security, and extra juice, in case the Master required it. They could have been carbon copies of Samuels. Same dark glasses. Same black suits and white shirts. Black ties. Short hair. The only differences were build and hair color. And the exact cut of their suits telegraphed pay grade for those who knew how to read those signs.

The Master was keeping Samuels waiting. Samuels could feel the rage boiling off of Hoover's white skin, tingeing his face with red, causing his neck to bulge against the white collar cinched in with a slim navy tie.

The Master scratched at a once pristine sheet of snowy paper, the nib of the calligraphy pen practically ripping holes as it laid black ink on the white.

Thoughts tumbled through Samuels' head as he stood at attention in front of the Master's large slab of a mahogany desk.

Cotton was next to useless. Oh sure, he would turn state's

witness if they needed. And he'd been a good plant. But the magic had twisted him too much. Drained his vitality. The black man might still be of use to Samuels, but he hadn't figured out how yet.

So Samuels had been called back to Washington DC. He fumed inside, keeping his emotions locked as tightly away as possible. But they must have still been leaking through.

The dark room was lit only by a single lamp tonight. The Master's desk was littered with discarded drawings. The sigils. All five of them.

Dried spittle marred the edges of the Master's mouth.

Setting his pen down, Hoover finally looked up, grimacing at his once favored agent. He raised his right hand in a mudra.

The tattoo under Samuels' arm burned and writhed as the Master pinched his fingers together, manipulating the magic.

Samuels hissed before clamping his lips together.

The stink of methamphetamine sweat was acrid and disgusting. Samuels swore it was worse than before. Had the Master increased his "vitamin shots"? Samuels wasn't around enough lately to know.

Damn, that hurt.

"You like that?" the Master said. He was truly losing it. His eyes looked weird and fresh sweat rolled down his doughy face, streaking through old sweat, dried hours ago.

"I need to get back to Los Angeles. Master," Samuels gritted out. "They are planning something. Those sorcerers. I can feel it."

"You can, can you? You think I can't? You think I can't sense all the ways you have fucked up this operation?"

The Master slapped Samuels across the face, flesh cracking on flesh. The Master's heavy ring jarred Samuels' teeth into his cheeks. He tasted blood.

But the smack didn't have the power it once had. Samuels acted as though the blow had rocked him on his heels. Any advantage.

"You disgust me," the Master said. "You put our Temple at risk. You give power to the undeserving. You are not fit to walk the halls of magic."

The Master paced away from him, leaving Samuels in the middle of the elaborate woven carpet on the floor. The hush in the lead-lined room felt suddenly oppressive. Samuels wished for sound. Any sound. Anything except the Master's labored breath and his own heartbeat.

"Master." Despite the tang of blood, Samuels mouth felt dry. He calibrated the edges of his aura with a breath and shored up the defenses of his mind. Show no fear. "I need operatives as backup. Things have gotten...larger than expected. My plant says they are training more people."

The Master whirled, white shirt sleeves rolled up on his stocky arms. "What do we care if they are training up a bunch of peasants and darkies. For what? To be cannon fodder?"

"No sir. They are training them in magic."

The Master stopped. Then walked slowly back toward Samuels, who remained rooted to the thick rug beneath his leather-soled shoes. His serpent rose within him, as though to show the Master that it was still there. A force to be reckoned with. Samuels only hoped that Hoover didn't see it as a threat.

The Master's pasty square face with its potato nose was inches from his own now.

"How is this possible?"

Samuels risked a small shake of the head.

"I don't know sir. All I know is that we need more people on the ground. The infiltrators aren't enough. I need agents."

A risk, to state things so boldly. But it was either that or die.

The Master snapped his fingers. Two operatives moved forward from the walls. They both wore serpent rings on their left hands.

Samuels nodded.

"Take the first plane out tonight."

"Yes, Master."

The three black-suited men bowed, then left the shadowed room.

49

JASMINE

I couldn't take it anymore. The lies. Helen putting us in danger. Terrance and his sigils and sickness, rocking the foundations of our sorcery, and more importantly, spilling out in ways that I was now sure were harming the very people I was organizing.

With every damn thread unraveled, it became more clear. The head of the Association was working with the Feds. And the Feds were at war with the people.

And no one going to do anything about it all, it seemed.

At least, not quick enough to suit me. And I couldn't let that stand.

We had big magic to do, and weren't going to be able to execute it while we had to worry about Terrance and Helen undercutting us at every turn.

And who knew what else?

With everything we'd already found out about Terrance, and with Helen turning traitor? Bringing a Fed to my parents' home?

It was high time someone challenged the man for real. Helen, too. So I was taking things into my own hands. Carol,

Ernesto, and most importantly, my mother, had all agreed to let me do this.

Because they didn't see any other way, either. I was more of an outsider, at this point, so a challenge from me was less politically charged.

We were supposed to wait for my mother to arrive, but Terrance was getting out of his car when Ernesto pulled up to the Mansion.

I shoved my door open as soon as we rolled to a stop.

"Terrance Sterling!" I called out.

He turned to me, eyes black and blank, as if his soul was far away.

I needed to get to him before he entered the Mansion. Who knew what magical artillery he had in there?

Doors slammed as Ernesto and Carol got out of the car.

Rosalia's blessing from the union hall still ran along my skin, mingling with the Elemental Water coursing inside me.

"Jasmine!" he said back, walking a few steps toward me. Trying to bluff. Like he was glad to see me. He hadn't been happy to see me in quite some time.

I didn't want to do this. But I had to. Going up against the Man was never easy, but I was always clear it needed to be done. But to have the Man turn out to be a person who'd trained me since I was seven?

It made me feel sick.

"I'm here to challenge you."

He paused. "I'm sure I don't know why. I know you've been unhappy about your Panthers lately, but..."

"Cut your shit, Terrance. We've had those conversations. And I'm done. I'm talking about the fact that you've betrayed your Association oaths. And sold our sorcery out to the Feds."

"Isn't that a bit paranoid?" he asked.

I threw a bolt of blue fire at his feet. He jumped. Good. Not expecting it. Though a man with his training should have been.

Something flashed in those black, blank eyes of his. A spark of intelligence. The old Terrance Sterling, before he'd gotten trapped inside a spider's web.

"I'm here to ask you to step down. We're calling for a general election, either way. But it will go better for you if you step down before all of this comes out."

He glanced at Ernesto and Carol, still standing by the car behind us.

"Are you going to fight me, then?"

"Only if it's necessary."

He shot a blast of red at me. Then green. The green bolt connected with my injured shoulder as I ran forward, rushing him. The man still controlled all the Elements, no matter who was controlling him.

A wall of energy surrounded us both. Ernesto and Carol had combined forces, trying to keep us contained. The front of the Mansion wasn't the best place for a magical fight.

We stumbled onto a patch of verdant green, surrounded by the half moon sweep of the long drive.

The lawn was slick from the damned sprinklers that kept the grass green in the desert hills of LA. At least I wore my Army boots. Terrance was in leather-soled shoes, but didn't seem to be slipping.

Yet.

His hollowed-out black eyes were freaky, but I couldn't let myself become distracted by that shit. The man was just a puppet now, not the man who trained me. Not the man my parents once called friend.

I sent another wave of blue fire toward him. He deflected

it, firing a braided bolt of Fire and Air my way. My shields held this time.

I was starting to sweat. He still looked perfect, every silver hair in place.

I blasted another bolt of blue fire at his feet, trying to get him to stumble. He just stepped away, grin slicing his pale white face.

Those eyes, that looked like he was straight tripping, weren't his own. Not at all.

The earth shook beneath my feet. He was using Earth power now. He'd been cycling through all the Elements, showing me he could. Laughing at me.

Carol had seen it in her vision. That some other force had taken his eyes. Some other force that had a signature like my snake's, but smelled different. Acrid. Chemical. Dangerous.

With the power of the Temple behind it.

That animated the man who stalked me on this mani-cured patch of lawn in front of the Spanish-style Mansion, a place that should have been both sacrosanct and a place of safety.

It was neither, now.

Okay, time to make it official. I was here to strip the man of his powers, or die trying.

And Jimmy didn't need to know about that.

"Terrance Sterling, I challenge you!" I said again.

He threw back his silver-crowned head and laughed, white teeth flashing in the sun.

"You cannot challenge me. You know *nothing!*" he said. His hand shot out a multicolored bolt of fire.

I grinned as I dodged it. He must be feeling threatened if he called upon the braided Elemental powers of the Quin-tessence this early in the fight.

Or maybe whoever was controlling him didn't know to not go for the big guns so soon. That even a skilled sorcerer like Terrance could be depleted.

Slowly, I built up the power of Water inside me. The slick grass was a boon. So were the few clouds gathered toward the west, hovering above the ocean that I couldn't see, but could taste and smell.

I had to take him down; even though I didn't give a shit about the Association these days, I needed to do it for the good of the people. And for my mother, who still wanted all of this somehow.

But I wasn't yet sure how. So I just kept fighting.

In the corner of my eye, I saw another car pull up. My mother had arrived. I could feel her. Then saw her race out of the car, heels clacking on the drive, heading toward Ernesto and Carol.

Terrance blasted toward my shoulder again. Aiming for my weak spot.

Grunting, I hurled a wave into his solar plexus. It connected, and he stumbled.

I hoped my mother and friends stayed where they were.

Someone needed to take the fall. It might as well be me.

Besides, all I knew in this moment, with the way things were building up, it was time to act. We'd done enough talking. We'd done enough strategizing. We'd done enough worrying. As Chairman Fred said, *We're gonna have to start practicing and that's very hard.*

"I know that you are possessed by something right now," I said. "And I know you've brought danger directly into the Mansion. And I know the Association is at risk." I'd said those things already, but whether he'd actually heard still wasn't clear.

We circled one another like prize fighters, which was

weird. We could have been fighting with our backs to one another, or on the astral plane, but we'd both chosen to be here, now. Face to face. As though the Mansion itself was contested ground, and the earth plane was the only important battlefield.

Maybe Terrance Sterling was down with the revolution in ways I didn't know. Something in his spirit still thought the earth plane was worth fighting for. Or maybe whatever sickness controlled him wanted earthly power. The man I knew had more than enough power on earth, and had been steadily more focused on the other planes in recent years.

He feinted toward my left and I sent a blast of blue, ocean-tinged fire at his head, knocking him back three feet. Throwing up a shield, he threw a rope of braided fire toward my ankles. I leapt into the air, but couldn't quite clear it. It whipped itself around my feet, tripping me onto the wet grass.

That pissed me off.

The ocean throbbed inside me. I drew and drew and drew upon the Elemental power. The fiery shackles around my ankles and feet burst outward, shattering with a burst of power.

Rolling up to my knees, I sent twin balls of flame at Terrance, one to his solar plexus, one to his head. He whipped his head out of the way, but the ball aimed for his center hit him in the shoulder as he moved. I felt the bolt connect with his aura, and the subtle body closest to his skin. He was tagged now. With a little *push*, the blue fire burrowed its way into his skin.

He shouted and pushed out a wall of colored fire, but my own warded shields were ready and pushed back with a wall of blue.

Then I felt it, some Powers-be-damned piece of magic sneaking around me from the back.

A slippery sigil, aimed at me like a dart.

Slamming my shields shut in the back, I felt the magic dart drop to the grass and heard it hiss out.

Terrance looked gray all of a sudden, instead of his usual pale white and peach. Something was wrong. The thing—whatever it was—was using up too much of his power.

Then I saw a glint in the sun, almost blinding me. A lapel pin. It was a silver pentagon.

Swirling my sorcery inside me, I formed a drill of blue ocean fire, flicked my pointer finger from my thumb, and sent it out. It caught, drilling a smoking hole through the center of the pin.

All of Terrance's shields collapsed. He clutched his chest. Staggered. Fell.

"Call a doctor!" I shouted. Carol ran into the Mansion.

I felt Ernesto taking down the shields around us, and found I hoped Terrance Sterling was already dead. But we had to make sure.

Never in my life had I thought killing a man would be the best recourse.

Welcome to the new world, Jasmine. Grow the fuck up.

I ran to the body splayed upon the grass. How low the mighty had fallen.

Ernesto ran to my side.

"Terrance!" Ernesto said.

The open eyes, with barely a sliver of blue iris surrounding the black pupil, stared at nothing.

But his chest still rose and fell.

"He's still breathing," I said.

I watched as some ragged remnant of Terrance's soul

rose like a vapor through the crown of his head. It was swept away, despite the lack of wind.

"Did you see that? How is he still alive?" I asked.

Ernesto looked at me, face like a stone. I heard Carol running toward us, shouting, "The doctor is on her way."

A doctor from the Association.

Carol dropped to her knees, panting slightly, and began feeding Earth energy into Terrance's body, trying to support his systems before everything shut down. I heard a heavy Mansion door shut. It must be my mother, heading inside to start making phone calls.

Which was strange. As an Earth sorcerer, she could have been helping Terrance.

I guess she'd made her choice.

And the Association must be told.

"But, Ernesto. His soul." I was still tied in enough for that to bother me. Traitor or not, Terrance was still a sorcerer.

Ernesto's brown eyes never left mine. "They're taking it, Jasmine. Whoever these people are—and I do think they *are* the government now—they're using up as much of him as they can."

I sat heavily on the grass, the dampness wicking its way into the fabric of my jeans.

Disabling Terrance Sterling had seemed way too easy, drilling his pentagon pin or not. It was as if whatever was protecting him had suddenly pulled away.

And I didn't feel like we knew nearly enough.

Not a Powers-damned thing.

And our main source of information, for good or ill, was in a coma now, his soul ripped from his skin.

50

CAROL

The crowd was huge, and growing, taking over the street in front of Rosalia's shop.

Carol just hoped the cops didn't show up before the Panthers were ready for them.

The Brown Berets were getting people into formation, giving the small cadres safety instructions. Carol and Jasmine would need to go through to do the same thing soon, talk to them about magical links and protections, and what they were going to need from the people on a magic and energetic level.

They needed another year to train these people, who were sipping water and Cokes, and eating tamales from the jingling carts that moved through the crowd, fortifying the people for the battle ahead.

They'd had nine days. Nine days to orchestrate the largest magical operation done in close to thirty years.

Carol knew they were never going to be ready in time, but every sorcerer in Las Manos—plus Ernesto, Rosalia, and Cecelia—insisted that the tides were right.

They had to move, and move fast. The full moon was coming up, and that had the power to change everything. Carol didn't know if the Feds were more tuned in to the full or the dark moon—like the panther shifters—or used some other system entirely. But most ordinary magics rode the powers of the astral tides, pulled on by the waxing increase of the moon's light.

Despite the sorcerers scattered through the crowd, mostly they were dealing with ordinary folks here. Folks who knew their moods changed, or things became more clear, the brighter the moon grew in the sky.

Besides, it would be good to get this done before Christmas. There were a lot of Catholics and Baptists in the streets this week, taking up the practice of magic like they were the Three Wise Men.

"How different will this be from the work we did in San Luis Obispo?" Carol asked Jasmine, who stood at her side on the crowded sidewalk, craning her neck to see if Jimmy had arrived. "Or what you and Doreen pulled off in Oakland, at the park?"

"Oh, girl, I don't know," Jasmine replied. "But this *feels* bigger to me, you know? Besides, look at this damn crowd! This is way more people than we've tried to organize before!"

More and more people poured into the streets. Carol wouldn't be surprised if they ended up with a thousand. Maybe more. All the people at the rally Jasmine had attended across from City Hall. All the people from the union hall. The people from the neighborhood. Everyone was here.

Jasmine spoke again. "And I just don't feel ready."

"Because of Terrance, or...?" Carol gestured to her leather-covered shoulder.

Jasmine just nodded. Sighed. And then said, "Both."

Carol looked at her friend, saw the purple shadows beneath her eyes. Jasmine looked tired. Not a good way to be heading into whatever it was they were doing today. But sometimes, a sorcerer had no choice.

"Well, no time to think about it now," Carol said. "Let's get these charged-up sashes to the marshals."

They gathered up heaps of yellow, red, blue, green, brown, and black sashes. Las Manos all wore purple sashes. The other sorcerers would wear sashes closest to their Elemental colors. The Brown Berets and Panthers? Well, that was obvious.

Jimmy ran up then, looking good in his leather coat and black beret, big smile on his face. A smile trained on Jasmine Jones. That made Carol smile in turn.

"Babe!"

"Jimmy! You made it!" Jasmine said.

The panther shifter drew Jasmine into his leather-clad arms for a deep kiss, then pulled back, resting his forehead against hers. "Missed you, Jaz."

"Missed you, too, Jimmy."

With a pang, Carol longed for Ernesto. She knew he was helping Rosalia in the shop. She also knew he didn't look at her the way Jimmy looked at Jasmine.

Maybe someday soon.

Smelling the familiar scent of cinnamon floating over Jimmy's musk, Carol backed further away from the couple and turned. Doreen and Cecelia strode through the crowded street, Drake and Patrice in tow.

Far out. They all came.

"You made it!" Carol said, when they were close enough to hear.

Hugs were exchanged all around, but they didn't have time to do much more than that.

"Carol and I were just about to pass these sashes out," Jasmine said, afro shifting in the breeze. "The local tailors and seamstresses worked all day to get them done. We charged them up late last night."

"What are they for?" Jimmy asked.

Carol replied, "They're for protection, to help keep people's personal shields up, but more importantly, they'll link our magic together, making us a solid force." She grinned, high on all of this despite the hell of the past weeks.

Despite the fact that Jasmine laid Terrance Sterling out in a coma, and they didn't know whether, or where, his soul had been taken. Or if he would survive.

"At least, that's the theory," Carol added. "Don't you need to get with local leadership?"

"Already done. They want a shifter with you all, just in case."

"Cool," Jasmine said, smile playing at her lips. She bumped his skinny hip with her own. They kissed again.

"Jasmine, we have to get these distributed now," Carol broke in.

She grabbed a pile of brown sashes and handed them to Jimmy.

"Take these. They go to the Brown Berets."

Doreen, Patrice, Drake, and Cecelia all had sashes in their arms already.

Carol pulled a green sash over her head.

Jasmine got on a bullhorn, blue sash slung across her own long leather coat, and started walking through the crowd.

"Comrades! Thank you for coming here today! We are here to say *power to the people!*"

The crowd shouted in response.

"We are also here to practice our magic together. To make sure our communities are strong. Some brothers and sisters are handing out sashes. They're keyed to the Elements. There are Elemental sorcerers here today, watching over you. You are under their protection, and the protection of our comrades in the Brown Berets, the Black Panther Party, and the Local Union 535. We rely on you.

"Tune in to whatever Element your sash color represents. If you've got yellow, think of the power of wind. If you have earth, think of the strength of trees and mountain. That will key you to the sorcerers. They will link us all together."

People put the sashes on, crosswise, shoulder to hip. As the charged cloth hit their energy fields, Carol could almost feel a crackling and surging. They needed to get these people all tuned, and quick, or something might explode.

"Linked together, we are strong! Take some sashes and pass them on. We need to get this together quickly, and we thank you for your help and dedication."

Good. That would get the magic up and running faster.

Members of Las Manos were also passing out the sashes. Carol hoped they heard Jasmine's suggestion of getting the people themselves to pass them on. Energy was building. Carol didn't want to get caught out in the middle of the process.

The racing tension along her skin alternated between excitement and fear.

Jasmine lowered the bullhorn and massaged the hollow in her shoulder, scanning the crowd.

She was looking for Feds. Carol trained her own eyes on the increasing mass of people.

They'd discussed it earlier. Just because they didn't see any black suits, didn't mean the suits weren't already here. It had been a quiet nine days on that front, but that likely meant the federal agents were building their own plan.

They'd be stupid not to be.

Carol just wished they knew what that plan was.

51

JASMINE

We had to pull this off. I needed to set my thoughts of Terrance Sterling and the Association aside. That was petty. Penny ante stuff.

What we were here for this day? Was the biggest damn piece of magic I'd ever even thought of. I knew even bigger magic was coming, but set that thought aside. It was going to be hard enough to lure that snake of a Fed to the park. We wanted to battle on our terms this time.

And we had our own serpent now, to match whatever he threw at us. Rosalia and the Aztec dancers were going to raise the ancient Feathered Serpent. Quetzalcoatl. The Guide. God of the winds at dawn and Venus riding bright in the sky. This serpent was apparently down with the people. Especially the people who still honored its power.

That Pentagon shit was going to have to wait for another time. Or maybe our work here today would make it unnecessary.

I sure hoped so. Frankly, I could use a break. I could stand to go back to feeding the children and making love to Jimmy. Maybe even school, though it was hard to imagine.

Straightening my spine, I lowered the bullhorn and slipped its strap over my head. My shoulder ached like hell. I ignored it, hoping it wasn't trying to tell me anything.

"How are you, hechicera?" Rosalia said.

Her green velvet skirts swirled around her legs. She had on extra rings and bracelets today, and a brightly flowered shawl wrapped around her shoulders, and a sash making a slice of purple across her narrow chest.

Avoiding her citrine eyes, I kept my own trained on the Aztec dancers, who were getting into position behind four tricked-out lowriders that had pulled up an hour before. The cars were as brightly painted as the dancer's feather headdresses, and just as elaborate.

"I'm cool."

She touched my chin. I jerked my head back, but her fingers grasped me, turning my head toward those eyes.

"You may be 'cool,' but I need to know if you are ready." She let my chin go.

"As ready as I can be. Which doesn't feel ready enough."

Who was I, admitting weaknesses to Carol and Rosalia? Who was I, to be this weak in the first place? I could feel the spit gathered in my mouth, a response to my sour stomach. Jimmy was going to catch on that I wasn't okay soon, too, if I didn't get my shit together.

"We never feel ready, hechicera. But that does not mean we are not strong."

I exhaled and shook out my hands. The magic was building in the streets as the sorcerers worked with the people. Some of the Black Panthers had already shifted. I could feel Las Manos doing some kind of spooky shit with the Brown Berets, but I wasn't sure exactly what it was. Good thing I wasn't the general here.

"We've got to get this started."

"Tell the people," Rosalia said. She was the general, but I was the messenger today.

I got on the bullhorn. "Comrades! Open your hearts and souls to the magic around you. This is your birthright. This is your power!"

Raising her arms, Rosalia sent the dancers a signal. The big drum started a steady beat.

"Feel the beating of the drum. Follow that beat. Do as it says. The dancers will lead us to the place we will take our stand and claim the power of all the people to fight the forces arrayed against our own."

"Maaarrrccch!" said the Brown Berets.

Ankle bracelets clacked and clattered as the dancers began to move, feather headdresses swaying and dancing through the air. The low riders crept forward, jumping their wheels, clearing the streets up ahead.

A small group of Gabrielino Indians followed the Aztec dancers, shaking rattles, heads bound with bandanas, wearing denim jackets, boots, and jeans.

And we all followed, shifters pacing at the edges of the crowd with the Brown Berets and union members. Black Panther security forces were arrayed at front and back of what was turning into a massive march.

Rosalia grabbed my hand. Together, we entered the crowd, crushed between groups in green and yellow sashes. I saw flashes of blue a few yards away. The Water people. Good to know. Even though it wasn't my gig today to keep track of their magic, I might need to call on them for a boost.

"Keep your eyes open," Rosalia shouted up into my ear. "But look on the astral plane as well. We are going to be in both places at once."

Holy shit. She wanted me to do this shit while walking

in a crowd? I felt cold, then hot, then cold again.

The small sorcerer jerked my hand. "Jasmine! You can do this! Pay attention!"

I rubbed at my shoulder again. It throbbed with sudden pain. Shit. *Okay, Jaz, you can do this. Slow your breathing down. Let your boots march down this East LA street. We're heading for the boulevard. The crowd will take your there.*

And Rosalia pulled.

And I was in that star-shot plane she had taken me to before. Back when she wanted to prove how powerful I was. Back before I got so fucked up by that snake of a Fed.

My boots were still on tarmac. I could still feel the bodies around me. There was pressure at my temples like a headache was coming on, and my stomach felt a little woozy with the dual vision. I hoped I would get used to it before things went down.

This was seriously weird shit. But it was kind of groovy, too.

"Look." The hechicera's voice was in my head. I followed the bracelets down her thin arm to the silver ring on the pointing brown finger.

Hovering on the astral, but also hovering just over the crowd, trailing the energy of the dancers as they swirled and leapt, crouched and stomped, was a massive serpent, made up of all the colors of the rainbow.

"Far out..." I whispered.

Bright feathers streamed from the massive serpent's head. Down in the crowd, a conch shell sounded three times.

The serpent bunched its mighty muscles, swimming through the æthers.

It was the most beautiful thing I'd seen. My eyes streamed with tears.

"What are we supposed to do?" I asked.

"Whatever the serpent tells us. Just follow."

The crowd turned a corner. Whittier Boulevard. The massive thoroughfare that stretched from Los Angeles all the way down to the sleepy town of Whittier itself, an hour's drive away. It was the lowriders favorite stretch of road. I knew they paraded up and down it Saturday nights, showing off their paint jobs and hydraulic tricks.

We were heading toward Laguna Park. Funny how all our major battles were ending up outside, in parks or on that hillside outside the prison.

Parks were the places people could still gather. The places that hadn't all been stolen by the rich.

The queasiness was abating, which meant I was adjusting to the astral vision and still seeing the misty shapes around me. It made me wonder if Rosalia had clearer vision in both planes. She must.

I wondered if I would, someday, too.

The feathered serpent shook its massive head. It looked more than big and bad enough to take on the snakes the Fed sent after me. I trusted that much.

What I didn't trust was that I could lure the Fed to the park. I was hoping that since he kept showing up wherever I was, he'd just be there. Rosalia and my mother both insisted that even though they'd cleared the dart from my aura, I could still use the entry place as a way to connect back to the sender.

Hoping that was true, because today's action depended on it, it also bothered me, deeply.

Because it meant that bastard still had a way to connect back to me, too.

52

SNAKES AND SPIDERS

The park was a depressing place. The opposite of the verdant green of Washington DC.

Patches of dried-out grass. A heap of garbage around an overflowing can. Trees with twisted branches. A metal swing set, empty.

The whole park was empty except for some wino sleeping on a green-painted bench, huddled inside a greasy black coat.

Samuels lowered the binoculars. They were hard to focus properly over the dark glasses, but the damn Southern California sun was relentless, beaming through the brown haze and bouncing off the cracked sidewalks around the parking lot where he stood beneath a fig tree.

His operatives were spread out around the park.

The Master had finally consented to sending five of them, plus Samuels had his remaining provocateurs and plants. Cotton from the Black Panthers. Samuels hadn't cut him loose yet, because he didn't have a replacement. A local cop, Fernando Sumaya, in the Brown Berets. And one member of the Union 535 rank and file, those bastards. They all marched with the crowd.

So Samuels had eight men plus himself to pull this off.

He grinned, lips pressed tightly against each other. That Panther bitch was going down today, no problem. No problem at all.

The twisted wire of the cincture cut into Samuel's right thigh. He smiled at that, too. He was a dedicated magician. A man who would be Master of the Temple someday, if all went well. The constant pain and pricking at his leg reminded him of what was at stake.

He had to remain disciplined. He had to remain strong.

The low rumble of the ridiculously gaudy Mexican cars reached his ears, followed by the clatter of some sort of shells and the booming of drums.

Then the sounds of people, moving en masse down the street. Shouts and whistles. The stomp and smack of shoes and boots on the ground.

And there they were, led by the purple and gold cars. Followed by tall plumes waving in the air. The dancers, crouching and weaving, rattling and shaking. Those damn Black Panthers.

Well, well, well, if there weren't shape-shifters stalking the sides of the crowd. Wasn't that intriguing?

Samuels gave a slight squeeze to the men marching with the crowd. He had trained them to squeeze back in response. One. Two...and the third.

The other Temple members, he linked to mind-to-mind. Rubbing the serpent ring on his left hand, Samuels sent a thought out to his agents. They sent back images of their positions around the park.

He directed the man on the southeastern corner to move back. He was too exposed.

"Perfect." Samuels said.

The crowd poured into the small park. The man on the bench raised his head and looked around before shambling out of the way.

Samuels began to chant the mantra in his head. The one the Master crooned and slobbered in the dark basement space where their magic took its form.

Come, Intelligence. Time is now! Prove your Power! Light my mind. Build the Temple! Rule the world!

He sent the energy that built inside him out to the other men, linking them in one purpose, one magical signature, one source of power.

The source of all.

Riding up onto the astral winds, he was smacked by a force equal to his own.

No. Greater than his own.

Ancient. Terrible.

The serpent rose inside of him, the pain of his cincture gripped his leg, and he almost fell to the cleared, dry dirt around the tree.

Fighting his serpent down, Samuels struggled to expand.

He needed to get bigger. He needed to be three times larger than he was. Four times. Five.

This thing was massive.

And all he had were five trained magicians and three plants.

And his own magic.

Which now didn't seem nearly strong enough.

"Raise the Temple!" he shouted out loud and in his head. He knew his men had heard. They had to.

Around the park, people still streaming in, Samuels felt the mighty pillars rise. One for each direction. Then one arch of magic formed a ceiling—that was his own. One arch for the ground below.

With a mighty boom, *he felt the Temple set itself, right itself.
He felt his own power increase.*

"And. We. Do. This. NOW!" he screamed.

And six serpents blasted forth to meet the crowd.

53

JASMINE

We were walking into a trap.

By the time I saw it, it was too late. There was no way to stop the juggernaut of lowriders, Aztec dancers, and the sheer mass of people who had all been told they were heading to Laguna Park.

I didn't have to lure the snake in after all. He was here. And had already raised a temple formation on the astral plane that overlaid the park. Damn it.

I hadn't thought he had that much power, especially after all the attacks we'd already pulled off.

"Rosalia!" I paused at the corner, people bumping into me and streaming past.

"I see it," she said. Then she grabbed my hand and yanked me all the way into the astral with a lurch. The damn serpents were streaming everywhere.

"I have to go back. The people need help!"

"They need your help up here. Let the other sorcerers do their jobs!" Rosalia shouted back inside my mind.

I sought out Carol on the earth plane down below, and did a sending that I hoped got through. I also hoped someone had gotten our physical bodies out of the way. I didn't feel like anything was wrong, but I sent a thought down the silver cord that tethered me to the base of my skull. Sure enough, some Brown Berets were carrying my body and Rosalia's to a big tree.

We must have just collapsed.

This was so not cool.

Carol sent back, *"We're cool. Everyone is almost ready. The drummers and dancers are getting ready in the center of the park. We're setting up warded stations at the outside corners."*

Blue, ocean-colored fire burst around the edges of my aura, crackling like a storm. The feathered serpent coiled around and around the Temple, smaller snakes biting at its sides. It didn't seem to feel them at all.

"What do we do?" I asked Rosalia.

"We watch."

Watch? She yanked me up here to just watch?

"Pay attention!" her voice snapped.

I stilled myself inside and looked. What was she seeing? Sigils glowed bronze and gold on the tall white pillars. Looking up, I saw that they formed one larger glyph together in the center.

"What is that?" I asked. "And what is the feathered serpent doing?"

Rosalia laughed. "The feathered serpent is doing whatever it damn well pleases, hechicera! The dancers are feeding it well. But look more closely and you'll see what it does."

I looked. All I saw was the serpent, flowing in a sinuous circle around the pillars, tracing the edges of the temple space with its massive form.

Then I got it. Every pass around the columns took a tighter loop. Tiny fissures appeared on the astral structure.

Cracks I wouldn't even notice if I hadn't been asked to look for them.

"The composite sigil at the top of the Temple is the key," Rosalia said. "Memorize it if you can."

I wished Carol was up here. She was the one who had the bead on these sigils. They just looked like squiggles to me. I did the best I could.

"I need to get around to all the pillars, to see the sigils before I can figure this out. Can you keep the snakes distracted?" I asked.

I wished I knew what in all the Powers was going on down below, too. I could feel my body tugging at me and wondered how long we'd been up here.

Rosalia nodded her head. "Go," she said.

I turned. Oh shit.

He was up there. On the astral plane. The Fed. Even up here, he wore those damn dark glasses on his face. His suit and hair looked perfect.

He raised a hand and shot another snake straight at me, heading for the sore spot on my shoulder.

I slammed him with a wall of blue fire that rocked the Temple floor. A chunk of one of the pillars fell behind me. I jumped as I felt it. I had no idea whether getting hit by astral debris would hurt, but instinct said get the hell out of the way.

"What do you want from us?" I yelled.

"Everything," he yelled back.

He wanted our power.

We circled one another. I was barely aware of Rosalia doing something at the Temple edges, and the continued circumambulation of the serpents.

"You don't have to work for the Man, you know! You could steal your soul back. Come join the people." It was a taunt, more than an offer. The man could die, for all I cared. And maybe that would happen today.

"My soul is fine," he said. And I felt a shift, like the astral slipping suddenly sideways. He was pulling power from somewhere.

I had to strike before it built.

He raised his arms. Then we were running toward one another, through the star-shot mist, across the heaving Temple floor. I threw out a blast of pure Water from my core.

Our powers slammed, one against the other, and then our astral bodies smacked together. I didn't even know that could happen.

A bell tolled.

And then we were falling, slamming hard into our bodies down below. Slamming into earth. A headache spiked my skull and I lurched up, coughing.

Where was he?

I could feel him, just outside the perimeter of the park. Could hear the dancers and chanting from some of Las Manos.

Rosalia still looked asleep. I hoped she could do without me on the astral for awhile. The re-entry headache made me want to vomit, but I coughed and spit on the dried-out grass instead.

"Water?" a voice said. It was a Brown Beret, standing above me, offering a canteen. I took a careful swallow. It was good.

"Thanks. How long was I out?"

She screwed the cap back on. "Around fifteen minutes. You both collapsed and we carried you in." She jerked her chin at Rosalia's resting form. "Is she...?"

"Still up there. Fighting. But I have some things I need to

take care of down here. Can you get me to Carol and Ernesto?" I asked. *And Jimmy,* I didn't ask. I was a little hurt he hadn't stayed with my body, even though I knew that was stupid. He was needed in the fray.

The woman gave me a hand up and led me through the crowd. Every boom of the drums shook my skull.

The people stood in concentric circles, colored sashes practically glowing in the winter sun. Their hands were raised to the sky.

They were pushing against the Temple ceiling. As we neared the edges of the park, I saw other people facing outward, also pushing. They must have figured out about the corner columns.

Good.

Good! A grin split my aching head. Power to the damn people!

Carol's blond hair shone in front of me.

"Carol!"

She turned her head, but didn't stop what she was doing, which was grasping strands of energy from the people behind her and forming them into one pulse of Air fire aimed at the pillars ordinary people couldn't see.

"Jaz!"

"Where's Jimmy?"

"I think he's with Patrice and Drake, helping Las Manos keep people organized. Doreen, Cecelia, and Ernesto all took the other columns. We can use you if you have time."

"I have something else I have to do."

"Before you go, take a look outside the park," she said.

My skin grew cold.

There was another black-suited white man looking right at us, sweat running down his face.

"How many?"

"One on each corner, as far as we can tell."

"Hold tight," I said. I had to take care of this.

And then all hell broke loose behind us, in the center of the park.

Whirling, I ran toward the shouting and the brightly colored flashes of magic. Then I saw the writhing.

There was another goddamned nest of snakes in there.

A panther shifter roared, holding a man down on the ground with its massive paws. Two other panther shifters ran in, taking down two men who'd been grappling with some Brown Berets.

Who were these men? They had to be plants.

Shoving into the swirling dancers, looking for a way through the feathers and muscled legs and shoulders, I found the pattern of their dance and broke through.

Powers be damned.

One of the men on the ground had a brown felt beret on his head. The other wore the black beret of a Panther. I recognized him. It was Cotton. And the third man? A white man. I thought I recognized him, too, from the union hall.

I wanted to kick them for their betrayal.

Instead, I threw up a shield of magic around the group in the center, keeping them from affecting the rest of the park. Those people had enough to deal with and didn't need cracks in their concentration.

Then I opened my third eye, honed in, and started yanking on the snakes that snapped and squeezed in the middle of the grappling men, trying to burst outward into the rest of the park. Sending bolts of blue fire at the backs of their diamond heads, I took out one, and then another. They kept coming, writhing into existence from a hole to nowhere.

This wasn't going to be enough. I'd made a mistake

putting up the wall of quarantine. I couldn't take out the snakes with humans in the way.

"Get ready to drag these traitors out!" I shouted, then dropped the wall.

The panther shifters grabbed shirts and shoulders in their massive jaws, human Panthers and Brown Berets grabbed feet. In a crazy tangle, they dragged the men out of the central circle.

I raised the magic curtain around me once again, then spared a glance up.

The veils between the earth and astral plane were buckling. I caught glimpses of the sigil powering it all, shining overhead. Then fog. Then dirty sky. Then the Temple vault again.

I needed to get to the Fed. My Fed. I had to take him out. But there wasn't time right now.

Then I knew what needed to be done.

Letting Ocean build inside me, I felt the people connected to Water throughout the park, especially the ones nearest me, who were focused on what hovered above.

Linking to their energy fields, I started to draw, like sucking lemonade through a straw. I breathed in power and breathed out solidity. Hands in front of me, I formed a mighty blue-green ball of fire.

There were dozens of snakes by now.

But I had the power of the people to multiply my magic, along with the entire Pacific Ocean off the coast.

Lifting my arms above my head, I slammed that ball of deadly energy down onto the writhing snakes. They exploded upward, in a column of blue fire. I kept drawing on the magic all around me and pumping that power back out through my hands. The column flared and flamed, torching its way through both earth and astral planes.

I imagined it burning at the sigils up above, damaging the magic wards that kept the Temple safe.

The mighty feathered serpent squeezed. The dancers just outside my inner circle spun and shook and rattled, the drums beating faster and faster. The column flamed. The people let out a mighty yell.

Then, *crack!*, a booming flare of light and sound.

And everyone in the middle of Laguna Park collapsed onto the dried grass, panting and heaving, some sobbing, some cursing.

The astral columns around the park crumbled in a slow cascade. I could feel Doreen, Carol, Ernesto, and my mother, all holding the magic steady until it was safe.

And then the a breeze shook the branches and leaves overhead. Las Manos cleared the park with the power of Air.

A conch shell sounded. The feathered serpent descended from the astral and waved its long body around and around the park, caressing backs and faces with rainbow-colored plumes. Blessing us.

Then it winked out, leaving only the scent of orange blossoms.

I breathed in the blessing of that smell, then looked around.

The people were weeping, rapt, ecstatic looks on upturned faces.

They were crying tears of joy.

54

JASMINE

Two Brown Berets helped Rosalia toward me.

I rose to meet her, folding her small frame into a hug. Her dark hair smelled of copal and ozone.

Something solid bumped my thigh. I looked down. Jimmy. His golden panther eyes gazed up at me. A purr rumbled from his throat.

I laughed and tugged gently on one soft ear. Then the laughter left me.

There was something I still had to do.

"The Fed..." I looked around. All I saw were people, weeping and laughing, holding each other close. Panthers. Sorcerers. And all the people from the community who took a risk on us.

"Let him go, hechicera," Rosalia replied. "If he isn't dead, we injured him enough that he won't return any time soon."

I looked at her. "But what if he isn't injured *enough*? What if he causes more harm?"

She put a hand on my arm.

"Sometimes we have to let the people have their victory. Look at them, hechicera. Today is one of those times."

Something in me rebelled against that.

Not against letting the people have their victory. She was right. We all needed some hope after all the shit that had gone down. After the assassination attempts, the bombings, the harassment…and the bad magic.

But the victory wasn't going to last long if that snake was still out there.

She grabbed my arm. "You aren't strong enough yet."

Tears pricked my eyes and I drew in a shocked breath.

"She's right," a voice behind me said.

I turned.

It was my mother, hair askew, yellow dress dirty from the park.

"You shouldn't have even been here today, but we knew there was no holding you at home," she said.

"You think I'm weak?" I asked.

"No. We think you are too strong for your own good, girl!" Doreen said. When had she arrived to the central space? Was I that out of it? Or was time moving funny?

Rosalia spoke again. "You did good work today, hechicera. Better work than I could have done on my own. But if you go after him now, when all their power is spent?" She waved an arm out to the crowd. "There will be no protecting you. And as you know, we have won this battle…"

"But we're still at war," I said.

We were always still at war.

I wondered if this war against the people would ever end. But I guessed I wouldn't find that out this day.

And they were right. I was tired to my bones.

So I did what I'd been wanting to do for a week. I knelt back down and wrapped my arms around Jimmy, inhaling his panther musk and placing a kiss on top of his black-furred head.

55

CAROL

The Mansion was quiet.

Helen had taken Terrance off somewhere to try and heal. She said she didn't trust anyone at the Mansion to care for him.

Well, no one at the Mansion trusted either of them in the moment.

The students had all been sent away for winter break. Even the ones who usually stayed behind found places to go.

No one wanted to be in the long hallways right now. Not until a major psychic and energetic cleansing happened.

Not until something changed.

"You think Helen will be back?" Carol asked Ernesto.

Carol was in Ernesto's bedroom for the first time in her life, lying on the simple, Mission-style double bed, curled under burgundy sheets and the white comforter with a burgundy stripe around the border.

An ancestor altar was set up on a Mission-style dresser against the wall. Silver-framed photos, a pocket watch. A handkerchief embroidered with delicate golden flowers.

Her eyes moved to Ernesto, fresh from a shower. A white towel wrapped around his brown hips, beneath the small mound of his belly. The whorls of dark hair that curled across his sculpted chest made her nervous.

She wondered what it would feel like beneath her hands.

Carol had never seen Ernesto naked before. She'd never seen any man naked in her life, sheltered in the Mansion as she had been, far from regular schools and home.

She shouldn't have been asking those kinds of questions. About Helen. The Association. Not right then.

But the thought wouldn't leave her. And she was stalling for time. Trying to act like being in her former teacher's bed was no big deal.

Like she was some groovy chick into free love, who slept with men all the time.

Ernesto shook his head, rubbing a second white towel over his dark, wet hair. His face looked so vulnerable without his glasses, but he was still the most handsome man she knew.

"I don't know, maga," he replied. "It's hard to know what's going to happen now. The Association of Magical Arts and Sorcery has not had to deal with a situation like this in probably one hundred years."

He crossed toward the bed. Carol scissored her way further down beneath the sheets.

Ernesto kept talking, throwing the white towel he'd used to dry his hair onto the hard wooden floor. "The Association has to meet now. Vote for a new head. Discuss the direction we're headed."

Then he smiled at her.

"But we don't really need to be talking about this right now, do we, maga?"

She shook her head, damp blond hair spread out over the pillow.

He leaned over her then, smelling of Ivory soap and Old Spice, and a breeze in spring, warm and soft.

Their lips met. Soft. Then firm.

The taste of fennel on his tongue.

Carol reached her hands up to Ernesto's face. His cheeks were smooth. Freshly shaved.

He pulled away.

"You sure you want to do this?" he asked, his dark eyes staring down at her. "We can just lie in bed and kiss awhile, you know. Take it slow."

After the magic in the park, after feeling how close they had all come to oblivion, Carol knew she needed this.

"No. I want this. It's like..." She reached for the towel and tugged, until it dropped to the floor.

He pulled back the sheets and comforter and crawled into the bed.

And then he touched her skin.

"What is it like?" he asked.

It didn't matter what happened. Whether the Association would implode. Whether the Feds attacked again. What mattered was feeling Ernesto. Kissing him. Drawing herself as close to his skin as possible.

And feeling the place where Earth met Air. It felt like a different kind of magic than she'd ever felt before.

His rich brown eyes stared down at her, his lips still too far away.

"It's like...I need to feel this, Ernesto," Carol said. "To feel you. Us. And I want you to show me everything. Show me how it feels when two sorcerers make love."

And he did. They did.

For hours.

56

DOREEN

Doreen and Patrice sat beneath the jacaranda tree in the back of Cecelia's home.

Doreen's sister, Cecelia, who was likely going to become head of the Association of Magical Arts and Sorcery if everything went according to plan.

Cecelia, who was having a well-deserved reunion with William.

And who knew what Jimmy and Jasmine were up to. Still plotting revolution, even after all they'd done that day.

You'd think they'd take a break.

They should have been having a sweet reunion of their own, but Doreen knew there was some debrief meeting with the Panthers downtown. She should have been there, but couldn't bear it.

"Doreen?" Patrice asked.

"Yes, baby?"

Doreen was tired. The high she'd felt after the working in Laguna Park had left her deflated, but content.

So here she and her lover sat, freshly showered, with a

cutting board of salami and cheese, and a loaf of bread they'd found in Cecelia's kitchen.

They were sitting in garden chairs in loose dresses, drinking red wine from juice glasses because they didn't want to risk Cecelia's fancy ones. And they shouldn't need to do any magic for a while.

"You ever think you'll get married again?"

Doreen looked across the table at her lover. Patrice's face was bare after her shower. Her lips were their natural deep brown against her slightly paler face. Her eyes looked tentative. Earnest.

Patrice had never looked more beautiful.

"You asking?"

Patrice nudged her bare foot with her own.

"Maybe."

All of a sudden, Doreen wasn't tired anymore. She knew what she wanted, and she wanted it now.

"I think if I was ever going to get married again, it would be to you."

Patrice's brown eyes lit up, and she smiled.

"Well then, future wife, you still tired?"

Doreen took a breath. Paused. And realized that no, she wasn't tired at all.

"Let's go find that spare bedroom, lover. Much as I would love to take you here under the tree, I'm not sure my sister's neighbors would approve."

The women gathered up the food and glasses, and walked across the grass toward the kitchen door, laughing.

There were still decisions to be made. Messes to clean up. Aftermath to be dealt with.

But for now?

Life was good.

And Doreen was damn well going to enjoy herself.

57

———

JASMINE

All during the debrief, I never once let go of Jimmy's hand. I needed him near me. Needed the feel of him. The strength of him.

I needed his love.

Then we went walking. I wasn't ready to go home to my parents' house, and needed to be away from the crush of Panthers, Brown Berets, Las Manos, and everyone else.

Rosalia had kissed both my cheeks and told me to go. Panther leadership wanted me to stay, but she fixed them with those citrine eyes of hers, and they shut up pretty damn quick.

That woman could run the world if she wanted to.

I hoped she could, some day. It had to be better than the one we'd been living with.

Jimmy and I wound our way through the streets of South Central LA. Past barber shops, boarded-up storefronts, corner stores, and single-room churches.

As we turned into the neighborhoods, some folks shouted at us from their front stoops. I nodded, smiled, and waved.

"Jimmy, I've got to get out of here."

He nodded, brought us back to the union hall and ran back out holding a set of car keys, pointing to a pale blue El Camino.

Unlocking the door of the low-slung truck, he waited until I'd slid onto the leather seat before closing it with a thunk.

"Where are you taking me?" I asked, once we were underway.

"Santa Monica. The beach."

I started to cry then. All the emotions of the past month. All the pain. All the joy. All the lovemaking. The planning. The sorcery. My fight with Terrance Sterling. It bubbled to the surface and spilled out of me. I sobbed and sobbed, bracing my hands against the dashboard as I cried.

Jimmy placed one warm hand on the center of my back.

He said nothing. Just let me do my thing.

That made me cry some more.

And then I saw it. The pale, shining ribbon, out past the narrow strip of golden sand. The sun was tilting toward the horizon, spilling salmon and peach across the pale brown sky.

Ocean. My ocean.

I swiped the tears from my face and cranked the window down, inhaling huge drafts of salty, briny air.

"Thank you," I said, not sure if I was talking to the ocean, or Jimmy, or both.

"I got you, Jaz. We're gonna take care of each other, dig?"

"I dig."

As soon as the car pulled to a stop in the small parking lot, I kissed him as hard as I could, grabbing the tight, nappy curls at the back of his skull, wanting to eat him alive.

"I love you, Jimmy."

"I love you, too, Jaz. Now get out of this truck and do what you gotta do."

Nodding, I fumbled with the latch, shoved open the heavy door, and ran toward the sand.

As long as there was Water.

As long as there was Earth.

As long as there was Air and Fire and the spirit that wove them all together...

As long as there were people who cared enough to risk their lives for what was right...

The world was a pretty groovy place, and I was happy to be part of it.

Some kids ran, shrieking, back and forth, dodging the small waves of foam that snuck their way onto the shore. Further down the beach, sandpipers hunted, dancing up and back, seeking out the tiny crabs that burrowed in wet sand.

People walked along the ocean, or stood, waiting for the sun to set.

Then Jimmy was beside me. I could feel him there, though my eyes were trained on the beautiful waves rolling in.

"You know, Jimmy, it's time."

"Time for what?" he asked.

"It's time for us all to rise. It's getting to be *our* time, you dig?"

"What do you mean?"

My eyes swept the beach again, looking at the children, the sandpipers, the gulls swooping overhead, the couples and families, all doing their own thing.

Then a magnificent vee of pelicans flew by. I threw back my head and laughed.

"It's time for all of this!" I said. "It's time for *all* of this."

Looking at my lover's face, I thought I'd never seen anything so pretty before.

"Those bastards have ruled this world long enough," I said then. "Let's take it back. For this. For all of this."

"Right on," my lover said, then kissed me, wrapping his strong, wiry arms around me. The power of Ocean pooled inside me. I pushed it toward him, and felt the panther in him answer back.

Pulling apart, we stood, forehead to forehead, and just breathed each other in.

As the sun began to set, the people cheered. Jimmy smiled at me.

"All power to all the people," I whispered.

"All power to the people, baby."

Right on.

58

———————

SNAKES AND SPIDERS

he Master wasn't pleased. Red-faced, he leaned in to Samuel's face and screamed.

"I gave you every resource and you squandered it! What kind of magician are you? I should strip your powers from your DNA and throw your husk to the monsters of the abyss!"

Samuels wiped the Master's spit from his face.

He felt calm. So calm. In their highly polished shoes, his feet were firm on the rug. His right hand held his left wrist. Calm.

Sure, he needed rest. After that bitch had blasted him from the Temple, he had fallen, but luckily, the operatives held firm until he gave the word, and Samuels was able to cloak himself from the Panther girl until the operation was complete.

He had already issued his report. Told the Master how much information he and his operatives had gathered on that girl, and the Panthers. On the Brown Berets and the union, too. The operation had been a success on that front.

But the bitch was still alive. And the Temple had been compromised.

Only mildly. The astral form that had crumbled barely

affected the main Temple, of course. It had only been a construct, built by Samuels and his men.

But the Master didn't care. Everything was an insult to him. Everything had become a threat.

Samuels throttled down a smile, schooling his face to seriousness.

When everything feels like a threat, it meant a person was weak.

The Master himself had taught Samuels that, many years before.

He must have forgotten.

Samuels felt the Master's magic probing at the tattoo under his arm. The one from his last "initiation." That tethered Samuels more firmly to the inner sanctum of the Temple. And to the Master.

Except the tattoo didn't itch or burn today.

The Master had miscalculated. Giving Samuels the authority to build an astral replica of the Temple that mirrored the structure of the thing itself? He should have known that gave Samuels the key to more magic than he'd ever had before. And the Intelligence recognized Samuels now.

And Samuels could wrap the power of the Intelligence around himself, as protection. And use the very sigils the Master had keyed as his own.

"I believe the operatives and I did everything within our power to take care of the situation, sir. And we gathered important intel, plus more magic to feed the Temple."

Samuels pushed back at the Master's probing. Felt the resistance. Saw the flash of surprise that crossed the close-set eyes set in the pasty face stained red with rage.

Samuels smiled inside, wanting to pump one fist into the air. But he kept all that locked down. The game wasn't over yet.

But it was getting to be time. The stinking, sweating Master had lost his grip.

Hoover's eyes flicked down. Just for an instance, but it was enough.

The Master knew he couldn't control Samuels right now. It didn't mean he wouldn't try again. Or come up with another way to get him back under control.

But for now, Samuels simply straightened up his spine, and looked the Master directly in his eyes.

"Will there be anything else, Master?"

"Get out of my sight!"

"Very well, sir."

Samuels smiled and walked out of the office.

He didn't care when or if he would be summoned back.

He had his own work to do now.

We were in Obregón Park, following the Chicano Moratorium march against the war.

The energy of the march still lingered, wild and strong.

The park smelled of fire and freedom as much as it did sun and patchy, dried grass. It seemed fitting to gather here, in this powerful place that the people had claimed as their own...

*If you enjoyed this book, please consider telling a friend, or leaving a short review at your favorite booksellers.
Many thanks!*

Also, Thorn has a weekly newsletter at thorncoyle.com if you want to keep in touch.

AUTHOR'S NOTE & BIBLIOGRAPHY

Author's Note:

This series came about because for many years I've wondered what racial justice in the United States would look like if Fred Hampton had not been brutally assassinated by the FBI and Chicago PD, and if J. Edgar Hoover's COINTELPRO had not purposefully decimated so many groups and coalitions working toward equity, autonomy, and justice.

With encouragement from others—especially from my amazing first readers when I wondered about giving up— what started off as a 10,000 word short story soon turned into a four book series.

There's a lot of history in this alt-history fantasy. 1968-69 was a time in which so much happened, it is almost impossible to keep track of events. The infiltration, assassinations, psychological warfare, disruption, and attacks on anti-war and civil rights groups by the FBI was far worse and more comprehensive than I could even being to include in these novels. Many of these tactics continue into contemporary times.

I chose only a few key events to highlight in the story, and concentrated on Oakland and Los Angeles, though events were going down in cities across the U.S.

When possible, I used the words of Panther organizers like Fred Hampton and Huey Newton. I also tried to remain respectful of the Panthers still living and doing good work in the world. That is why so many key historical players are barely mentioned, or appear as only very minor characters. I didn't want to put words in their mouths. That is not my place. Many of them have told their stories, and you can find a few in the books below. There is a wealth of information not included here.

If you are interested in more actual history, here is a resource list to get you started:

Film:

- Black Power Mix Tape
- 1971
- The Black Panthers: Vanguard of the Revolution (this film is controversial among some of the remaining Panthers).

Books:

- The Fire Next Time - James Baldwin (not about the Panthers in particular, but a great background that frankly, everyone should read.)
- To Live and Die for the People - Huey P. Newton
- Revolutionary Suicide - Huey P. Newton
- The Nine Lives of a Black Panther - Wayne Pharr
- A Taste of Power - Elaine Brown
- Seize the Time - Bobby Seale

- The Ten Point Program of the Black Panther Party
- Assata: An Autobiography - Assata Shakur (Panther history after the time period of this series).
- J. Edgar Hoover: a Graphic Biography - Rick Geary
- Chicano Movement for Beginners - Maceo Montoya
- Youth, Identity, Power: The Chicano Movement - Carlos Muñoz, Jr.

And of course, the repercussions from this time roll forward.

Additional key resources:

- The New Jim Crow - Michelle Alexander
- The 13th Movie - Ava DuVernay
- From #BlackLivesMatter to Black Liberation - Keeanga-Yamahtta Taylor

Many members and associates of the Black Panther Party continue to do public work in the world:

- Fred Hampton and Deborah Johnson/Akua Njeri's son, Fred Hampton Jr, founded the Prisoners of Conscience Committee.
- Elaine Brown is an activist and author.
- Ericka Huggins is an activist, speaker, and spiritual teacher.
- Bobby Seale is an educator, author, and activist.
- Angela Davis is a professor, author, and active in the prison abolitionist movement.

- Tarika Lewis is a violinist, artist, activist, and art teacher.

ACKNOWLEDGMENTS

Every published book requires both an author working alone, and a host of friends and community.

Thank you and love to Robert and Jonathan, for helping me build a home all these years.

Thanks to first readers Leslie Claire Walker, Thealandrah Davis, and Luna Pantera. Thanks also to Al Osorio for the occasional consultation on the series! These would be lesser books without all of you.

Blessings to the Sorcery Collective, my amazing advance team who directly contribute to the success of this series.

Thank you to Dayle Dermatis, editor extraordinaire.

Thanks to my first and third Saturday writing cohort. It's great working with you.

Thanks to Kris Rusch, who told me this wasn't just a short story, but a novel series.

Most of all: thanks to all of the activists and justice organizations who do the work day in and day out. May your lives and work be blessed.

ALSO BY T. THORN COYLE

FICTION

The Panther Chronicles (Complete)

To Raise a Clenched Fist to the Sky

To Wrest Our Bodies From the Fire

To Drown This Fury in the Sea

To Stand With Power on This Ground

The Witches of Portland (complete)

By Earth

By Flame

By Wind

By Sea

By Moon

By Sun

By Dusk

By Dark

By Witch's Mark

The Steel Clan Saga

We Seek No Kings

We Heed No Laws

We Ride at Night

Seashell Cove Paranormal Mysteries

Bookshop Witch

Haunted Witch

Tarot Witch

Short Story Collections

A Hint of Faery

A Touch of Faery

A Spark of Magic

A Flame for Yuletide

A Hope for Winter

A Speculation of Stars

A Speculation of Hope

Risk It All: Queer Stories of Love, Suspense, And Daring

Thresholds: Queer Stories of Love, Suspense, And Daring

Non-Fiction

Evolutionary Witchcraft

Kissing the Limitless

Make Magic of Your Life

Sigil Magic for Writers, Artists & Other Creatives

Crafting a Daily Practice

ABOUT THE AUTHOR

T. Thorn Coyle worked in many strange and diverse occupations before settling in to write novels. Buy them a cup of tea and perhaps they'll tell you about it.

Author of the *Seashell Cove Paranormal Mystery* series, *The Steel Clan Saga*, *The Witches of Portland*, and *The Panther Chronicles*, Thorn's multiple non-fiction books include *Sigil Magic for Writers, Artists & Other Creatives*, and *Evolutionary Witchcraft*.

Thorn's work appears in many anthologies, magazines, and collections. They have taught magical practice in nine countries, on four continents, and in twenty-five states.

An interloper to the Pacific Northwest U.S., Thorn stalks city streets and talks to crows, squirrels, and trees.

Connect with Thorn:
www.thorncoyle.com